Between Each
Line of Pain
and Glory

GLADYS KNIGHT

Between Each Line of Pain and Glory

My Life Story

HYPERION

NEW YORK

For my precious children, grandchildren,
and those who may follow,
I leave you this chronicle
of the pain and the glory for posterity.

ACKNOWLEDGMENTS

First and foremost, I give honor to the Lord for giving me my life and His infinite blessings. "The Lord is my light and my salvation, of whom shall I be afraid?"

There were many people who were part of the pain, and even more who contributed to the glory of my life story. Among those whom I must thank personally for their enormous contributions toward helping me document my life are, as always, my closest friends and my family.

Lloyd Terry, one of my earliest musical mentors, came through for me—as always—when I needed him by not only providing, but taking, many of the priceless photographs that appear in this book.

Zora "Blondie" Brown, one of my dearest and oldest friends, not only lived through more than a few of my "experiences," but helped me through many of them. Her memory was invaluable when it came to helping me recollect long-forgotten facts and details. Likewise, I am forever indebted to my big brother Bubba for that same helping hand and for so, so much more.

For pitching in when I needed their assistance, advice, and plain old moral support, I thank my younger brother David Knight and his wife Cindy, who helped me with the photo gathering and always made sure I had the latest copy of my manuscript-in-progress with me so I could work on this book on the road. I also thank my "wiser than her age" hair and makeup artist, Vicky Turner, who has been my right arm on the road for years and years. Without a doubt, this book simply would not have been if not for the careful attention it was paid in all of its various stages by Denise Miller, my son Jimmy's assistant.

In the publishing world, I owe thanks to many. To my agent, guardian angel, and sister, Jan Miller, I give thanks for your dedication to this project; for lending me your ears when I needed to talk; your shoulder when I needed to lean on someone; and your hands to lead me through the literary world. Thanks as well to Jan's right hand gal, Elizabeth Grant, who helped to keep all the loose ends together, which I know wasn't easy.

To my editor, Maureen O'Brien, thanks for believing in me and for convincing others along the way that my life has value. Thank you for your inexaustable and invaluable store of advice and guidance, and for always going that extra mile to make things happen as I felt I needed them to be for this book. Thanks for your consistent but gentle and respectful nudging, without which there would have been no closure to this life story, and most of all thanks for becoming a friend.

To the staff at Hyperion, thanks for making me feel special and for the very, very high standards you hold to and stand for. You've already made me feel like family. Here's to making it happen.

Many thanks as well to Luchina Fisher, who was infinitely patient and invaluable in helping me gather information and my thoughts early on, while writer Wes Smith jumped on board just when I needed him toward the tail end of this journey. Thanks, Wes, for helping me coordinate my thoughts when the deadline was knocking on the door, and especially for your strong sense of calm and peacefulness, which helped me get through a very difficult time of personal chaos.

Gratitude, in all honesty, must also be paid to Les Brown for ultimately badgering me, way back when, into finally agreeing to write this autobiography.

I thank my children—Jimmy, Kenya, and Shanga—for who they are and for always being there for me.

Finally, I thank my mother, Elizabeth Knight, my number-one mentor. Thanks for your love, your laughter, your sacrifices and your wisdom. You've been the leader and the follower. Thanks for setting the pace and the example for us to live by. Thanks for everything. And, for the record, I love you and I am so very glad that you're my mom.

PROLOGUE

$\mathcal{F}$or almost as long as I've drawn breath on this earth, I have been singing, and nearly every song I've performed has contained some pieces of my life: its ups and downs; its pain and its glory; its endless challenges and its countless blessings. I have attempted to put my life down in the pages that follow and to fully communicate it, I should sing this tale for you too. After all, without the songs, it would be an entirely different story.

How intertwined is my life with my songs? In 1998, I will celebrate my fifty-fourth birthday as well as my fiftieth anniversary as an entertainer. I find it hard to believe there is even four years' difference. When did I not sing?

Consider that I began performing and touring as a guest soloist with both the Mount Moriah Baptist Church Choir and the Morris Brown College Choir in Atlanta before I was six years old. At eight, I won the *Ted Mack Original Amateur Hour* contest on national television by singing Brahms's "Lullaby" and Nat King Cole's "Too Young." At eight, I joined my brother, my sister, and two cousins in forming The

Pips. Before I turned twelve, we were traveling the country on the Chit'lin' Circuit as the opening act for the likes of Sam Cooke and Jackie Wilson.

By the time I was a teenager, I was getting makeup lessons from Tina Turner, audience-reading lessons from Sammy Davis Jr., and show business–survival lessons from B.B. King, whom I loved and called Uncle B.B.

I sang through kindergarten and grade school and then The Pips had to drag me away from javelin-toss practice in high school to get me to sign our first recording contract. I still had on my graduation dress—and my first barf-inducing liquor buzz—when we got on the plane to New York to lay down the tracks for our first record.

I sang through two marriages and two divorces. I sang through three pregnancies and one terrifying miscarriage. I sang through love affairs and abusive relationships, through addiction and recovery (both mine and others'), through bare-floored poverty and marble-tiled affluence.

Carrying my dolls, my homework, or my babies, I sang in country churches and national cathedrals. I sang in gospel choirs, honky-tonks, juke joints, gay bars, city stadiums, concert halls, recording studios, and the White House.

I sang for preachers, parents, princes, and presidents; for drag queens and mob kings; for regal audiences and drunken fools. I sang for my husbands, for my children, for my band members, my managers, my record companies, my debtors, and, of course, my fans.

On March 30, 1989, I sang purely for myself.

Let's go there.

On that night, at the age of forty-four, I made my world premiere as an adult solo artist before more than 2,500 people in the main room at Bally's in Las Vegas—the biggest house in town.

It was a bold move, but I felt that it was long overdue. Not everyone agreed, of course. *Who the hell do you think you are, Miss Diva? Where are The Pips?*

I had been performing with The Pips for thirty-seven years at that point, and just a few months prior to the Bally's show I had stunned them, my family, and many of my fans by announcing that I was stepping out on my own. It was not something that I had been planning. I simply had come to the realization that it was time for me to really challenge myself—to take my talent to the next level.

I called a meeting at Bubba's house in Atlanta. My sweet Bubs. I knew it was going to be hardest on the guy I love so very, very much. My big brother, who has been with me through it all. Bubba was my sidekick, tennis partner, dinner partner, partner-in-crime, my Jiminy Cricket, and my friend. We had shared so many wonderful times.

I loved all the guys in this group. Edward Patten and William Guest are my cousins. I look at the pictures of us together on stage at the Apollo and I think about how we drove all the way from Georgia to Harlem to make that show in 1963. We were so hungry for success back then.

Now it seemed that Edward and William had become more complacent. They were preoccupied with other business interests and even Bubba was distracted by his real estate dealings.

I wanted to continue to grow as a performer, and I'd decided that I had to leave *them* to be *me*.

I prayed about it and it occurred to me that this was about maturing as an artist and as a woman. It was time to make a solo run. I had shared long enough. I wanted to take flight. I wanted to do a show that did not have to be approved or voted upon or divvied up.

Each one of us in Gladys Knight & The Pips had shared equally in decisions and in pay. I was the lead singer most of the time, but we were a group. I felt sincerely that every contribution was important to the whole. God knows we each had made sacrifices and we each had paid the price and reaped the rewards. Our loved ones, too, had paid dearly, and their rewards were less palpable. As men, The Pips had left their children with their wives to watch over and guide them. Because I was usually a single parent, my children had been raised by me and my mother, who was a dynamo. I surely could not have done this without her tenacity, guidance, and wisdom.

The most compelling thing that pushed me to go solo was the survival of my immediate family: my kids and me and my mom. And I do mean survival.

The public generally perceives entertainers as highly paid and extremely well-off. In our early days as a young group, we were often so hard up that the featured acts would take pity upon us and feed us. I swear that everytime we saw "Uncle" B.B. King on the road, his first words to us were, "Ya'll hungry?" We most often were, and he always fed us.

But we kept singing and striving and after twenty years of living from gig to gig, we were not only surviving, we were thriving. But I wanted to build something lasting so my children would not have to struggle as long and as hard as I did.

By 1989, I felt it was time that I moved up to the next level as a solo performer. I hadn't always been the sort of woman who could step boldly forward and demand her due, but two marriages and two divorces and a lot of years on the road had strengthened me. It was time. Two of my three children had reached college age and I knew that was going to be quite a financial challenge. I owed my children so much.

Although by the time I opened at Bally's I had signed a half-million-dollar solo recording contract, that money was mostly already gone. The IRS was claiming that I owed them more than $1 million in back taxes, penalties, and interest. While the government is supposed to be an extension of the people, I feel it has no moral conscience. The IRS had jabbed its hand into the deepest pocket, or so it thought. The agents hadn't even looked for my ex. "You're Gladys Knight and we know you can pay," one of them told me.

I had just gone through a five-year divorce and custody battle with my second husband, who had taken our son. I'd paid hundreds of thousands of dollars to private detectives and to lawyers. My cash reserves were shot, and in my panicky effort to replenish them, I had begun accumulating debts of an even darker sort. These collection calls would not be coming from Visa or MasterCard. These calls came from casino credit departments.

I was out of control. My personal life was falling apart. There were all sorts of pressures on me at that point, some of which I've never before made public. So, in truth, the driving force in my decision to take the stage alone and to break up the group was the need to regain control over my life. We had only recently come off our 1988 Love Overboard tour, which had been a smoking, smoking national road trip, our best ever. We had played intimate theaters and small arenas with a group of backup singers named Apollo and an opening act called the Deal, which featured an incredible young singer who would rise to fame in the coming years as Babyface.

Our act was as strong as it had ever been, but we were all working on projects outside Gladys Knight & The Pips. It was as if we each needed something else to challenge us and hold our interest. I'd just gone through the challenge of undergoing a hysterectomy that I had put off for a long time. I was eager to get on with my life and to take it up a notch or two.

While everyone else was distracted, I took it upon myself to organize that tour. The guys were more than willing to let me do it, and I found myself enjoying the responsibility and the independence. After the tour proved so successful, I felt a greater sense of accomplishment and self-assurance than I'd ever experienced before. I'm sure that success contributed to my decision to break out of the group and to make my declaration of independence.

When I told The Pips that I wanted to go my own way, they were concerned and disappointed and even somewhat angry with me. I knew this would create challenges for them, but they were men who could stand on their own two feet and I knew and respected that. We had succeeded in reaching and staying at a very good earning level as a group, and they were more than happy to remain there for many more years. I told them I loved and respected them, but I told them that it was what I wanted and needed to do.

I was worried about Bubba the most because he more than any one of us had invested his entire life in Gladys Knight & The Pips. He was the group's spirit and its heart. He had lost a wife because of his devotion to the group and its welfare. At first, he was the most hurt and openly angry, and I understood. It wasn't so much that I'd hurt him personally. He had invested wisely. His view was that I was destroying a legendary group that he had helped create. We exchanged some emotional words and it was probably our biggest confrontation in many years. I told him that I would always be grateful to work with him, but that one of my concerns was that he had invested so much into the group and had such deep loyalty to The Pips that he had not developed his own talents fully.

Bubba, who today serves as the head of my company and as my opening act and road manager, is an incredible singer, dancer, and comedian and my hope was that if I left the group, he would focus on his own career. He had always pushed me to the forefront in the group, and now my stepping aside could allow him to move forward.

I told all the guys that for me it was a matter of becoming a mature woman who could stand on her own. I felt it was time for me to make a run. It was a very serious moment because each of us understood that our lives were going to change dramatically. And they did.

As soon as I allowed myself to think about making the break, I began dreaming of flying free as a performer. I dreamed especially of the songs I could sing: great songs, contemporary songs, and old songs. The theme of that breakout performance came to me as I dreamed. It would be a love story, a search for love, with the underlying idea that my love was the audience, as usual. I wanted to continue to pour my heart out to them. To make the break a clean one and the declaration a clear one in this first solo appearance, I did not want to do a Gladys Knight & The Pips show minus The Pips. Instead, I chose to showcase mostly material written and performed by others—songs

MARK'S DISCOUNT GROCERIES

Open: Mon. thru Fri. 9:00-5:30 PM; Sat. 9:00 AM - 4:00 PM; CLOSED SUNDAYS

4487 York Road, New Oxford, PA | (717) 624-7619

Fruit Gushers Tropical 6-0.8 oz. Pouches **$1.49** OR **4/$5**	**Herr's Chips** Regular Size **$1.00**	**Chunk Light Tuna** 4 lb. 2.5 oz. **$7.99**	**Fiber One Chewy Bars** Oats and Chocolate 10 bars **$2.99**	**Great Northern Beans** 40 oz. **99¢**	**Mountain Dew** 2 Liter 4 pk. **$4.99**
Mixed Vegetables with Potatoes 28 oz. can **$1.19**	**Honey Bunches of Oats with Almonds** 14.5 oz. **$1.49**	**Malt O Meal (Several Varieties)** 12 oz. bags **79¢**	**Malt O Meal Fruity Dyno Bites with Marshmallows** 35 oz. **$1.99**	**Hidden Valley Ranch Dressing** 40 oz. **$4.99**	**Red Path Granulated Sugar** 4.4 lb. **$2.69**
Kraft Mozzarella String Cheese 12 oz **99¢**	**Pillsbury Sweet Hawaiian Grands** 16.3 oz. **99¢**	– COOLER BUYS – **Immaculate Organic Crescent Rolls** 8 oz. **59¢** OR **2/$1**	**Pillsbury Brownie Dough Peanut Butter** 16 oz. **59¢** OR **2/$1**	**Kunzler Slab Bacon** 10 lb. **$32.99**	**John F. Martin Cream Cheese** 8 oz. **$1.29**
Buy One Get One Free! **Edy's Peppermint Ice Cream** 1.5 qt. **99¢**	**Chunked and Formed Beef Sandwich Slices** 10 lb **$14.99**	– FREEZER PLEASERS – Buy One Get One Free! **Ben and Jerry's Ice Cream** 1 pint **99¢**	**Drumstick Dulce de Leche'** 8 cones **$3.99**	**Breaded Onion Rings** 5 lb. **$7.99**	**Organ' Bulga' Red** **X**

that I had always wanted to sing as much for the message as the music. And I wanted to sing them as I had never sung them before.

We spent months in rehearsal. Bubba selflessly put aside his emotions in order to help me. As my older brother he has always let our love be the overriding factor. With his encouragement, I also called upon one of our show business mentors and our "Pops," Cholly Atkins, who over the years had helped mold us from a group of Atlanta choir kids into a professional act. Before I was even born, "Pops" had been a member of the Copacetics, with his tap partner Honi Coles. They were a top act on Broadway and around the world. His work in training and refining the moves of The Pips was so respected that Motown had hired him to tutor all of its top acts, from the Temptations to the Supremes to the Jackson 5.

Just having Pops and Bubba there boosted my confidence even more. These two highly creative and energetic men in my life gave me their approval to assert control at a time when I was finally ready to be on stage . . . solo.

With my name standing alone on a Las Vegas marquee for the first time and with a standing-room-only crowd in the biggest room in town, I opened that night with the Pointer Sisters' "I'm So Excited," and followed with the Doobie Brothers' "Sweet Freedom."

When I saw the waiters and waitresses stop to listen, I knew I was reaching them. In the middle of that exhilarating second number, I did something else that I'd long wanted to do but had always been afraid to try. I sang scat, jazz-riffing in homage to my early mentor and idol Ella Fitzgerald. It was incredibly liberating to break free of words, to lose myself instead in the language and emotion of the music itself.

Sensing the significance of that moment, the audience roared. I beamed.

I did look over my shoulder for the guys a couple times. Yes, I missed them, especially Bubba because I was used to him taking care of the right side of the room all those years while I worked the left. I had to cover twice the stage so I felt like I had to move in double time. I was one movin' sister that night.

I soared through the rest of that breakout performance and when it was over I collapsed into the backstage embrace of my longtime friend and fellow entertainer, Patti LaBelle, who, like me, had left her own group, Labelle, to fly free.

"Girl, you were dynamite!" she said.

"Oh, you're just crazy," I protested.

It did feel good. I felt like I had stepped out and I wanted to keep growing. Having Patti there to celebrate my first performance in decades without The Pips also gave me the sense that I had finally won acceptance in the ranks of the great female solo artists who were my contemporaries, my competition, and, with a few notable exceptions, my lifelong friends.

As much as I have lived inside the world of show business, I have never felt completely a part of it. In some measure, I know that is due to my "good girl" image, and my relative naivete about the darker sides of the entertainment world. I have seen it all, to be sure, but rarely participated in it. I've always been the girl on the bus who the guys in the band were careful not to curse in front of, even as they hung out the windows to entice cooing groupies and camp followers aboard.

While other performers explored the moral backwaters, I played solitaire, or slept in a corner, pretending not to hear, while they sought the forbidden fruits. When I got older I hung out with their wives and children. They boogied. I cooked. I'm a natural-born homebody, always was, always will be. That's me.

Although I have certainly lost my way from time to time—sometimes for long and painful stretches—I've always sought to follow God's way, to do the right thing, and to be a good person even aboard a rock-and-roll bus that was often rocking and rolling with all *sorts* of carrying on.

My faith and my belief in the Golden Rule were also big reasons why it had been so difficult for me to break away from The Pips.

Without a doubt, much of what I had learned, experienced, and reaped, I owed to them, but I owed myself and my family too.

Since my first performance at the age of four, I have been torn by the conflicting desires to make the most of my God-given singing talent and, on the other hand, to live a "normal" life. I've sought to live in both worlds, but often I've found myself caught between them.

Some of the happiest and most fulfilling periods of my life have been those spent as a woman at home, blissfully tuned into the rhythms of housework and child care, nurturing, cleaning, cooking, giving myself up to those I love. Yet, my gift will not and should not be denied, because to sing is also to nourish and provide for others. It is a southern tradition to feed friends and neighbors and loved ones as a sign of caring. Singing is like that for me. It is a way of sharing my spirit in song. I believe the songs in our lives nourish our souls in hard times and elevate them in good times. I will never lose the joy in providing that for others, and for myself too.

This then, is my life story with all of its pain and all of its glory.

Gladys Knight
July 1997

CHAPTER 1

Ladies and gentlemen . . . Little Miss Gladys Knight . . .

The first time I heard those words I was four years old and standing at the pulpit of Mount Moriah Baptist Church in Atlanta, Georgia. It was my first recital, but already I was accustomed, though not really comfortable, with being placed atop a pedestal because of my "big voice."

Even as I child, I was a belter, not a vocalist. I guess you could compare my style of singing to that of Aretha Franklin or Janis Joplin among women contemporaries, or James Ingram, Michael Bolton, and maybe Rod Stewart among the men. I admire the range that singers such as Whitney Houston, Celine Dion, and Mariah Carey have but I cannot complain. I've been blessed with a voice that has served me well in spite of my lifelong aversion to rehearsing.

I'd blame it on the fact that I started so young, but in truth, I've always hated to practice. My momma tried to work with me early on when she and other adults grasped that I had a special gift. One of the things she built into my brain was to never ever "flake out" on a note. She told me that if a note is high but within your natural range you have to go for it instead of chickening out and going to the falsetto. I don't have great range. My top note is about a B-flat, so to hit the high notes that are considered within my range, I have to *sing ugly*. You can't be worried about looking pretty when you are pushing your voice to hit those high notes. You have to strain and push and so often you look like your poor face is being squeezed by a giant set of pliers. That's singing *ugly*. Keep the cameras away when I've got that going on.

My momma has told me that I instinctively knew how to sell a song from the first time I sang, although no one seems to know exactly when that happened. It is on record, or at least on tape, that I was belting out gospel by the age of three.

My mom's brother-in-law, Uncle Ben, owned an early version of a tape recorder, which had a needle that pressed grooves into a disc as it recorded. Another family member, my uncle Alvin, figured out how to use the machine, so one night while everyone was visiting, he recorded me singing the gospel hymn "Just a Closer Walk with Thee." That was fifty years ago, and that was for the family, so there were no royalties for that one, but I'm still waiting for the others.

When I was so young, I really couldn't understand all the fuss that folks made over my voice. "I'm just singing," I'd say. It was just something that came out of me. My mom told me I was an "old soul," and so I gathered I had an old voice in there that took all those wide-eyed adults by surprise.

It wasn't such a big deal to me and I was much more interested in climbing trees with Bubba or making mud pies with my cousin Gwen, my best friend growing up—and still today.

If anything, all the attention I got when I sang in those early days was embarrassing. I didn't like it when adults made me feel as though I stood out from my brothers or my sister. I remember Mrs. Clack, a minister's wife, coming to visit and fussing over all of us, pinching our jaws and calling us "baby." It was one thing to be part of a group pinch, but another matter to be singled out. *"Well, there is little Gladys. Oh baby, we just love the way you . . ."*

I accepted her words politely, as I'd been taught to do, but when she was finished, I gave her a quick "Thank you, Ma'am," and blew that pop stand. I had trees to shinny and mud to bake. Now there is where my real childhood passion was. As a little girl surrounded by great and avid cooks, I was much more into cooking than I was into singing, and mud was my favorite entrée in the early days.

I first came to understand the culinary magic of mud while playing one day with my distant cousin and childhood friend Janice. We were at her Atlanta house in a wooded area of tall trees surrounding a brook that ran through her family's side yard. We set up this little table near the brook and put out a play tea set and got to pretending that we were cooking twigs as carrots and mud as potatoes. Once we had our meal all laid out on the table and our "bread" was in the oven, we decided to go get our dolls to join us. When we returned about a half hour later, we found the table steaming with a huge meal of real cooked carrots, potato cakes, and bread. We were amazed.

While my aunt watched from her kitchen window, we sat right down and ate that magical meal, and I have no doubt that experience is one of the reasons I've always gotten as much of a kick out of cooking as singing.

I loved hanging out in the kitchen with my momma, my aunts, and their friends. At five years old, I was already duplicating the recipes from my *Little Girl's Cookbook.* In our family, you weren't considered a real woman until you could whip the cake batter 500 strokes. I am woman, watch me whip!

I'm not going to come out and claim that the Knight family of Atlanta, Georgia, actually invented soul-food cooking, but we certainly played a role in refining it into a fine art. My aunt Velma made a corn *off* the cob with bacon and onions and peppers that was known to make grown people smile in their sleep for a week after they'd eaten.

Our Sunday dinners featured fried chicken to die for and the all-day eating frenzies came to a grand finale with lemon pies, spice cakes, coconut cakes, and my aunt Velma's famous fried pies. I can testify as to the fresh ingredients because I was usually involved in the creation. I specialized in cracking coconuts open for the coconut cake. Sitting out in the yard, I'd punch holes in the "eyes" of the coconut with an ice pick, drain the juice, then wack it with a hammer. Then I'd lift out the pulp with a knife and put the chunks in a bowl. I scraped my knuckles every time I grated those coconuts and to this day there are those who would swear that it was Gladys Knight's knuckle skin shavings that gave those coconut cakes their distinctive flavor!

Among my fellow entertainers, I've long been known for my ability to whip up home cooking on the road. Over the years, I've cooked for everyone from Luther Vandross to Linda Hopkins to Jamie Foxx, Tom Jones, Stevie Wonder, and B.B. King. Sammy Davis Jr. once went into a conniption because he came late for dinner one night in Las Vegas and all of my black-eyed peas had been gobbled up. I cooked the doo-doo out of those peas that night too.

Since childhood, I've enjoyed every aspect of cooking. Strange as it may seem, in the beginning the magic of singing was more elusive to me, until I matured and realized what a great gift I'd been given. Often, singing seemed more like work or a responsibility. I've struggled over the years with that feeling, but I've come to experience the true joy in my own singing.

Don't get me wrong; I have enjoyed nearly every moment *while* singing, but often I have felt torn or ambivalent about the thought of having to rehearse or perform when I really wanted to be with my playmates or my loved ones. Sometimes it takes maturity and the perspective of many years to fully appreciate God's gifts to us.

As a child, and even into adulthood, it often seemed that I was always being dragged away from play or from other things I wanted to do in order to sing for my supper. While I have always been grateful for my talent and the life it has given me, the magic of it was sometimes hard to capture under the pressure of making a living and providing for all who have depended on me.

I think this is due in part to the fact that it is not my true nature to seek the spotlight. My momma, who was not so much a stage mother as a cheerleader for my singing, would often appear out of nowhere while I was deep into play, watching television, or hiding with my brother and sister. To her credit, she didn't demand that I perform. She was more tactful than that.

"Baby," she'd say, "they are having a party in there for Uncle Ben and we were just talking about some of the things you have done. They really want to hear you sing. Could you do that for Uncle Ben?"

Usually, I preferred just to be an ordinary kid. I was shy and unlike many performers who begin their careers in childhood, I was no showbiz wannabe. I was no show-off. These command performances and the Shirley Temple curls inflicted by my momma on my dark, nappy hair were the bane of my existence back then. To get me to perform, my mother would have to coax me away from the television set or the board game or my dolls. Momma never bribed us with goodies, but she knew how to appeal to my sense of giving and morality. Bubba and my big sister Brenda would eventually tire of my mother's shadow over their activities and shout, "Just go!" before returning to their play.

While singing was not always a priority with me back then, music was as natural to our lives as dogwood and honeysuckle. One of my earliest memories is an image of the old piano in the hallway of our home at 224 Merritts Avenue in Atlanta near the Fox Theater.

Bubba and I used to bang on that piano like we were child prodigies performing at Carnegie Hall. When I was only two years old, Bubba, who is just sixteen months older, would scrunch down behind me to get leverage on my baby behind and push me up high enough to get a handhold on the piano bench. Then we would both scramble up and get to playing—a term I use loosely.

You know, no one in our family could really play that piano. But singing was sure a talent we all shared. Many nights after the dinner dishes were cleared from the table, we returned to our seats to sing in thanks and in praise of God. My parents were members of both the prestigious Wings over Jordan and Mount Moriah churches choirs. Bubba and I were in the Sunbeam Children's Choir. At the age of four, I was the youngest member and while I don't remember what it was that prompted me to sing at such a young age, I do remember that I had a finely tuned ear that was regularly offended by the choir's piano player. She was a plinker. You know, plinkety-plinkety-plinkety-plink. To this day the memory of that sound makes me crazy.

We would be up there wailing: "This little light of mine, I'm going to make it shine . . ." and Miss Williams would be plinkety-plinking away. We'd just look at each other and think, "We gotta get a better piano player!"

Later, when we formed the Youth for Christ Choir, we got a very hip new piano player named, appropriately, Margaret Ivory, whom we nicknamed Mona for her beautiful smile and saintly demeanor. That woman could *play*, let me tell you, and her talent filled us with higher expectations for our voices. I would like to think that we rose to her level.

My first recital as a soloist at the age of four was actually a paid concert to benefit the church. Pastor Smith and his family were frequent dinner guests at our house and the recital was his idea. I remember feeling a little overwhelmed by all of the planning and arrangements that went on for weeks. I couldn't believe that people would pay to hear me, but the biggest surprise was that they had asked members of the Atlanta Boys Choir to be the ushers! They were celebrities in our community. Most came from the black elite of Atlanta, which even then had a well-developed black professional class of doctors, lawyers, politicians, preachers, business leaders, and educators.

Ours was a very nurturing and supportive community in which even the less affluent parents like mine instilled their children with high expectations for their lives. Among the members of the Atlanta Boys Choir back then were Maynard Jackson, who would become the first black mayor of Atlanta, and his successor, Andrew Young, who would march beside the Reverend Dr. Martin Luther King Jr. and serve as U.S. ambassador to the United Nations. There was also a very ambitious fellow whom we came to call Hustle McMuscle because he was always telling us that we should work harder and play less, even though he wasn't much older than us. "Hustle makes muscle!" he would yell to us. His real name was Marvin Arrington, and today he is president of the Atlanta City Council, and running for mayor.

My father, Merald Woodrow Knight Sr., was one of the first African-American post office employees in the city. He was not a wealthy or prominent figure in Atlanta, but our family was typical of the city's emergent middle class. Although we lived in the Gray Street public housing projects when I was born, my father took on two side jobs, making drugstore deliveries and doing gardening and yard work, to get us into our first regular home when I was not quite four years old.

Today, Atlanta is considered a thriving center of the black professional class, but then, it was a magnet for poor African-Americans seeking to elevate their lives, raise a family, and strive for their share of the American dream. Atlanta had jobs that were rapidly disappearing in the rural South as more and more blacks were pushed out of farming and into blue-collar jobs in the city.

My daddy was born in Cordele, Georgia, a rural town about 100 miles south of Atlanta. Like many rural blacks, and whites too, he moved to Atlanta seeking the promise of a better life. His first job was as a delivery boy for a drugstore on Northeast Peachtree Street. My mother, Sarah Elizabeth Woods, who had grown up in the Atlanta suburb of College Park, worked across the street as a nurse's aide. My father first called upon my mother while accompanying a friend who was in pursuit of my mother's sister Velma, who had considerable drawing power among the young men of Atlanta. My father cut a dapper figure in his come-a-callin' suit, his crisp shirt, Windsor-knotted tie, and glossy shoes. His father, Kid, whom I never met, was said to be a full-blooded Cherokee, which accounted for my daddy's thick and wavy black hair (although his father was bald late in life). He kept his long front curls in place with a daily dab of Royal Crown pomade.

My mother's father, Bee Woods, abandoned her family when she was very young. It wasn't until I was eight or nine years old that she saw him again. Her brothers found him living in New Jersey and they brought him back to Atlanta briefly. I remember him crying and apologizing to his family for deserting them. He returned to New Jersey with the intention of moving back home to Georgia, but sadly, he died before he could rejoin his family.

My momma's mother, Susie, raised her. She died before I was born. My mother's upbringing was largely focused on services and activities within the Mount Calvary Baptist congregation in Atlanta, which was lead by the Reverend Martin Luther King Sr. Momma often told us stories of the reverend's son, Martin Jr., who would lead the fight for racial equality from a quiet struggle by individuals into a massive and undeniable national movement.

Atlanta, which was heralded as the seat of the New South, had a reputation even then for racial tolerance and understanding, though it was highly segregated in many areas. Racism did exist there, to be sure, but so did neighborhoods like ours, where black children were closely monitored by all adults in the community. We had neighbor ladies who monitored our every activity from their kitchen windows and porch stoops. If we misbehaved on a bus, there were always plenty of adults on board to straighten us out. We were expected to develop our gifts and to follow our dreams, and many of us strived to live up to those expectations.

As our family grew, we all benefitted greatly from all of the love and support our community provided. My sister, Brenda, was born on March 27, 1941. Merald Jr., who came to be called "Bubba" because I had difficulty saying "brother," was born the next year on September 4. I followed on May 28, 1944, and our youngest sibling, David, was born three years later, on August 22, 1947.

I was known as Little Gladys for a long time because I was named for my aunt Gladys, a strong and dynamic woman who lived "up north" in a cabin in the woods on the outskirts of Detroit with her husband Fred and their two big black dogs, Jet and Ebony. (Do you suppose there were any white folks with big white dogs named Time and Life back then?)

We spent every summer visiting Aunt Gladys and Uncle Fred throughout my childhood. On one visit when I was about nine years old, I established my reputation as a mischievous child. My aunt and uncle had gone to work, so Bubba and I decided to clean all of the junk off the back porch of their cabin. While undertaking that ambitious task, we came upon a box of old 78 records (an early form of the CD, for you younger readers) and instead of tossing the box into the trash pile, we began winging the records in the air like Frisbees. When Aunt Gladys came home, she was astonished to see that we had cleared the porch and thrown away all of the "junk."

"Where's the box of records?" she asked nervously.

"We took them in the woods and zoomed them," I said.

"Oh, your Uncle Fred is going to kill me," she fretted. "Those were collector's items."

In our very first exposure to the record industry, Bubba and I had managed to throw away about $100,000 worth of product. It was not a good omen.

While we were mannerly children most of the time, we also had a mischievous streak. Even in Bible class.

While attending Bible studies one Saturday at Aunt Mary Gaither's house, I felt a terrible temptation coming over me. I noticed that Aunt Mary, a heavyset woman, was spending more time seated than usual as she taught the class. Instead of staying at her blackboard to discuss the lessons she had written, she kept sitting down. Then she would return to the board, point a little more, and go back to her chair. After noting this, I began scooting my chair closer to hers every time she left it. Her niece Jackie noticed that I was up to something, but she didn't warn her aunt. When Aunt Mary called everyone up to the blackboard, I quickly moved her chair back out of its usual position and then joined the group. After she finished the lesson, we all went back to our seats. As was her practice, Aunty Mary backed into her chair, or where she thought the chair was supposed to be. Thanks to me, her chair was no longer there, and she hit the floor. Hard.

When I saw the stricken look on Aunty Mary's face, my little joke didn't seem so funny. Some of the other kids had snickered but Jackie and a few others ran to help her get up. I was too mortified at my own recklessness to move. Aunt Mary did not say anything, but I could tell that she had been hurt. Her spirit seemed to lose some of its strength.

That night, as Jackie and I sat on Aunt Mary's front porch swing, she confronted me.

"Do you know that it was really dangerous today when Aunt Mary fell, because she is pregnant?"

Tears came to my eyes.

"You know I did it?"

"Yeah, I know you did it."

I monitored Aunt Mary's pregnancy very closely in the months that followed, and I was extremely relieved when she had a healthy baby girl. That was the last of my chair-moving pranks even though I still managed to get into my share of mishaps. For reasons that only the heavens might divine, I once applied a thick coat of Vaseline to my uncle George's white dress shoes and my aunt Rose's cotton bedspread too. I was just trying to make them shine a little more.

That prank was hard to explain, but relatively harmless. On another occasion, when I was about five years old, there was an incident that very nearly took the songs out of my mouth forever.

One Sunday, my mom had just finished making a cake and Bubba and I dropped our mop-handle horses and came looking for any cake bowl and spoons in need of a licking. Momma must have left the kitchen for just a moment and though she was usually a very cautious and protective parent, this time she left a big knife in the cake bowl on the edge of the dinner table.

Bubba and I both wanted to get at the cake frosting in that bowl and we began scuffling over who was going to get the first lick in. Being bigger, he snatched the bowl away. I couldn't even reach the top of the table, but I was determined to get in on some of that bowl. I clambered up a chair and hoisted myself on the tabletop. Grabbing the knife in one hand, I lunged for the prize in Bubba's hands, but he moved it out of range.

"Fine," I said defiantly. "I don't care. I have this."

I was just about to take a lick of the cake frosting on the sharp knife when Bubba grabbed for it, shouting "No!", startling me and making me fall off the table. When I hit the floor with the knife still in my grip, it had sliced into my tongue.

My screams brought the whole household running. Bubba was terrified. Seeing the blood gushing from my mouth, my momma was certain that I had severed the tongue and cut off not only my budding singing career, but my ability to speak. As it turned out, the tongue was badly cut, but with a few painfully placed stitches, it healed right up.

I think poor Bubba still has nightmares in which Little Gladys tries to sing but she sounds like Elmer Fudd on a weeklong drunk.

Along with being the scene of at least one horrifying childhood accident, our kitchen table also was the center of our family life. When we were doing well as a family, the table was alive with our dinner-time replays of the events of the day and our plans for those days ahead of us. It was a huge table with thick sturdy legs. It served also as my dollhouse and as my shelter when I was in trouble. Momma couldn't get me out from under there. On school nights, after dinner was cleared, the tablecloth would come off and we would do our homework at that table while Momma did her mending in a nearby chair. But usually, we would sing a while first.

Daddy had a melodious baritone and he would lead us in church songs. He wasn't real enthused about us singing popular tunes of the day like "Drinking Wine Spo-Dee-O-Dee." But if it was a weekday, he would let us have our fun with our favorite tunes from the Four Fresh-men and the Hi-Los. The weekends, however, were generally reserved for the Lord's music. Then we would gather around the piano and sing gospel. Daddy would try to play along, even though he had never taken lessons.

On Sundays, of course, we took our songs into church at Mount Moriah, where each of us children was baptized at the age of five in a baptismal pool that to me looked like a miniature swimming pool. To sing in the choir, we had to be at church by ten-thirty on Sunday mornings. After the service, there were Baptist Training Union meetings in which we were schooled in the principles and traditions of our faith. Often, we had our meals at the church and took in a night service before going home. It was a very secure feeling to worship as a family. I believe our shared religious background and the principles that were instilled in us in those early years helped to nurture us through childhood and then guided us in relative safety into our adult years. When you think about all that we were exposed to as young people traveling the Chitlin' Circuit and around the wilder sides of Atlanta, it is a wonder that we survived, and, I'm proud to say, we thrived too.

My first solo recital at Mount Moriah was but one of many showcases that parents provided for their children in order to build their self-esteem. One of my mother's friends, Dorothy Alexander, whose husband was a real estate broker, made my outfits for that recital in her house, which we regarded as a mansion. Two other members of my early support team were my accompanist, Dr. Wright, and Dr. Hubert, the director of music at Morris Brown College in Atlanta. He was the first to teach me that my voice was really an instrument, if a relatively limited one. He told me I was a "contralto," which made me think I was in trouble until he explained that it described the quality, tone, and range of my voice. A contralto, he said, does not have the high range of a soprano but does have a lower range than an alto. But I made up for that then, and always, with sheer lung power. "Presentation is ninety percent of performance," my mother often told her little belter.

Dr. Hubert taught me about breath control, phrasing, and structure, as would my high school mentor, Dr. Hampton Z. Barker, choral

director at Archer High, who also strengthened my four-year-old repertoire, even adding the Latin religious classic "Ave Maria." In preparation for the recital, my mother had to teach me the correct
pronunciations to the Latin words. For two weeks, I climbed into bed
with her and Daddy each night. She would say a phrase of the song
and I would repeat it until I'd memorized the whole thing without
really understanding a bit of what it meant. Daddy snored through
most of it, as I recall, and some mornings he would awaken with me
asleep between them.

"Ave Maria" was the first selection in my first public performance in front of the village composed of my parents, Bubba, Brenda,
and our newborn baby brother, David, as well as many of my relatives—my grandmother, aunts, uncles, and cousins—friends, and
neighbors. Mount Moriah was filled with members of the church and
folks from all over Atlanta. They were my first audience, and in my
heart and mind, they are always there when I perform. I owe them so
much for their early love and support, even at a time when I was too
young to fully appreciate my own voice and all the blessings it would
bring. On that day, and in the days of my protected childhood, they
gave me a gift that far too many of our children do not have today: a
safe and supportive environment in which to grow and flourish.

Like most towns back then, Atlanta was a segregated city but we
had few direct encounters with racism that I was aware of. I never
paid any attention to whether I drank out of the "Negroes" water
fountain or the "Whites" one. My parents, who had many white
friends, didn't make race and racism much of an issue in our young
lives, preferring, I guess, to let us live as long as we could without that
burden. My mom, who is still a major part of my life and lives within
shouting distance of me in Las Vegas, tells me that when I was six I
stood pondering the signs over two water fountains that said WHITE
and COLORED and then I asked her, "Momma, what color is water?" I
never got an answer.

I'm not even sure the one incident that stands out in my memory
was a nasty racial prank, an honest mistake, or just a trick played on

children by a couple of mean-spirited men, but I definitely remember it. After school we always walked home past a sweet-smelling factory where Baby Ruths, my favorite candy bars, were made. One afternoon, as I walked home with my sister, Bubba, and a couple of neighbor kids, two white workers asked us where we were going.

"We're just going home," we said.

"Well, we got something for you," they said.

We told them that we weren't allowed to take anything from strangers. But we stopped in our tracks. After all, this was a candy factory.

One of the men went inside and returned with two boxes.

"I thought you might like to have these because we know how much kids like candy. We have so much, we were going to throw this away," he said, offering us the boxes.

That seemed reasonable enough to a bunch of candy-crazed kids. When we accepted the two boxes, Brenda announced that she was going to tell on us. "Ya'll know you aren't supposed to be taking candy," she reminded us.

When we arrived home, Momma spied the boxes and demanded to know where we had gotten them. We told her the story of the candy factory employees. Eyeing us in disapproval, she opened one of the boxes and took out a Baby Ruth. She opened it, then broke it in half. A squirmy swarm of little white worms spilled out from inside the chocolate bar.

"That's another lesson," she said calmly as she tossed our rank "gift" into the trash can.

We would learn many more in the years to come.

CHAPTER 2

$\mathcal{I}$t was shortly after my seventh birthday that my momma announced that she wanted to send in my name to be a contestant in the children's competition on *Ted Mack's*. My daddy promptly vetoed the idea.

"She don't need to be on no television show," he ruled.

Ted Mack's Original Amateur Hour was one of our favorite shows when we were growing up. It was the *Star Search* of our era and the biggest thing going, first on radio and then for twenty-two years on television. More than 10,000 "amateurs" appeared on the program and it's said that at least 500 of them became professional entertainers. It was *the* showcase. Frank Sinatra made his first television appearance on *Ted Mack's* as a member of a quartet known as the Hoboken Four. Others who were on it included Ann-Margaret, Pat Boone, the great opera singer Maria Callas, singer Jerry Vale, and comic Jack Carter.

Ted Mack's might have been all right for those folks, but my father was no fan of television or any other public display that was not church-related. He thought my voice was God's gift and that it should be used only in God's service. Singing in the church choir was his idea of the best and highest use of my talent.

Daddy had moved to the city as a young man but his beliefs and view of the world were still very much rooted in rural Georgia where he grew up. He was a soft-spoken country man suspicious of modern things, even when it came to basic household appliances. For a long time, Momma pushed him to get a real refrigerator instead of the old ice box we had. In Atlanta's hot and sticky summers, it had to be filled twice a day by the ice deliveryman. She reasoned that the money we paid for the ice to be delivered would be far better spent on a new refrigerator.

"We're fine with what we've got," my father said. "Ain't none of this food spoiling."

My momma respected that my father worked three jobs to support us, but she also had an independent streak, which I inherited, that was more than a match for Daddy's stubborness. One day while he was working, she had a refrigerator delivered and the old ice box hauled away.

As a compromise, she had not purchased a new refrigerator that my father would have to pay for outright. Instead, she'd purchased one that you had to put a quarter in every time the door was opened. At the end of each week, a guy would come and collect the quarters as our payment on the refrigerator.

As you might imagine, my father wasn't happy when he first saw the new appliance in the kitchen, but when Momma explained to him how it worked as sort of a pay-as-you-go thing, he went along with the program. It was a pattern in their relationship that Momma often did as she pleased. Daddy mostly gave in once the deed was done, but over the years Momma's independence took a toll on the relationship.

It was no surprise to anyone then when Momma went against my father's wishes and submitted my name to *Ted Mack's Original Amateur Hour*. She and her longtime friend Ann, whom we knew as

Aunt Ann, wrote and boasted that I could sing "Ave Maria" and Brahms's "Lullaby" since I was four years old. They bragged about me quite a bit and their letter must have struck a chord, because in very short order an invitation came from New York City. A producer for the show said that they were going to allow me to audition, even though there had been a lot of other children in line ahead of me. They even sent enough money for train fare for Momma and me and my brother Bubba to travel to New York.

My daddy may have been stuck in his ways, but he didn't hold a grudge. He went with us to the train station in Atlanta to see us off to New York City. As he gave me a hug good-bye, nearly making me spill my lunch in my shoe box that Momma had packed, he whispered, "I want you to do good now, you hear?" He meant it, too, and I loved him for it.

The Southern Railway took us up through the Appalachians and into the Carolinas and Virginia, past the cotton and tobacco fields of the Southeast and into the urban grit of Washington, D.C.; Philadelphia; and New York. It was along much the same route back then that black "race" music mixed with soulful gospel "church" music and flavored by a touch of country-and-western "hillbilly" rhythms was making its way north too. This new musical mix followed southern whites and blacks as they migrated, like my father had, from the farm fields toward more plentiful and higher paying jobs in the northern cities.

In the same year that I appeared on *Ted Mack's*, a gospel group called the Royal Sons became a Chitlin' Circuit R&B band called the 5 Royales. Also that year, a group previously known as the Gospel Starlighters stepped out of the choir loft and onto honky-tonk stages across the Southeast as the Fabulous Flames. The lead singer of the Flames was a young guy born in the piney woods of North Carolina and toughened in the streets of Augusta. His name was James Brown.

The appearance of one big-voiced little black girl from Georgia on *Ted Mack's Original Amateur Hour* in New York City was but one small harbinger that change was in the wind, in music and in society too. Of course, I carried none of that awareness with me at the time. I had my little shoe-box lunch filled with Momma's mouth-watering fried chicken, a bag of toys to keep me busy, and a child's open-eyed wonder at the world expanding outside the train window.

The greatest thrill for me was simply riding the train. We had never been on one before, so Bubba and I spent hours exploring every car. We'd been from the caboose to the engine and every place in between and I still could not figure out where we were going to sleep.

On that trip, we slept in our regular seats but on a return to New York a few weeks later, I was amazed when the Pullman porter led us to the sleeping coach and pulled our bed down out of the wall. I never would have guessed that a bed could go up and into the wall of a train. I got the top bunk and I know they say it's easy to sleep on a train, but I was just too excited to sleep much that trip.

After almost a day and a half on the Southern Railway, we arrived at Grand Central Station. Our little train station on Mitchell Street in Atlanta was a busy place, but it still felt like home. Grand Central Station was a whole other world. I was amazed at how none of the people hustling by would look me in the eye or bother to speak to us. They kept their eyes focused and their mouths tightly closed while they moved swiftly to their distinations. If I did manage to catch someone's eye and then spoke to them, it seemed to make them suspicious, like "What's up with that little girl?" Down south, I was used to folks being more friendly. These northern folks were cold.

Traffic, too, seemed to move at twice the speed, but somehow in the mass confusion, our cousin Bishop Crockett found us and took us to the famous Oscar Hammerstein Theater, where the auditions for *Ted Mack's Original Amateur Hour* were being held. The theater had been the home of the show since it was a radio program called the *Major Bowes Amateur Hour*. Just as the radio program became a television show, the radio theater had been converted into a television studio just a few years earlier. I loved that big old place. We used to spend a lot of time between rehearsals and shows, exploring its nooks and crannies. Today, it is known as the Ed Sullivan Theater, and it is home to the *Late Night with David Letterman* program.

Most of the other kids in the competition looked to be ten to fifteen years old. I was definitely the youngest, not to mention the darkest and the shortest. Bubba and I watched the others perform and they all seemed pretty slick, whether they were dancing, singing, juggling, or playing an instrument. I wasn't all that nervous when my turn came because I figured I'd already gotten to ride on a train to New York City and that was prize enough for me. I sang my old standby "Brahms's Lullaby" just like I'd been singing it for three years already and it seemed to go over pretty well. The producers told Momma that they were scheduling me to compete in the next show but since that was several days away, we returned to Grand Central and took the train home. I got to be very familiar with that train trip because I won the first round and then had to return to New York for two more preliminary rounds before the finals. This stretched out over a long period of time because back then, they had to wait for the viewers to send their votes in by mail. Then the votes had to be counted up.

It shouldn't surprise you that a lot of my votes came from Atlanta, Georgia. My parents weren't about to leave my fate and future as a singer up to strangers. They started a campaign to get people to vote for me. My daddy, who had temporarily put aside his misgivings about television, even handed out preaddressed postcards so people wouldn't have an excuse not to vote. He mailed them to friends to sign and put them in restaurants and businesses around Atlanta. Bubba, Brenda, and my cousins and friends took them door-to-door in the neighborhood. Our relatives in other states were doing the same thing, as were family friends and fellow gospel singers at Morris Brown College and at Mount Moriah. You can bet that the supporters of the other competitors were doing the same.

I could tell that all of this was a big deal to my parents and the other adults around me, but at the tender age of seven, I had little understanding of the significance of $2,000 and nationwide television exposure. Between the excitement of going to New York and competing, I'd simply return to being a normal kid playing with my friends and going to school. On at least one occasion, Momma had to bend over backward to get me to go back to New York. Even the train rides had become routine. She persuaded me by agreeing to take Bubba and Brenda and my little brother David along so I could play with them. More than anything else on those trips to the big city, I enjoyed being with family, and I am still the same way today.

While the idea of going to New York and being on television certainly sounded like a lot of fun, there was actually a lot of downtime between shows, and worse still, rehearsal time. There were three days of rehearsals before every show. I didn't understand the need for practice. I'd been singing for half my life (granted, that's a short span for a seven-year-old). I found it hard to concentrate or to go all out in rehearsals so it's a good thing the folks back home couldn't see me during those practice sessions. Still, Momma worried that the producers and stage crew might decide to send me packing because of my lackluster rehearsal performances, so one day she pulled me aside.

"Baby, look," she'd say gently. "I know you can do this. And I know you're going to do just fine when the time comes. But these men need to know what you can do. You've got them nervous with the way you are rehearsing. So you need to show them just one time what you can *really* do."

I got the picture.

My next time up during rehearsal, I brought down the house. Even the stage hands broke into applause.

"I was gonna do that when the time came anyway," I said under my breath as I marched off the stage.

Looking back on that time, I remember that one of my secret motivations for wanting to keep coming back to New York and the theater was a friendship that I'd developed with a group of ladies unlike any I had ever known before—or since.

They were the famous Old Gold Girls.

Old Gold cigarettes was a sponsor for *Ted Mack's Original Ama-*

teur Hour, and its commercials, like most in those days, were done live. The Old Gold Girls would come on stage and dance like the Radio City Music Hall Rockettes during the live commercial breaks. It was quite a spectacle since they were beautiful women wearing white stockings, tap shoes, and Old Gold cigarette boxes over their torsos.

I was fascinated by those women.

"Is it hot in that box?" I asked one of them one day.

That got a big laugh, so I tried another question.

"How long does it take you to put that thing on?"

Maybe it was my old soul voice, or my southern accent, but the Old Gold Girls were tickled by me. They made me an unofficial young Old Gold Girl, and even asked me out to lunch one day.

I accepted, and then decided I had better check with my momma.

"My friends are going to lunch and they want to know if I can go with them," I said.

"What friends are you talking about?" she asked.

"Why, the Old Gold girls," I replied.

Just then, the girls, minus their cigarette boxes, walked over. "We want to take little Gladys to lunch with us. We're just going to the restaurant down the street. We'll take good care of her, we promise."

How could my momma refuse?

I remember it as a grand lunch, but what I remember most was the vision I came upon on the way back, at a corner on Broadway in Times Square. There, I froze at the sight of a billboard in which a ten-foot-tall man was blowing perfectly shaped smoke rings from a cigarette.

Others may have marveled at the Empire State Building or the Statue of Liberty. The smoke rings blown by that Camel man made Manhattan a magical place for me.

Along with showing me the wonders of the Big Apple, the girls welcomed me into their dressing room before each show. Once they'd gotten ready, they would make a fuss over making me up by powdering my face and putting a little dab of lipstick on me. I'm telling you, I was feeling awful pretty when I walked out of there with my girls.

I had to return to New York for three preliminary rounds leading up to the final. Our expenses were paid each time by Mr. Mack's people, although we continued to carry our meals on the train in shoe boxes. When we were in New York, we usually stayed at the Brooklyn home of a distant relative named Bishop Crockett. He was a renowned minister there. People from all over New York City came to worship at his church.

Of course, I was less impressed with his church than I was with the candy store and soda fountain that he owned just down the street on the corner. Now, that was heaven to me. Ice cream sodas, jars packed with candies, and racks of comic books so high that I couldn't reach those on top without standing on tiptoe.

I can't remember how long exactly it took to reach the championship round of the Ted Mack competition held at Madison Square Garden. I do know I won three consecutive rounds, performing Brahms's "Lullaby" and "Because of You" in each of them. By the time I got to the $2,000 final, it was 1952 and I'd lost a front tooth and turned eight years old.

It was a big deal to appear on *Ted Mack's* because it was one of the most popular television shows on prime time, almost as big as *Bonanza*. While I regarded it as kind of a lark, some of the other kids and their parents were more serious about the whole thing. I remember one of my competitors was a little blond girl named Helen Hess. She was a violinist. She was also very intense and she refused to talk to me.

I realize now that there must certainly have been those who didn't think very much of a little black girl beating out everybody else. It helped that Mr. Ted Mack sort of adopted me. He would invite me into his office and talk to me before each show. He made it clear that I was one of his favorites. He was friendly and kind and he always made a special point of complimenting me on my singing.

He must have been in his late thirties, but he seemed ageless to me. He was always encouraging to me, as was his sideman and announcer Dennis Edwards. Each show would open with a big wheel of chance on stage spinning around and the introduction from Dennis: "Round and round she goes, where she stops, nobody knows."

I don't remember being nervous on the show, but I was in awe of the whole spectacle of it, the lights and cameras and all of the people running backstage. Not to mention the audience. When my turn came to perform, I would walk onto the stage and take a position next to Mr. Mack, just as we had auditioned. He would ask my name and where I was from and after I replied, it was time to sing.

I would step up to the microphone and just do what came naturally. The competition was at Madison Square Garden. There were nine finalists remaining. I was feeling sharp in another creation by Mrs. Alexander, a seamstress and family friend from back home. It was decorated with ivory ribbons and lace, with ribbon straps and a big satin bow in the back. Momma had also put a satin bow in my hair. I was wearing white gloves, white socks with satin and lace fringe, and white Capezio shoes that looked like ballet slippers.

I felt like a princess, even though I wasn't aware of what a big deal this show would turn out to be. Performing had come so natural to me that I took for granted that I could deliver what they wanted. The thought of winning a big prize, or any other rewards, was far from my mind. I was told to sing, so I did.

That night I sang Nat "King" Cole's "Too Young" while standing on a box because the microphone was too tall for me to reach. I was feeling a little scared up there, particularly since they had turned out all of the lights except for a spotlight on me. How remarkable it seems now to think of myself in Madison Square Garden—a first grader from a middle-class black family, singing on national television in the 1950s. Yet, then I took it as perfectly natural.

I just got up there and belted out my song. And the audience just brought down the house.

After each finalist performed, we were corralled together backstage. Still clueless as to the significance of this show, I grew antsy. I'd sung my song; I couldn't figure out why we were still hanging around. I wanted go back to Bishop Crockett's big house in Brooklyn and hang out with my family. I tried to talk with some of the other kids who were finalists. They would have none of it. They all ignored me as if I were invisible.

At last, it was announced that the votes had been tallied and that the winner was little Gladys Knight of Atlanta, Georgia. I was ushered out on stage and they presented me with a huge trophy that was taller than me. Momma came out on stage, hugged me, and tried to congratulate the other competitors. Bishop Crockett came out, too, and he was crying all over the place.

Not everyone was so delighted. Several of the other parents and some of the competitors refused to congratulate me or to even look at me. A publicity photographer for the show asked some of them to help me hold up the trophy for a picture, but they refused to do that too. The unpleasant situation was resolved when Mr. Mack himself stepped in to help me hold the trophy and he posed with me for a photograph that played in newspapers across the country.

At this point it finally began to sink in that this was a pretty big deal. Newspaper and radio photographers were all over us even after we left the auditorium. They were posted outside Bishop Crockett's house. They were at Grand Central Station to see us off. They were at the train station in Atlanta when we arrived, along with a big crowd of familiar faces yelling my name: "We're proud of you Little Gladys!"

I felt I had been successful because of them. It was like I was their representative. I never was a great one for handling all the attention, but I took it in stride. I really didn't realize that I had done anything so extraordinary. My whole focus throughout the competition was getting it over with so that Bubba and I could go to the candy store and get a vanilla milkshake.

At one point in the middle of the preliminary rounds of the Ted Mack competition, I had even refused to get out of bed to leave the house in Atlanta and go to the train station. I'd been up late that evening for a recital and I was worn out, and the thought of leaving my warm bed in the middle of the night for another long trip to New York was more than I could handle. I begged Momma to let me sleep through the night and after she and Daddy talked it over, they'd agreed to catch a train the next day instead. As I noted earlier, even as a child, I would occasionally find myself fighting to hang on to a normal life.

That is why I took the Ted Mack victory pretty much in stride, without giving much thought either to any social implications it might have. But others, with a greater frame of knowledge, understood what it represented for a black child from the South to win the competition on a nationally televised program before the dawn of the Civil Rights Movement. And they have never forgotten.

Just as I was writing this book, in fact, I was stopped in the Atlanta airport by an elderly black woman in a wheelchair. "Hello, Gladys. I voted for you when you won on *Ted Mack's*," she said. "I was so proud when you won, and I have followed you all these years." I have often been stopped by folks with similar memories and it helps me to keep in mind that while I may be up on stage alone now, there are many who have shared in the development of my career.

Upon my return from winning the Ted Mack competition, we went from the Atlanta train station straight to a tea-party reception at the home of a well-known southern deejay and community leader, Graham Jackson. Most of the other deejays around town who had urged listeners to vote for me were there as well, including Roosevelt Johnson, Pat Patrick, Zilla Mays, Zenas Sears, and Dr. Robert Scott. The local black newspaper, *The Atlanta World*, took more pictures that appeared the next day with an article entitled "Little Gladys Returns."

The head of the Atlanta NAACP chapter presented me with a lifetime membership during the reception and I was made to feel like the pride of the city. It was truly a great day and I reaped the benefits of winning that competition for a long, long time. For the two months after the victory, I joined Mr. Mack's traveling road show and performed for mostly white audiences at some of the classiest hotels in and around New York City. At one show, I overheard a man ask my mother if I was a midget.

"No, she is really just eight years old," she told him icily.

At another engagement around this time, I had returned to my momma's table after performing at a dinner banquet and a waitress came over to tell us that someone wanted to meet me. She pointed to a white man across the room. Momma was leery but since she could see the man from her chair, she let me go over. "Mind your manners," she said as I skipped off to his table.

After I said hello, the man offered me a soda, but I politely declined, remembering Momma's warnings about never taking things from strangers.

"Aw, a little soda ain't gonna hurt you," he insisted.

He then got up and went to the bar and came back with a glass. To be polite, I accepted it, thanked him, and walked back to my mother.

"You know better than that," she said, looking at the glass in my hand.

"I wasn't going to drink it. I was just being polite," I replied.

"Let me have it," said Momma, who put it to her nose and then made a face. "Just what I thought."

It wasn't ginger ale. It was pure booze.

It was my first taste of the pitfalls that can come with being in the public eye. Over the years, I've become accustomed to being asked for autographs and to being photographed with people. Most of the time, I am glad to do it. I did draw the line a few years ago, though, when I was in a restroom stall in an airport and a woman's hand appeared at my feet holding a pen and a paper.

"Would you mind autographing this?" she asked from the adjoining stall.

"When I've finished my business," I said as I stared in disbelief at the strange but well-manicured hand that had invaded my space.

CHAPTER 3

CHAPTER 3

$\mathcal{A}$ few months after I won on *Ted Mack's Original Amateur Hour*, my mother took me to Detroit, where local television executives had approached my parents with an offer for me to do my own show. My career might have veered off into television at that point, except for the fact that these guys used the worst possible approach with my hard-nosed momma.

They mistook a proud mother for a stage mother.

From the start of the meeting in a Detroit office building, the television guys kept talking about how much they would pay my parents and how much better they would make my life. It was as if they were just going to step in and take over for the poor, stereotypical black folks. They talked about the great support crew they would hire, the private tutor, the nanny, and all of the other things they would provide to make my allegedly miserable life so much better. Believe me, it did not go over.

My momma listened politely, as was her manner, and when they had finished painting their picture of her little girl as the black Gidget, she grabbed my hand, rose from the table, and made a beeline for the first train back to Atlanta.

"Thank you very much, but Gladys is not a starving child. She has a father who is quite able to take care of her and she does not need to be separated from her brothers and sisters and other loved ones," she said.

And so to my gratitude, my life returned, at least briefly, to the routine of a normal nanny-deprived childhood.

Oh, there were a few celebrity interludes during my youth, such as the night I was invited to be guest of honor at an Atlanta performance by Nat King Cole, Sarah Vaughan, and Billy Eckstein. They invited me because of my Ted Mack victory. After introducing me to the audience, they let me sit in the front row during the show and then come backstage to meet all the stars. Miss Sarah, I remember, was haughty and gruff but that was just her nature, and it didn't do a thing to dampen my admiration of her. She was thin then, and very striking with a poodle haircut. I remember she wore a red-and-white off-the-shoulder satin gown with rose buds all over it. But she didn't seem to care much for children and she waved me away. Billy Eckstein, on the other hand, was more friendly and he sure was handsome in a sharkskin suit, but it was Nat King Cole who stole my young heart. I was already singing his music then, and to me he was the epitome of sophistication and cool. He was quiet-mannered, but very attentive. He even had me come into his dressing room for a little chat.

"I hear you've been singing my songs," he said, referring to the fact that I'd sung his "Too Young" in the Ted Mack competition.

Then he told me that he had a little girl about my age, Natalie, who later would become a singer in her own right and a close friend of mine. After Mr. Cole and I talked a while in his dressing room, someone came in and said there was a man backstage to talk with him, so he took my hand and had me walk out to greet the man with him. While we were out there, a publicity photographer took our picture together and it is one of my favorites from that time in my life, a time when I was lucky enough to meet and get to know some of the performers that I most admired.

During my early grade-school days, aside from the occasional performance, or random meetings with the stars, I was able to spend a little more time being a regular child and going to school. We were living in a working-class neighborhood where many of the men, like my daddy, held two or three jobs. My momma decided that we were now old enough for her to go to work, too, and so she began doing housework for a few wealthy white families in the fancy part of town. My daddy didn't want her to work, but she brought home not only a paycheck, but also hand-me-down clothes from those families for us to wear.

Grandma Sally and Aunt Ruth moved into our new place to keep an eye on us while our parents worked. Grandma Sally took over the cooking and my father began keeping chickens in the garage for her. We used to help Grandma go into the garage and pick out dinner, although it sometimes involved a little chasing around when the selected entrée failed to recognize the honor of being chosen. I lost my taste for fried chicken after watching Grandma do the neck-snapping thing. My sister and brothers, who loved fried chicken, didn't share my misgivings about knowing supper before and after.

We were a close-knit family, focused on church, school, and music. We sang in the church choir with our cousins, schoolmates, and other kids from the neighborhood. With the move to the new house, we had switched to a new school, English Avenue Elementary, where some of the kids seemed not to like all the attention I had received after winning on Ted Mack. For no good reason, as far as I was concerned, one girl in particular, Elaine, decided that I was her enemy. It seems like women have this problem all of their lives. Nearly every woman I know has a story about being picked on by one natural-born you-know-what in childhood and adulthood too. Girlfriends, what is with the back-stabbin' girl-foes?

I'll tell you a little later about one of my celebrity sister antagonists, whose transparent manipulations probably did me more good than harm in the long run. But my childhood girl-foe was more in-your-face. She had moved to Atlanta from Chicago, and she was honed to a hard edge compared to most of the more ladylike southern girls I grew up with. Unfortunately, she was also a lot bigger than me. I suspected that she was fully capable of kicking my behind six ways to Sunday. Let me tell you, Elaine was a scary girl!

My parents had taught us the grace of turning the other cheek, but they had also instilled in us the sense to defend ourselves if it looked like a whupping was coming. Elaine and I played cat and mouse for the first few weeks of school until a showdown became inevitable.

She kept taunting me and bugging me over nothing until finally I tired of her threats. "Well, come on, then," I told her. "Let's get to it!"

The fight was set for a street corner near the school. We met there after the final bell and with a heavyweight crowd urging us on, the two of us hot-blooded girls came to blows. Elaine swung and hit me once. I nailed her with a roundhouse in return, and then it was toe-to-toe, blow for blow. She may have had a lot of size on me, but I was holding my own. This old soul still had some fight in her. We were on the ground going at it like a couple of barnyard roosters when suddenly Elaine was pulled up and off me.

The cavalry was Charlotte, another classmate whom I had be-friended. She didn't have many friends, in part due to her own rough ways. She was kind of chubby with short hair and she dressed like a boy in vests and high-top sneakers. I'd always gotten along with Charlotte, though, and she'd told me in the past that if Elaine ever messed with me she would take care of her.

She made good on her promise that day, that's for sure. Once she stepped in, Elaine decided that she had had enough fighting. She was still willing to mouth off to me, though, and we were trading words hot and heavy when Bubba finally showed up on the scene and dragged me away.

"Come on, girl, you got no business up here on the corner fighting," he said. "That ain't ladylike."

I told Momma what had happened and much to my surprise she didn't punish me. She believed in her children standing up for themselves. There was no more trouble with Elaine, who apparently had decided that I was not an easy target. In fact, like many childhood enemies, we became friends after that, and it's a good thing, too, because I soon had plenty of other things that demanded my attention.

Bubba's tenth birthday was September 4, 1952, and, as it turned out, it was also the day The Pips were born. You might say The Pips were the birthday gift that just kept on givin'.

Momma and Daddy were both working at their jobs on Bubba's birthday, and so, while he was at basketball practice, I took it upon myself to plan his surprise birthday party for that night. With the help of some of our neighborhood pals, I scraped together a few dollars in change and then we headed down to Barry's grocery store. Wanting to do this in style, we bought a big stack of bologna, three loaves of bread, and a few packs of grape Kool-Aid. Just what you need for the perfect party—ask any group of kids.

After we got back home with the party goodies, we mixed up the Kool-Aid, putting in every bit of sugar we could find in the house. Wouldn't be Kool-Aid if it wasn't good and sweet, you know. Next, we whipped up our favorite party hors d'oeuvres—bologna sandwiches cut up into little triangles. (If Martha Stewart had only seen me back then.)

My older sister Brenda, whom I'd begun calling "Bren," felt it was her responsibility to remind us that Momma had not pre-approved any aspect of what was rapidly developing into the social event of the year at the Knight house. "I'm going to tell Momma ya'll been in here making sandwiches," said our party pooper.

I figured I would face my momma's wrath later. By that point, I was deep into a birthday planning frenzy. Like a field general plotting a surprise invasion, I dispatched my troops on strategic missions. I ordered up a covert operation by sending two girlfriends to go to the playground, where Bubba was playing. Their assignment was to secretly recruit the other guys on the basketball team for the party. Not being one of those leaders who commands from an armchair, I marched down the block to borrow a record player from Garfield, a neighbor, and I invited him to come to the party along with it—a strategic mistake that would pay long-term dividends.

By the time Bubba came home from practice with all the other guys, we were ready to *get down*. We did the "surprise!" thing, then plugged Garfield's record player into the outlet in my bedroom and put it out the window so we could dance under the chinaberry tree in our backyard. I remember bopping to "Money Honey" by one of our favorite groups, Clyde McPhatter and the Drifters. After we worked up a good appetite, we broke out the bologna hors d'oeuvres and the Kool-Aid. To us it was better than caviar and champagne.

When Momma came home she wasn't upset at all, other than being a little peeved about the disappearance of all the sugar in the house. She thought it was really nice that we'd planned a party for Bubba. She even told me to call our cousins William and Eleanor Guest and some of our other friends from church and invite them over too.

The party had just gotten rolling when the music came to an abrupt halt. Garfield was insisting on playing some record that he'd brought, but nobody else wanted to hear. (No, it was not a Pat Boone song, but for the life of me I can't remember who it was). Garfield, meanwhile, insisted that since it was his record player he should be able to play whatever he wanted. "If I can't play that song, I'm taking my record player and going home," he said. Little did he know that his huffy little walkout would one day be part of music history.

Garfield and his record player were sent packin'. But that didn't stop the action. To take up the slack in the entertainment, someone suggested that we put on a talent show. I don't know where that idea came from, I swear. It was getting dark, so we moved the party inside and gave everybody ten minutes to work up an act. This crowd was up to the challenge, believe me.

Since our cousins Eleanor and William Guest and Tabby Smith were in the choir with Bubba, Bren, and me, we decided to sing together. The others opted to tell jokes, dance, recite poetry, and play the piano. When our turn came, we sang "In the Still of the Night" in harmony. We sounded so good that we voted for ourselves! Of course, everybody else voted for their own selves too. I don't even remember who won, but I do remember thinking that we sure had put out a nice sound.

After the talent show wound down, the party broke up, and soon it was just us Knights and our cousins William and Eleanor left sitting around. They were the children of my father's first cousin, whom we called Ma Margaret. William, who was then about twelve years old, was nicknamed Ba-bro or Ba-brother because he was the baby brother of Eleanor, who was then about fifteen.

As we all rehashed the wonderful party we'd given Bubba, my parents joined us and so did Ma Margaret. The adults said that we had sounded remarkably good singing together and then my momma threw out a proposal: "Would you cousins like to continue singing as a group?"

We looked at each other and nodded. It was agreed that we would start a singing group, but to make sure we didn't all succumb to temptation, we would continue to sing in the church choir too. So, every Wednesday after church choir rehearsal, we would practice as a doo-wop group similar to acts today such as Boyz II Men, only with girls too.

At first, we weren't performing anywhere; we were just getting our sound together. As word spread through our extended family, one of our older cousins, James Woods, who had some connections to the local club scene, was hog-tied by my mom into being our manager.

We had always looked up to him as a cool guy. He worked for our uncle Ben as a plasterer and we used to marvel at the transformation he would make after work each day. He would go into the house covered in plaster dust and grime but a few hours later he would emerge as the slickest, hippest dude in the neighborhood. He always had nice clothes and he drove a souped-up, two-tone Chevrolet with mufflers that rattled windows all over the neighborhood when he cruised by.

Our slick, street-smart new manager was known all over town by his nickname: Pip.

After he volunteered to help us get started, we began practicing at Pip's house, rehearsing our favorite songs on the radio, such as "Moonrise" by the 5 Royales and the Drifters' "Whatcha Gonna Do," and working on dance steps so that we weren't just up there standing stiff and boring like some DAR glee club. Pip went to work and got us our first engagement, a performance for a ladies' auxiliary club tea at the local YMCA. After that, we played everything from fish fries to fraternity parties and family reunions. If liquor was being served, Pip always made sure to get our young child behinds out before the fighting started. For several months we were a group without a name until Pip entered us in a talent show at the El Morocco Lounge in Atlanta. The first prize in the show was a two-week contract to perform at one of the hottest clubs on the Chit'lin' Circuit—the famous Royal Peacock Supper Club, where all of the top acts in jazz and rhythm and blues appeared.

This was a big deal, let me tell you, and we couldn't just go up on stage as the The Three Knights and Two Guests or The Two Guests and Three Knights, so we needed to come up with a name for our act fast. We spent an entire evening trying to decide if we wanted to be known as the Singing Wrens or the Daff-O-Dils or the Chev-Ro-Lettes, but it seemed like everything we came up with either was already taken or sounded too close to an existing group or was just too plain dumb. I don't remember who said it first, but over the course of the night, we had discussed taking on the nickname of our manager and by the end of the night, we decided that was what we would do. Neither fowl nor flower nor four-doored wonder, we would become The Pips.

It seemed like such a perfectly natural choice back then, and since Pip was so well-known in Atlanta, most folks around town understood its origins, but as we began performing across the country and over the years, it has made for some interesting conversations, particularly with white folks.

"Gladys Knight and the who? Did I hear you say you call yourself *The Pimps?*"

"Do tell me, dear, just what is a pip? Is it some sort of ethnic name?"

Well, my dictionary defines a pip as (1) *a disorder of a bird marked by formation of a scale or crust on the tongue;* (2) *one of the dots used on dice and dominoes;* (3) *a small fruit seed;* (4) *the act of breaking through a shell or egg;* (5) *a diamond worn to indicate rank in the British army;* (6) *a short high-pitched tone;* (7) *one that is extraordinary.*

I like that last one, but I have heard them all. One thing about our name, nobody ever forgot it. Except poor Dick Clark, who made a blooper highlight just on his problems with our name. From our first appearance on *American Bandstand* and to this very day, I think he knows our name in his mind, but every time he says it, it comes out "Gladys Pip & The Knights." That's okay, Dick. Call us anything and call us anytime. Just keep callin'.

The road to *American Bandstand,* for us and for many performers of our day, began at the Royal Peacock, which stood on Auburn Avenue along what was to become a legendary row of clubs that included the Zanzibar and the Poinciana. These were the clubs where all of the greats in rhythm and blues and rock and roll cut their teeth. Little Richard, Sam Cook, Jackie Wilson, Aretha Franklin, Chuck Berry, the Drifters, the Platters, the Coasters, and Bill Doggett; all of them made the rounds of these clubs where they first proved themselves and then kept coming back throughout their careers.

It was something to be only nine years old and involved such in a competition. There were no other groups in the contest that were as young as us—not even close. Even compared to Frankie Lymon and the Teenagers, who were super hot back then, we were toddlers. Most kids my age were still dreaming about being a princess or a cowboy. I was modeling myself on Ella Fitzgerald and Sarah Vaughan.

The talent show at the El Morocco made Ted Mack's look like a 4-H cooking contest. Believe me, there was some stuff going on backstage, in front of the stage, and in the parking lot out back. One of the groups in the competition was the Overalls. They were a bad-boy group that all the teenage girls swooned over. They were known for cutting school and having minor troubles with the law. We pretended we weren't scared of them, but we stayed out of their way.

Our biggest concern was the Continentals, a group of boys from Morehouse College who were led by another of our cousins, William Butts, who was about eighteen. Those dudes could wail, let me tell you, and they had musical training that we lacked!

To win the Royal Peacock gig, we had to win for three weeks straight against some incredibly tough competition. You have to figure with so many great artists living nearby in Atlanta, Macon, Memphis, and Muscle Shoals, we weren't going up against a bunch of the one-note harmonica blowers. We were in the heart of the Chitlin' Circuit and there wasn't a performer around who didn't want to make it to the Royal Peacock.

If I do say so myself, we did all right for a bunch of cousins out of the church choir. Singing "In the Still of the Night," "Canadian Sunset," and "Is It Yes, Is It No," we won the first and second weeks and we were feeling confident going into the third, but you know how the word gets out when there is a hot new group in town. All the big groups came gunning.

In the third week of competition, we ended up in a three-way tie with the Continentals and a group called Barbara and the Dellos. (Don't ask me what a dello was, I can't even find that in the dictionary.)

Since they weren't about to give all three groups the Royal Peacock contract, it was decided to hold a second round of competition on that final night. The Continentals went up first and gave it a good run, but the applause for them had definitely fallen off so that left us and the Dellos. We took the stage and laid the audience out with one of our best numbers, "Is It Yes, Is It No."

The Dellos rose to the challenge and sang a Jackie Wilson song that had folks standing on tables and pounding the ceiling. The judges ruled that we had tied again.

So, back on stage we went. This time, we really sang our booties off—"To Be Loved" by Jackie Wilson, which was a signature song for us—but it seemed to us that the audience response had dropped a bit. Maybe they were just worn out, we thought. Disappointed, the five of us went out to Pip's car with our heads hanging. We thought the Dellos would probably give another blowout and we couldn't bear to watch. Brenda and Eleanor started to cry. I was nine years old, thinking my singing career had already peaked. Washed up before the seventh grade, I thought.

But then there was a knock on the window. It was Pip, and he was beaming.

"What ya'll doing in here? They're asking for you on stage. You won!"

I'm not sure if I flew out the window of the car or just exploded through the door, but the next thing I know, we were back in the El Morocco singing a victory song. My career was saved. I still had a few good years left. This time I gave the lead to Eleanor, who sang her smash rendition of "Easy Baby."

Winning the El Morocco competition was wonderful, but claiming the prize was to be even better. This was not some quick gig in the basement of the Odd Fellows Hall, mind you. This was show business, and we felt we had to prepare ourselves for show time.

Our prize was two weeks at the Royal Peacock at the pay rate of $10 a night for two shows a night. Not a super proposition, but it was great exposure for us, and a lot of fun even though we were too young to get into some of the more adult pleasures of the Royal Peacock.

On our first night, we opened for Bill Doggett, a piano and organ player out of Philadelphia who was best known for a hot dance instrumental called "Honky-Tonk," and a blues shouter named Big Beulah Bryant. We opened that night with "Whatcha Gonna Do?" I guess the audience thought we were asking a question, because they responded by acting like they were gonna throw us out of there. Like I said, this was a tough crowd. One guy in the back of the room yelled "Look at those guys in them sissy shirts." Bubba and William, who were decked out in gold lamé, began to regret their costume selection. I noticed they started singing in a lot lower key. We were all nervous, but slowly we won the crowd over by showing them that we had the goods. More important, we won the approval of the owner of the Royal Peacock, Henry Wynn. By the end of our two-week tryout, we were in with Wynn. He made us the house group at the Royal Peacock even though we weren't old enough to get in the front door.

It's hard for me to look back at that time and comprehend how young we were. I didn't feel like a kid then. I felt like I belonged on that stage as much as anyone in the place, but I have to admit, I don't think there were many other performers who had to go out in the parking lot and do their homework by dome light inside their manager's car. Lots of times Pip would take us out to eat at Henry's Grill, the Two Spot, the Rainbow Inn, or the Varsity, a place famous for its hot dogs, and still standing today. We couldn't just roam the joint, and we didn't really want to, although the guys were more inclined to check out the audience. Oftentimes, in those early days, we would fall fast asleep in Pip's car and he would have to wake us up and give us a wet washcloth to splash water on our faces to get our sleepy-eyed selves ready to go back on stage for the last show.

Our steady gig at the Royal Peacock brought invitations to appear all over Atlanta and the Chit'lin' Circuit of the Southeast, and for the next few years we were a very happening group on the circuit, even if we also happened to be a bunch of churchgoing kids. There we were playing to packed crowds in honky-tonks and roadhouses, even though just a couple of years earlier Bubba would get upset if anyone played a blues record in our house. He thought the blues was the work of the devil. Well, we soon found ourselves in some devilish places, I can tell you that.

The Knotty Pine Nightclub was one of our regular gigs, and it served as my introduction to a unique form of artist compensation.

This Atlanta joint was one of the few in that time where black and white folks mixed in the audience. It had an "anything goes" atmosphere, and that carried over to the method in which performers were paid. At the Knotty Pine, the audience paid you by throwing money at you while you sang. In our first appearance there, we thought for a while that they were throwing things to get us offstage. When I saw it was money, I bent over to pick it up, but Pip yelled at me from backstage, "Girl, put that down." Later, he said that we were supposed to wait until the end of the performance to sweep up our earnings. It was a heck of a way to make a living, but at least we were getting paid.

Of all those early clubs we played, none was more fascinating and otherworldly to me than Ben Reid's, a legendary gay nightclub in Atlanta. I know it may seem strange that my churchgoing, God-fearing parents would allow us to enter such a dark den at so young an age, or any age for that matter, but my parents were very familiar with the entertainment business which, in general, is far more open-minded than most. They also understood that their children had their act together long before we were ever together as an act. We could go into a place like Ben Reid's and do our songs and maybe even see some strange goings-on, but that didn't mean we were going to fall to temptation. We were such a modest bunch that we girls learned to dress and undress from the top down, which meant we never showed anything to anybody whether we were sharing a dressing room with the guys or with other women. We were well-grounded and my parents knew it. We also had Pip watching over us, and he didn't want to have to answer to my momma if something happened to us.

Located on Simpson Road all the way across town from the Royal Peacock, Ben Reid's was a showplace with a mostly black clientele that was open to all types of people. It wasn't exclusively gay; straight couples came there, too, particularly late at night after other places had closed. It was known as a gay club primarily because it featured a lot of men who performed as women, and sometimes vice versa.

When we first went there to perform, we weren't really aware of just what sort of place Ben Reid's was. Pip was not the greatest for explaining certain facts of life to us. He was uneasy about explaining anything of a sexual nature to us, although believe me, Pip knew plenty. When we asked him questions about things we saw or had heard, his stock reply was "I don't know what to tell you." When it came to preparing us for Ben Reid's, the best he could do was, "This club is a little bit different; we're just going to be cool about it. You all go out and do what you usually do and they are going to love you."

Being only nine years old, I was curious about what sort of place this was. Bubba and William were just plain nervous. They knew more about Ben Reid's than we did and they had the teenage boy's fear of being guilty by association. If any of the transvestite dancers came up to Bubba or William back then and said hello, the two of them would run to the nearest exit. But there was really nothing to be afraid of. The drag queens considered us part of their family and they were always very supportive of us.

I particularly enjoyed Mary Jo, a drag queen and exotic dancer, who was one of the prettiest women I've known, even if she was a man. RuPaul is pretty and stylish, but Mary Jo was drop-dead gorgeous. That child had the prettiest skin of any human I've ever known.

The boys didn't know what to think of Mary Jo because this drag queen was so good-looking they couldn't help but stare. Then they'd get to feeling guilty and embarrassed. At first they thought they could take shelter in the company of the emcee at Ben Reid's, a handsome, dapper guy named Billy Wright. But Billy Wright was wrong too. He may not have dressed like a drag queen, but he was one of the most well-known homosexuals on the Chit'lin' Circuit. About the only giveaway that Billy was a queen in king's clothing was the mascara he wore in his mustache, a makeup trick shared by another famed show business legend, Little Richard.

I may get in trouble for putting those two men in the same book because they sure did have a great rivalry.

"Billy who?" Richard would say.

"Ain't nobody here thinking about Lil' Richard," was Billy's standard line.

I didn't choose between them, but Richard, who is originally from Macon, just south of Atlanta, has been a good friend of mine over the years. He even crowned me his "queen" once. I don't remember the exact year, but I'm sure it was in the early 1960s. We were opening for him at the Apollo Theater in Harlem and Richard had a show set up in which he was carried out on stage on a throne by a group of guys dressed up like Buckingham Palace guards, with the fur hats and all.

The king act was no fluke. Richard has always made no bones about claiming that he, not Elvis or any other, should be rightfully known as the King of Rock and Roll. I and many others agree he does have a legitimate claim to the throne. Many of the songs that he wrote or popularized, from "Tutti-Fruitti" to "Long Tall Sally," were covered by other artists, from Elvis to Jerry Lee Lewis to the Beatles, and many of them also mimicked his high-energy performing style.

On that night at the Apollo, I was backstage when Richard stopped his show and started telling the audience that he had watched my act since I was a little girl and that he, as the *real* king of rock and roll, wanted to pay tribute to my talent as the "queen of soul." To my surprise he then had his royal guards pick me up and put me on his throne on stage, where he then put a crown on my head and proclaimed me the true queen of soul "no matter what anybody else says."

Thank you, King Richard! I am honored to wear the crown.

CHAPTER 4

$\mathcal{I}$n all of the discographies and histories dealing with my musical career, which includes four Grammys and such memorable hits as "Midnight Train to Georgia" and "I Heard It through the Grapevine," I have yet to find one so comprehensive that it included the Parker House Sausage jingle.

Can you believe it? It could be because we only sang it live on radio from a restaurant booth in Detroit and never recorded it, but that jingle did lead to our very first record, which has also escaped many music historians. It was called "Whistle My Love" and it, too, came out of Detroit.

In the summer of 1955, we once again returned to the "country cabin" at the edge of Detroit owned by Aunt Gladys and Uncle Fred, who had forgiven us for turning his record collection into Frisbees. By that time, though, we had music, not mischief, to keep us occupied.

I was eleven years old, and The Pips were well on their way to becoming a nationally known live act. My momma, who was always on the lookout for ways to make us better, had also been scouting for a music mentor for us and a voice coach for me in Detroit, and as luck would have it, she found a man who was already on his way to becoming a legend in the business himself.

Maurice King was a well-known figure on the Detroit music scene because of his job as musical director at the hottest nightclub in Detroit, the Flame Show Bar. He was also holding down a similar job at the Fox Theater, but unofficially, he was known as the man to see in the Motor City if you had music on your mind. Talent agents, recording company scouts, singers, songwriters, anybody in the music industry who came to Detroit made sure they checked in with Mr. King.

Momma, who knew as many people in Detroit as she did in Atlanta, had gotten to know him through mutual friends and she immediately sensed that this was a man who could take us to a new level. My momma was way ahead of the pack in recognizing his value as a mentor. In the years to come, his successful work with us earned him a reputation as a star-maker. Mr. King would become the guru to a whole generation of Motown performers, including the Temptations and the Supremes. I consider myself a product of his teachings and I've tried in recent years to pass on to other young entertainers some of the wisdom he shared with me and many, many others.

A graduate of Tennessee State University, Mr. King had moved to Detroit in the 1940s as an arranger for "society bands" that entertained the auto industry elite in their mansions and country clubs. He also became the manager of an all-female orchestra called the International Sweethearts of Rhythm. Its members were black, white, Jewish, Chinese, Mexican, and Native American, and Mr. King had taken them around the world on a U.S. State Department tour to build up the country's image overseas at the end of World War II.

By the time we hooked up with him, Mr. King had been back in Detroit five years and he was at the center of its rapidly rising reputation as a hothouse for rhythm and blues, jazz, and anything else happening in the music industry. Drawn by good-paying jobs in the auto industry, blacks from all over the country were moving to Detroit, and many great musicians were also drawn to town. The Flame Show Bar was an all-day and all-night black-and-tan club where you could hear Ella Fitzgerald sing scat, Johnny Ray (a white guy with the sound of a black woman) sing soul, and all the jazz greats like Dizzy Gillespie, Charlie Parker, Miles Davis, and Count Basie's big band shake the rafters.

After Momma hooked us up with Mr. King, we moved from the amateur category to the professional rank as singers. He taught us the science of singing, things that street corner doo-wop singers just can't teach themselves. He worked with us four or five times a week that summer, and for many years after, honing our voices and constantly pushing us to "Do it again. Get it right!"

We could already harmonize when we hooked up with Pops, but he taught us to do it with love. It became art with him. His work did not stop there. Once we had reached the level of sophistication that he demanded, Mr. King went to bat for us and got us work around town too. Some of it was for the experience; some of it was for breakfast. He set us up with a gig singing jingles for Parker House Breakfast Sausages, which paid us to do the live commercials from a Detroit restaurant a couple times a week while a local radio station did remote broadcasts from an adjoining booth. We'd eat, sing, and then go back to eating some more. As a bunch of hungry teenage singers, we couldn't ask for anything better.

But Mr. King kept trying to find us something better anyway. He found us a song that summer called "Whistle My Love," and arranged for us to record it as a single at one of Detroit's few record companies at that time, Brunswick Records, a subsidiary of Decca. In spite of Mr. King's sponsorship and some good play on local radio, it went no-where fast. Its lack of success, and the wear and tear of so much travel and so many late nights, led to the departure of two of the original Pips, my sister Brenda, and our cousin Eleanor, who wanted to start families and finish their schooling. I wasn't even a teenager yet, and if Bubba was going to keep on singing, I was going to be there with him. He and William and I believed that we had only begun to blossom under Mr. King's training, but we definitely needed two more singers.

Although most people think of me only as a performer, I am also an avid sports fan and I have enjoyed seeing how the Chicago Bulls have had success in recent years by recruiting players who previously had given them a hard time while playing for rival teams—particularly bad boy Dennis Rodman who at one time had been a thorn in the Bulls' side while playing for the Detroit Pistons. Some sportswriters had a hard time believing that the Bulls would invite a former archrival onto their team. I've got news for them: That's how we built The Pips into a top group too!

When Eleanor and Brenda left the group, we went to the bad-boy group that had given us a real run during the El Morroco competition, the Overalls. Like all of the other groups around town, these guys had made it clear that they were out to beat The Pips. It was a healthy kind of competition because it made us better, but the Overalls were a little too big for their britches, as far as I was concerned. The member that really bugged the heck out of me was Edward Patten. All of the guys in the group were good-looking and cocky, but he was by far the biggest rooster of them all. He always wore blue sunglasses and a cream-colored cashmere coat, and it seemed like whenever they weren't performing he would be leaning against a wall with his hand in his pocket like he was posing for a clothing ad in *Ebony* or *Jet*. I could not stand him.

So, when Pip announced one day, "I asked ol' Patten to come rehearse with us sometimes," I knew exactly how Michael Jordan must have felt when he found out the Bulls had signed Dennis Rodman.

"You asked who?" I said.

"Edward Patten," he said. "He is my wife's cousin."

William and Bubba had known that, but I hadn't, and I still didn't care for him—a point that I made with Pip and both the guys. But they brought him in anyway and like the Chicago Bulls fans, I found myself liking him in spite of all the bad thoughts I'd had about him in the past. Once he got out of the Overalls and the attitude that came with them, he turned out to be a very friendly guy who fit right in.

After Edward joined the group, he helped us recruit another former rival singer, Langston George. We had some reservations about Langston because he had always been a lead singer and he had a real independent streak, but he seemed to want to be part of our group, and his voice added strength, so we became a quintet again, with me as the only female voice.

Because our first record hadn't done very well, Pip decided that we needed to get out on the road more in the summer months when we didn't have to be in school. Unfortunately, Pip concluded that he couldn't go with us. He had four children and he needed to get a full-time job to support his own family. We were hardly making enough to pay our living expenses. But through Henry Wynn, owner of the Royal Peacock, we managed to get on the Supersonic Attractions road tour, which featured a couple of Brunswick's top recording stars—and two of the most dynamic, and ultimately most tragic, figures in the history of rhythm and blues.

I was twelve years old when we joined the Supersonic Attractions tour with the wild and wicked Jackie Wilson and sexy, soulful Sam Cooke, who was ice cool to Jackie's white hot. They were the biggest stars of that era and, sadly, each of their careers was marked by violence.

Sam, who was known as a gentle soul, was shot in an L.A. hotel room in 1964 by a hotel clerk who claimed he had burst into her office searching for a woman who had fled his room. There were rumors, never substantiated, that he'd really been "hit" because of his growing popularity with white audiences.

I knew Sam only a short time and never grew close to him, but I spent many hours with Jackie. He was my teen idol as a performer and as a person who never neglected to reach out and help those coming up behind him. A former Golden Gloves champion prize-fighter, Jackie became a headliner at Detroit's Flame Show Bar, where he met Berry Gordy, who would become the founder of Motown Records. Then a struggling talent promoter and songwriter, Berry wrote Jackie's first hit record, "Reet Petite."

One of the early great soul singers, Jackie was so handsome and sexy that all he had to do was walk near the edge of the stage and women, I swear, would start fainting. I remember performing with him in a show in Philadelphia and it was one of the wildest things I'd ever seen. He would sweat through four or five outfits during a concert, unless the women ripped his clothes off before he could change them. Some cops in Louisiana once became so upset about the way white women were swooning over Jackie that they arrested the whole band, took them to jail, made them strip naked, and refused to release them until they performed their entire act that way. I'm telling you, that handsome man could sure sing!

Long before Elvis made his female fans so berserk, women were fanatical over Jackie Wilson, whose hits included "Lonely Teardrops," "To Be Loved," and "Doggin' Me Around." He could make women go rabid even when singing the Irish ballad "Danny Boy." And I do mean that women went *rabid* for Jackie. I was having a business meeting with Jackie once in his dressing room back in the early 1960s, while we were touring with him, and we were interrupted by his bodyguards knocking on the door. They had met some women who were having a fit in their britches over wanting to meet Jackie so they brought them to the room. Sitting in a corner, I watched in awe as these three women came in and practically draped themselves all over him. We tried to continue the meeting with them hanging on him, but at one point one of the women apparently decided that she was not getting enough of his attentions so she leaned down and took a big bite out of Jackie's arm! I don't know who was more shocked, Jackie or I.

Howling in pain, he jumped up from his chair with blood pouring out of his arm and all over his clothes, the furniture, and the floor. His bodyguards rushed him to the hospital, where it took a bunch of stitches to close the wound that woman had made. I liked Jackie a lot—even my momma thought he was wonderful—but neither one of us had ever considered taking a bite out of him.

Like Sam's murder, Jackie's death in 1984 was one of the saddest but most rarely told stories in show business. One of the sobering things about the entertainment industry is just how quickly a major performer can rise, fall, and then be forgotten. That is what happened to poor Jackie, who was a huge star in his day and a model for many of us who followed.

In 1960 and early 1961, Jackie had eleven records at or near the top of the charts, but then he got shot just like Sam, in a hotel room. In Jackie's case, it was a woman fan who shot him. She didn't kill him, but it took a long, long time to recover. No one gave him much of a chance to survive, but Jackie was tough. He made it back and he even had a couple more hits, including "Your Love Keeps Lifting Me Higher" in 1967. But he never completely recovered his health.

Slowly, his career faded to the point where he was singing in lounges instead of main rooms. In the fall of 1975, at the age of forty-four, he was performing in Philadelphia as part of Dick Clark's *Good Ol' Rock 'n' Roll Revue*, when he suffered a heart attack that crippled him. Sadly, Jackie was put in a nursing home, where I understand that he was not treated very well. I was one of a small group of performers who kept track of Jackie and supported him in those final years, but I admit that I kept putting off going to see him and I feel badly about that. His experience serves as a reminder to me that the joy is not in the material rewards, or the fame, but in the sharing of our songs.

This beautiful and talented guy whose fans were absolutely crazy about him died penniless and all but forgotten in 1984. Jackie, who was as popular as Michael Jackson at his peak, contributed so much to the development of our music, but then his life just wasted away. He died alone, broke, and sick in that nursing home. What happened to him is so typical of our industry. We may get a lot of accolades and recognition during our careers, but it is here today and gone tomorrow in many cases. You can be famous today, and tomorrow you are alone, sick and dying in a hotel or rest home somewhere. I've never forgotten what happened to Jackie, which is one reason that I have worked so hard to develop an act and a public image that has staying power. So many performers today are like supernovas that burn hot for a brief period but then disappear. There is a lesson in the lives of Sam Cooke and Jackie Wilson.

Joining the Supersonic Attractions tour made a big difference because it put us in the company of major stars such as Sam and Jackie, who always treated us kindly and sometimes even invited us off the bus, where the opening acts had to ride, and into their Cadillacs and Lincoln Continentals.

I know that Patti LaBelle wrote in her book of a bad experience with Jackie, after he had been drinking, backstage at the Apollo, but he was always a gentleman to me, perhaps because of my age and the presence of my protectors, The Pips. He gave me a huge boost after one performance on the tour when he invited us into his dressing room, complimented us on a great show, and then said, "And you, little lady, you are really something with that old powerful voice you got."

On another night on that memorable summer tour, we were playing the stadium in Atlanta and Jackie said he wanted us to come out like stars in our hometown, so he had his driver pick us up from our dressing rooms and chauffeur us in his Cadillac to the front of the stage in front of the audience. Just as the band rolled into our opening number, we jumped out of the Caddy and ran up on stage. We were big-time that night, thanks to Jackie's thoughtfulness.

Of course, I wasn't so big-time that I didn't still have an early bedtime. I also had a chaperone. I had always been closely guarded by my brother and all the other guys who accompanied us on the road. I didn't vip or vop without someone keeping an eye on me. If I went to the restroom, there was usually someone guarding the door. Since Bubba and the boys were older and increasingly inclined to wander off in search of adventures that were off-limits to me, old soul or not, I was assigned at one point to the care of my cousin Mildred, who was Pip's young and wild wife. As it turned out, she was more vulnerable to the temptations of show business that I was at that tender age. When she began showing up at parties that Bubba and the guys had sneaked into, it became all too clear she wasn't watching over me.

In truth, I didn't need much supervision at that age, and that is God's honest truth. Even though I was becoming a well-known entertainer, I was known as a "good girl" and I still had visions of going to college and majoring in home economics one day. Parties, pills, drinking, and drugs held no allure for me. I was more inclined to go into the kitchen and talk recipes with the cooks or the wives of the other performers. I'd been brought up to be a lady and my momma had always said if you acted that way, you would be treated that way and it was true. Even if you were acting like a lady in a den of sin like a Supersonic Attractions road-tour bus, which was my first real exposure to the wilder side of show business.

One of the acts on the tour was known less for putting on a performance than for taking off their clothes. The Spence Twins were a couple of hard-core shake dancers. I hadn't been introduced to sex yet, but even I could see that the Spence Twins weren't exactly a tumbling act. When they performed, they did the bump and grind until they'd bumped and grinded off every stitch of clothing on their twin-toned bodies. I swear!

Aboard the bus, they were every bit as down and dirty. They could outcurse any of the men. They would sit in the front of the bus with their legs sprawled across the aisle, inviting and offering taunts of the worst kind. But even as the guys traded gross insults and obscenities with the Spence Twins, they would be apologizing for their ripe language to the quiet little twelve-year-old with her face buried in a comic book. "Sorry, Gladys. Didn't mean for you to hear that."

The Spence Twins were not the only rough-and-ready riders on the Chit'lin' Circuit. It seemed like the tour-bus driver always knew which corner they'd be waiting on as we came into town to pick up groupies who wanted to hitch to a star or two for a brief ride. Often the guys in the other bands would mistreat these groupies terribly. I remember one horrible time on the road, I think it was in Alabama, when one of these girls fell asleep on the bus with her mouth open and a few musicians amused themselves by flicking cigarette ashes in her mouth.

The Pips protected me as much as they could from the coarser realities of life on the road, though sometimes, I still saw and heard things that frightened the daylights out of me and made me yearn to return to my family home and a more sheltered life.

In the late 1950s we were on the road touring with Joe Tex, one of the original soul singers who was also known as one of the first rap-style singers. Joe had invited The Pips and me to ride in his Cadillac with him and some of his band members. I'd been asleep but woke up when we pulled over along with another carload of Joe's band members. Apparently we were lost, or at least Joe or some of the guys in his band wanted to seem lost so they could ask directions from a teenage girl in a tight skirt, white top, and bobby socks whom they'd spotted walking down the street. I heard them ask her directions and from her giggling response, I could tell she was flattered by their attention. I feared what was coming and I wanted to yell *Run girl, run* . . . but she seemed to be willing prey.

"Hey, if you know where the hotel is, why don't you get in and show us the way?" came the invitation.

In a wink she was on board, sitting on the lap of one of the guys in the front seat, surrounded by a bunch of other leering fools as she giggled and laughed. *Where's your mother, girl?*

We were somewhere in the deep South, though I can't remember where exactly. Joe was a big star, so he was able to get a big two-bedroom suite at the hotel, but they wouldn't give the rest of us rooms, so we waited until he checked in and then sneaked us in to sleep on the floor. The guys took a mattress off one of the beds and put it down for me to sleep on in a corner. I was so sleepy I didn't pay much attention to Joe's band members, who were whooping it up with the girl they had picked up. I must have fallen asleep because I remember waking up in the middle of the night in the darkened room.

I could hear several of the guys in one of the bedrooms with the girl. I knew from those sounds that the party had taken a different turn.

I couldn't see Bubba and the other Pips, but I could hear them sleeping nearby and I took comfort in that. I was still frightened, although I had no reason to be. No one in this group of guys had ever treated me like anything other than a daughter or little sister. Still, I was only twelve years old, and I was seeing a side of life that I had never been exposed to before. It made me feel vulnerable in ways that I did not then understand.

I don't know who all participated that night, and I can't say that the girl was raped. She was gone in the morning and there was never another word said. I saw a lot of women like that on the road. As I got older, I would sometimes get angry at them for letting themselves be used and abused by these guys. When I was feeling particularly bold, I'd ask them what they were thinking: "Don't you have a man in your life? Why are you messin' around with these guys? They will be out of here tomorrow!" I just never did understand, but then maybe I'd seen so much by then that there was nothing magical or mysterious about road musicians, or the road, to me.

If I had stayed at home in the protective realm of our family and our neighborhood, I probably would not have felt the sting of racism until much later in life, but it, too, was part of being on the road in those days.

Often we had to go to the back door to be served food at restaurants, and most hotels and motels put out the NO ROOMS sign when we pulled into the parking lot, although I believe we may have been the first to integrate a Holiday Inn in Greensboro, South Carolina. The Pips and I were riding in our little beat-up six-passenger black Nash Rambler that we called the doodlebug, when we hit a snow blizzard, something southern roads and southern drivers are not equipped to handle. We pulled off the highway and found a Holiday Inn. In those days, black folks generally were not welcomed at such places, but maybe the night manager was a fan, or perhaps he just took pity on us in the snowstorm. He gave us the keys to a place in the back and cautioned us not to tell anybody that we'd been given a room.

Generally in those days, you could count on being turned away, even if you were just looking to use a restroom. We had just filled up the doodlebug at a gas station in North Carolina when I went into the office and asked for the restroom key. I was all of thirteen years old, but I knew no fear.

"We don't let niggers use our bathrooms," the guy said in a slow drawl.

"You mean I can spend my money in your little raggedy gas station but I can't use your bathroom?" I said defiantly.

I walked away and told the guys, but it was nothing new to them. They knew what I was going to walk into inside that gas station, but they thought it was something I needed to learn to deal with on my own. Like them, I dealt with it by developing an incredible mastery of my personal plumbing. When you grow up as the only girl in a carload of guys on the road, believe me, you learn how to hold it.

One of the early lessons we learned on racism on the road in those early days was that even the lawmen were not to be trusted. We drove in caravans for fun and sometimes for protection. In the early 1960s, we were touring in the South in a caravan of cars with Smokey Robinson and the Miracles, Jerry "Iceman" Butler, Chuck Jackson, Dee Clark, Shep and the Limelights, and a couple other groups when two policemen stopped us. "Where you niggers going?" the tallest and fattest one demanded.

The next thing I knew, we were being ordered to follow the policemen. They led us off the freeway and into the countryside for several miles deep into what looked like a forest. Finally, we pulled in front of a big, red-brick house. The cops led us all inside to a waiting room in the front hall. It didn't look like a jail, but that's sure what it was. All of the men were ordered to go down a hallway while they told the women to go back outside. I went with Smokey's wife, Claudette, one of my best friends, who was also the only female singer in her group. She and I were milling around outside wondering what the heck was going on while inside the police were making the guys give them their jewelry, watches, and wallets. Then they locked them up.

When we found out what was going on, we were beside ourselves. We were out in the middle of nowhere. Finally, Claudette went inside and used the telephone to call their manager for money to bail them out. They wired it to us in the nearest town and we drove in and got it. I think it cost $75 to get the guys out of jail, although the only crime they seemed to be charged with was the infamous DWB, driving while black.

One of the scariest road encounters with racism in those early days occurred in Little Rock, Arkansas. After playing one show for a white audience and a later show for blacks there, we somehow managed to get a room in a hotel, but if the clerk was color-blind, there were others who were not. Right after we had unpacked, the clerk brought a note to our room from the local police chief. It told us that we would not be allowed to spend the night in his town.

There was some discussion among the guys about refusing to leave, but caution prevailed over anger. We were just starting to reload the bus when several carloads of police officers pulled up. They told us we had a time limit for getting out of town, and that time was running out fast.

We made a show of walking calmly into the hotel and once we were out of their sight we ran back to the room. They followed us inside to make sure we were hurrying. We got so nervous we started throwing things out the window. The mood was turning uglier and uglier. When we brought the last of our bags down, they started yelling at us to get out of town. We hustled onto the bus and started rolling, but even then they put on the sirens of their squad cars and virtually ran us right out of Little Rock.

Years later, when the Pips and I performed at a fundraiser for then governor Bill Clinton, I gave him a playful hard time about what had happened to us that night.

"Gladys, it wasn't me; I didn't do it," he protested.

I forgave him, and a few years later, we danced together at the White House. He and I, and the country, too, had come a long way.

CHAPTER 5

$\mathcal{D}$addy was pushing away from us and I had to get him back. I was his little girl. He needed me. What could I do? What did he need? What had come over him? Why had the light left his eyes? Even I couldn't seem to bring it back.

While we were on the road performing in the late 1950s, during summer vacations from school, it seemed that my father had become another person. He had lost his prized job at the post office because of erratic behavior and because he kept having accidents in his delivery trucks. This was not the man who had always been a top-ranked worker. This was not the man who had always taken pride in everything he did. I was thirteen years old and he was changing dramatically, but we remained close.

After being fired, he briefly worked as a handyman until he got a full-time job as a busboy captain in the cafeteria of Rich's Department Store. But even that seemed too much for him. He seemed to be overwhelmed by the world and incapable of communicating his despair. Instead, he slipped away, and the fabric of our close-knit family began to come apart at the seams.

The dining room table, which had been the focal point for our family life and the scene of so much laughter and song, fell into silence and disuse as Daddy slipped away from Momma, from us, from the world.

Eventually, he moved out of the master bedroom and into the living room, where he boarded up the doors and windows to cut himself off from us and whatever was causing his inner pain. This meticulously groomed man suddenly began living and looking like a homeless hermit. He cut his own hair into a raggedy mop. He quit pressing and starching his shirts. He lived in our house, but in his own squalid cutoff room.

One day while he was at work, I pried the boards off the door to the living room that he had turned into his hermit's nest. I wanted to understand. I wanted to help. I couldn't believe what I found.

It was a mess. I went to work cleaning up, scrubbing and sweeping. Then, suddenly, there he was in the doorway, staring at me, but the merry gleam was gone. There was no anger either, only a dull glaze.

"What you doin' in here?" he asked without emotion.

"I was just cleaning up a little bit because this place is such a mess," I said meekly.

He did not respond either in anger or regret. He did not thank me or scold me. He just walked in and sat down and stared into the hole that was swallowing him up.

While the excitement of being a young entertainer was often tempered by the challenges of constant travel and the pitfalls of life on the road, the truth was that life back home in Atlanta was no longer as comforting and secure as it once had been.

In those early days, we joined road tours only in the summer months and then returned home during the school year, doing shows on weekends and the occasional week night. Our singing careers seemed to be taking off. The Pips and I were in great demand as an opening act and we were even beginning to get some calls to be the featured act in smaller clubs along the Chit'lin' Circuit. A small measure of fame was coming our way. Fortune, however, continued to lag stubbornly behind.

On the big summer tours, The Pips were paid a total of $250 per show, but our expenses came out of that and by the time it was divided up, we were lucky to keep the doodlebug doodling down the road. My parents were supportive of Bubba and me and our singing, but it was tough on them to have us coming and going all the time. We were not yet self-supporting and that, too, took a toll, particularly on my father.

We didn't know much about stress in those days, but I have to think that working three jobs without a vacation all those years contributed to my father's deterioration. It was sad, and not a little frightening, to see this proud man slide. He never really had a complete breakdown, but our closely knit, loving, churchgoing, gospel-singing home life deteriorated along with him.

Still only in the eighth grade, I dealt with it with the resilience of youth and the power of prayer. It is amazing to consider now how normal my life was in many aspects even while it was certainly extraordinary in others. I went to school, played with my friends, did my homework, flirted with boys, and lived a typical teenage existence on the one hand. Then, on the other, there was increasing recognition as a performer, summers of adventure on the road with performers who were either already legends or well on their way. And at home, always waiting, always in the back of my mind, was the tragedy of my father's slow psychological slide.

My momma suffered the most from his decline. Their marriage and partnership was but a shell. It had been breaking down since I was about nine years old. They were both strong-willed and they clashed with increasing frequency as we got older. Often they would send me out to play or to my room to do my homework when their words began to heat up, but the sound of their battles could not be contained by walls and windows.

The sounds of their raging battles remain vivid in my mind to this day. The stress of his work and his troubled marriage must have eaten Daddy up from the inside out. When I recognized what was going on, I tried to step in and put him back together. I would sneak in while he napped and take his dirty clothes and wash and iron them. Since he no longer ate with us, I'd make him meals and set them up on a little table in his room.

The rest of us took to eating in the kitchen.

Just before I graduated from the eighth grade, Daddy moved out of the house. He took a place in the University Apartments. Momma encouraged me to visit him there and at work. He welcomed us, and our relationship remained close. We laughed together; he even would take us shopping in Rich's, where he had a 20 percent employee discount. He would offer us sweets. We would sit and talk and it was pleasant, but then we would take the bus back home without him.

I think Bubba missed him more than any of us. My father's departure came at that crucial junction when Bubba was entering manhood. He resented being pushed prematurely into the position of man of the house, but Bubba is not a vengeful or resentful man, and when Daddy got him a job working in the Rich's cafeteria, they formed a new bond.

My father's decline and departure had a huge impact on the quality of our lives. For the first time in our lives, bills went unpaid. Utilities were cut off. The bank threatened to take our house. There were times when we had no food in the refrigerator and we had to go to bed hungry. It hurt my momma to be poor. She worked two jobs for a while. She made army pants for Fulton Trousers for a while before moving to the Scripto plant to make writing pens from six A.M. until three P.M. After working there each day, she would come home to sleep, cook us a meal, and then leave to work the late shift as a cook at the Rainbow Inn drive-in until four A.M.

Many nights we would go over there while she was working. The carhops would ask us to sing and while we did, they'd bring us food.

On her days off, Momma would be so tired she often just stayed in bed all day. She was wearing out too.

During the school year, we took on part-time jobs in addition to our singing to help out with expenses at home. Brenda worked at a service staion owned by Uncle Ben. Bubba, who has always been one of the hardest-working guys I've ever known, held down jobs at a grocery store, a meat market, the gas station, and the drive-in. After school, I cooked in the little restaurant owned by Uncle George and Aunt Rose. In high school, I joined a professional jazz group led by Mr. Lloyd Terry, the band director at school. We played all over the Southeast. We got jobs around town for $15 a night and I would put the money under my pillow. Some mornings, I'd wake up and it would be gone. I knew Momma was taking it and I told her all she had to do was ask for it.

Momma was prideful and I could see it was hard for her to ask for help. "We didn't have any butter. We didn't have any bread. What am I supposed to do? I'm sorry."

I didn't fuss with her about it anymore. She was too proud to ask for what she needed, what we needed. I will say, however, that my mother never pushed her babies up on stage to make money. Unlike so many sad cases today, where you see child stars and their parents in courtroom battles over paychecks, my momma never thought of the money; she only wanted us to develop our gifts to the fullest. In fact, that $2,000 prize I won on the Ted Mack show at the age of eight remained secure in a bank account with my name on it for years and years, until Momma reluctantly allowed me to withdraw part of it as a teenager to buy a dress and some shoes to perform in. The rest of the money stayed in the bank for many more years. "That is your investment for the future," Momma would tell me.

In spite of those rocky times and increasing money problems, we still loved each other and that love came through. Momma found ways to fill our bellies and our hearts. She would make us hot oatmeal milkshakes by filling a mason jar with oatmeal, milk, butter, and sugar.

Then we would gather across her bed and listen to stories from her childhood until we'd finished our shakes and fallen asleep.

We learned to live creatively, I'll say that. When the heat was off, I'd sleep in my coat. My momma was more inventive. She would heat up the iron, wrap it in a towel, and put it by our feet. If it was the water that was cut off, Bubba would go to the backyard, find the main water line, and turn it back on. Then we would fill every bucket and tub we could find. I took "bird baths" by heating up a pot of water, pouring it in the sink, and then washing myself. Brenda and I did our stockings in the sink, too, and then we hung them in front of a little heater. Sometimes they'd overheat or fall on the hot coils and fill the house with the rank scent of toasted nylon. We'd wash our panties the same way and then put them in the oven to dry. If we forgot to come back within ten or fifteen minutes, the panties would have grill marks on them. Try explaining that in gym class. "Gladys, girl, you must be smokin'."

We survived by laughing at those things that were laughable, and by praying for those that were not. Like many people we knew, we were poor in goods but rich in spirit. We didn't have the ten cents for the bus so we walked and sang as we went. We didn't have lunch money so we found other things to do over the lunch hour. Sometimes, a friend would share a meal.

High school and singing were my refuge and my salvation during those stressful times at home. While I knew we could not afford to turn down work, I wanted to be a normal teenager. School and all of the activities surrounding it did give a comforting measure of normalcy to my life. And I pursued that life with a vengeance.

You name it, I joined it at Archer High School in Atlanta. I was on the track team, the choir, the yearbook staff, and the cheerleading squad. I had a gang, too, a solid pack of friends that swallowed me up and gave me a place in that teenage world. There were ten of us, five boys and five girls, and we *ran* that high school. At least we thought we did. The teachers and even some of the other students started calling us the Big Five Boys and the Big Five Girls. We adopted that name gladly. We were the achievers, the goal-setters, the instigators of deeds both positive and mischievous. I realize now that this was one of the few times in my life that I ever felt like I was really "in" with the "in" crowd and, I have to admit, it was wonderful!

One of the guys, Jessie, was student body president and a major brain. Winston, Larry, Frank, and Elmo were the other guys. Jackie and Edith were the biggest jocks among the girls. Edith McGuire later ran track on the U.S. Olympic team. Mevelyn was the best student and Connie, who would marry Bubba, was the star dancer in the school's Goldlarama Talent Show. We were all cheerleaders. Go team!

It was a sign of my yearning to be a normal kid, I suppose, that I was willing to risk my singing voice to be a screaming, yelling, jumping-up-and-down cheerleader. Miss Stockard, the track coach and cheerleading sponsor, could not believe it when I showed up for the tryout.

"What are you doing here?"

"I wanna be a cheerleader too," I said.

Miss Stockard cared about me, so she worked out a plan that would let me cheer and sing. She put me on the half-game program. Half the game I yelled and screamed like every other bubble-headed cheerleader. The other half, I sat next to her and rested my vocal cords.

The band director at Archer High, Lloyd Terry, was also exceptionally caring toward me. He stepped into the gap that my daddy had left, and he opened my eyes to a far greater and more diverse musical world than I had imagined. It was Mr. Terry who introduced me to the sounds and songs of Ella Fitzgerald, Sarah Vaughan, Yousef Latiff, Oscar Peterson, and others.

"Take this home and listen to it, Gladys," he would say, handing me record albums from his own collection.

He also taught me how to sing jazz, and he added great numbers like "Doodlin'," "The Masquerade," and "Round Midnight" to my repertoire. Then he invited me to join his own nine-piece jazz band, which performed all over the Southeast on weekends.

Momma was leery at first. It was one thing to send me out under the protection of Bubba. It was something else to have your thirteen-year-old daughter playing late night gigs with her music teacher and a bunch of strangers. But Mr. Terry won her over too. He personally picked me up for each engagement, kept me always within his sight, and took me home. My talent flourished even more under his care. I did all right by his band too. We became the top jazz band in the city and soon I was rubbing shoulders and trading solos with many of the greats of the jazz world who came through Atlanta. We worked with Cannonball Adderly, Jimmy Smith, and Jimmy McGriff in the clubs around town. It was through my work with the after-school jazz band also that I first met Aretha Franklin.

I knew of Aretha before I met her in person because of my momma's many ties to the gospel singing community. She went to every gospel show that came to town, and she knew many of the performers, including Clara Ward and Mahalia Jackson. She also knew the Reverend C. L. Franklin, the Detroit minister and preacher who could command $4,000 for an appearance and whose thundering, steeple-shaking sermons were sold on Chess records to eager fans around the world.

Known as "the man with the million-dollar voice," Rev. C. L. Franklin was Aretha's father. Obviously, he passed his gift on to her, with interest.

I first heard of her when my momma came home from one of the reverend's appearances and told us about his little daughter coming out to sing a gospel song during the program. "Baby, that little girl sang her heart out, just like you, but she plays the piano too," my momma said as she took off her finest Sunday hat and her matching but heavily mended kid gloves.

Momma told us that Aretha's own mother, Barbara, had deserted her when she was only six years old and then had died four years later. My momma felt so sorry for her that she'd even thought about bringing Aretha home to live with us, which might have been interesting, considering the somewhat delicate nature of the relationship that she and I would have later.

I first heard her voice when Momma bought a record that Aretha and her father made together. It was a song called "Never Grow Old," and I loved her voice as well as the song, which I quicky memorized. When she moved from gospel to pop songs, I bought all of those records and memorized the songs too. I became known for my rendition of "Dr. Feelgood," which I had learned from her recording.

Although she was only two years older than me, I looked up to Aretha, and I was thrilled when Mr. Terry told me that she was coming to Atlanta to perform and that we were going to open for her. At our first rehearsal, though, I found myself scared at the thought of introducing myself. She had arrived with her sister Erma and her sister-in-law Earline and I had spotted them as they strolled into the room.

I was with my friend Connie, and I told her that I really wanted to tell Aretha how much I admired her, but I was shy and a little scared of this big-talent city girl.

"Do you want me to go with you?" said Connie.

Together, we made a cautious approach. Summoning my courage, I walked up to her and stuck out my hand, "Hi, my name is Gladys Knight . . . welcome to Atlanta."

Aretha looked at me like I had been dropped from a spaceship. Without saying a word, she turned back to the other gals and rejoined their conversation.

Over the years, our relationship hasn't warmed but a few degrees from that icy introduction. There have been times when we have hung together and talked on the telephone, but there is always a distinct chill in the air. Sometimes, it goes in the deep freeze and she simply ignores me. One year at the *Grammy Awards Show*, Bubba and I were walking down the hall to the auditorium, getting ready to go on when we met Aretha.

"Hey, Ree, how are you?" I said.

Aretha just kept on walking. Not a glance. Not a word. She could sing it and spell it, but she wasn't interested in giving *any* respect to me.

I'd told Bubba about her previous snubs and he'd thought I was exaggerating. Now he was my witness.

"See, I told you," I said to him.

He turned and called out to her.

"Hey, Ree-Ree," he yelled.

She stopped in her tracks, turned, and came back and gave Bubba a hug.

"Gladys was just speaking to you too," my brother said.

"Oh," she replied, acting as though she had just realized I was there.

I took it in stride, and to this day, I don't take Aretha's snubs seriously, even though I wish there were a way we could be closer, since we have shared so many of the same experiences.

It's always bothered me that I haven't been able to establish closer ties to Aretha because we have so much in common. I was good friends with her brother Cecil, but to this day, she and I have yet to overcome whatever lies between us.

While I have many friends among women performers, there are those, too, who find it difficult to share the spotlight. Its understandable in some ways, because it is so difficult for women, particularly black women, to succeed and to stay on top, especially in show business. Even those who make it sometimes develop a mind-set that says there is only so much to go around. But we should not get stuck on that. Someday I want to write a book on unity and power among our people in show business.

While growing up, I was lucky to have a great group of friends outside of show business, and a very active life that was not all that different from theirs. You might think that because of my singing career and my travels with the jazz band and with The Pips, that I was fairly sophisticated as a teenager but in truth, I was lagging behind most of my friends in both social and physical maturity. Compared to my girlfriends, who were rapidly blossoming into young women, I still looked like a little girl. They were getting curves in all the right places. I was so shapeless they'd tease me and call me "white girl."

Ch
Sc
O

Real Champion—Mowing down competition all over the nation, eight-year-old Gladys Maria Knight of Atlanta, Ga., came out on top, and last week was acclaimed national amateur radio champion of 1952. Gladys sang her way to the finals of the Ted Mack Original Amateur Hour radio program and won hands down in New York's Madison Square Garden. She won the $2,000 first award and a four-foot gold trophy.—Layne Photo.

Here I am with the huge trophy I won on the *Ted Mack Original Amateur Hour*. News of my win made the front page of our hometown paper, *The Atlanta Daily World*. (*Courtesy of the author.*)

My paternal grandfather, Kid Knight, was said to be a full-blooded Cherokee. (*Photo courtesy of the author.*)

My paternal grandmother, Sally Knight. I can almost hear her now saying to a neighbor kid, "Child, go clean your nose!" (*Photo courtesy of the author.*)

That's me on my daddy's lap surrounded by my older sister, Brenda, and my older brother, Bubba. (*Photo courtesy of the author.*)

Momma in a picture taken right after I won the Ted Mack competition. (*Photo courtesy of the author.*)

Bubba, David, and I standing under a peach tree at our house in Atlanta on Chestnut Street. Look at Bubba trying to be buff! (*Photo courtesy of the author.*)

Merald Woodrow "Bubba" Knight Jr., David Leon Knight, and smiling Gladys Maria Knight. (*Photo courtesy of the author.*)

A widely used publicity photo taken of me on the Ted Mack stage right
after a show when I was eight years old. (*Photo courtesy of the author.*)

My "look" as I grew a little older. This shot was taken in Birmingham, Alabama, at an early engagement by The Pips. (*Photo courtesy of the author.*)

Me in high school with Lloyd Terry's jazz band. That's my first husband, Jimmy Newman, second from the left. (*Photo by Lloyd Terry.*)

Me and my fellow classmate and singer Winston Meadows, the year we graduated from Archer High School in Atlanta and were voted Most Talented. (*Photo courtesy of the author.*)

Most Talented

Lloyd Terry's jazz band in 1960 at a gig at Atlanta's famed Royal Peacock club. That's Jimmy with the sunglasses. (*Photo by Lloyd Terry.*)

My high school choir, led by music director Hampton C. Barker (at piano), who was one of my many mentors. I'm second from the left in the third row. (*Photo courtesy of the author.*)

Another one of my many musical mentors, Lloyd Terry. He was our high school band instructor and the first person to introduce me to jazz. (*Photo courtesy of Lloyd Terry.*)

Here I am with the world at my fingertips in a photo from our high school year-book. (*Photo courtesy of the author.*)

My high school graduation picture, taken when I was sixteen. That same year The Pips signed our first record deal and Jimmy and I got married.
(*Photo courtesy of the author.*)

Here I am right after Tina Turner gave me a beauty makeover at the Howard Theater in Washington, D.C. (*Photo courtesy of the author.*)

This picture, featuring a classic pose from my "wig" days was taken at the Apollo in New York City in the early 1960s. (*Photo courtesy of the author.*)

Me at some Chit'lin' Circuit club somewhere in the 'hood in Philadelphia in 1963. (*Photo courtesy of the author.*)

Here I am holding my daughter, Kenya, and her big brother, Jimmy, during a welcome break from the road. That's my nephew Chetley and niece Valesia on the right. (*Photo courtesy of the author.*)

An early promotional photo used in the days when we were managed by Willie Mays's ex-wife, Marghuerite Mays. I'm wearing one of her dresses. (*Photo courtesy of the author.*)

Here I am decked out in full 1960s attire at the famous Twenty Grand Club in Detroit. Look at that puffy hair! (*Photo courtesy of the author.*)

Me and the guys
in the lobby of
the Apollo. (*Photo
courtesy of the
author.*)

My sister, Brenda (left), and
me on the road again. (*Photo
courtesy of the author.*)

I used to sign all my autographs back in the 1960s, "Stars belong to everyone, but I belong to you. Love, Gladys Knight." Ain't that corny! And again, look at that puff! (*Photo courtesy of the author.*)

Lord knows, to this day, I still have a reputation of being more down-to-earth than "sassy." What can I say? It's just how I was raised.

As far as my appearance, I still remember Bubba being embarrassed for me, and for himself, after I wore a leotard in front of the school assembly for a modern dance performance.

"Momma, please don't ever again let that girl be in something where she has to wear a leotard," my brother said.

Some things never change. I've been battling my weight all of my life. I've tried every kind of diet known to man and woman, and while I still try to exercise regularly and watch what I eat, I've given up on ever looking leotard-friendly.

Even back then, when I tried to look more grown-up, nature refused to cooperate. One night, Brenda offered to take me and my best friend Osalee to a real nightclub, the Railroad Club, with her and her friends. I had been to a lot of nightclubs as a performer by then, but I hadn't actually been "in" a nightclub to enjoy myself offstage. The one condition that Brenda laid down was that I had to let her make me up so that I looked old enough to get into the club. I was fourteen years old, but looked more like twelve, if that. She gave me the full maturity makeover. Bright red lipstick, liner, and press powder—the works. I put on a straight skirt, which I thought made me look older, but acting older was another thing altogether.

Once we got into the Railroad Club, I felt like a lost caboose. Osalee and I were so nervous that whenever a man came within five feet we'd start giggling and, yes, snorting. Brenda nearly walked us out when she went to the bar to order a scotch and water and we tailed along and asked for two Shirley Temples straight up—thinking, of course, that we were way cool.

"Why don't you two at least put a cigarette in your hand or something so you won't look so much like teenyboppers," barked big sister Brenda.

Osalee and I took the cigarettes as props; then we headed for the restroom. The props must have worked.

"Hey, baby. Baby, come here," a guy posed in a corner called out to us.

The male attention flipped us out so much that we dropped the cigarettes in midflight. Brenda must have regretted that she'd brought us along, particularly when word spread through the club that there was about to be a police raid in search of underage drinkers.

We panicked.

"We're not going to jail, are we?" I asked Brenda.

"Shut up and bring your butt on this way," she said. She led Osalee and me out a back door, put us in her car, and grudgingly drove us home while we giggled over our adventure in the back seat.

Momma didn't know about that little excursion because she was working. Normally, she kept me in tight rein. Like most teenagers, I resented it. On one occasion, she refused to let me go to the after-school hangout the Canteen, even though my friends had come to get me. I even sent in one of them, Mary Swain, whom my mother liked, to charm her. It didn't work.

I told my friends good-bye, and then I went to my bedroom and cried for hours. I was furious. I wanted to live a normal life and be a normal kid and do the things my friends were allowed to do. Obviously, I was mature enough to do that, as I demonstrated that night by taking a bright blue crayon and writing in huge letters "I hate my mother. I hate my mother" all over the linen bedsheet.

I am sure Momma saw it because we used to change the linens every three or four days, but for some reason, she didn't change mine. She let me sleep on them for two weeks, without saying a word.

Her strategy worked. The more I looked at my angry scrawled words on the sheet, the worse I felt about what I'd done.

In my immaturity as a teenager, I often blamed my singing career for interfering with my social life. I didn't give much thought to how many other people wished they had a gift such as mine. I was too young to fully appreciate it, and blinded by a teenager's narrow view of the world.

Often, I would rebel at the demands and responsibilities that came with the gift of song. I didn't want to rehearse every Wednesday night with The Pips. I didn't want to perform with them at every gig. I didn't want to sing every Friday, Saturday, and Sunday night with Mr. Terry's jazz band. I wanted to hang out with my friends and go dancing.

This frustration built in me until one night I did something that in retrospect seems almost sacrilegious now. I was sitting in a big stuffed chair in the hallway of our house. I was crying again because there had been yet another dance or party missed because of my "obligations."

I remember praying to God, and this is one prayer that I hope he tuned out.

Please take this voice away from me. I don't want this voice. I don't want to sing. It's getting in the way of the things I want to do. It's causing too much trouble. Please God, just take it away.

In His wisdom, I am sure God did tune me out, because from that point on, my voice seemed to grow even stronger, and slowly, so did my understanding and gratitude for His gift.

CHAPTER 6

*T*here comes a point in every life when the innocence of childhood is lost; either it slips away, or it is stripped away. The end of my innocence came abruptly and it was marked by a terrifying moment that I have rarely discussed, though it haunts me to this day.

I was fifteen years old, a sophomore in high school, and I'd come home late from a performance with Mr. Terry's jazz band at an Atlanta ballroom. I was particularly cautious that night after being dropped off in front of the house. There had been reports of a rapist preying upon our neighborhood. There had also been talk of other crimes, break-ins and vandalism, creeping into the area.

My daddy had moved out by then, but with Momma, Brenda, Bubba, and David at home, I had not felt unprotected. Not that I wasn't still my scaredy-cat self. I've always been afraid of the dark, and even today if I find myself entering a blackened hallway, I'll either find another route or bolt through it at a dead sprint, which is a good description for the sort of sprint I do.

As I came into the house, Brenda was on the small bed watching

TV and Bubba and David were asleep in the back bedroom with Bubba's friend Robert Fanning, who was staying over. Momma was still at work. I was tempted to curl up in the room and watch the movie with Brenda but I was tired. Brenda wanted to keep watching, so I went to our room on my own. Exhausted, I undressed and put on a long-sleeve flannel nightgown, jumped into bed, and burrowed under the covers after switching off the table lamp. I'd learned to do that at Brenda's insistence, since I generally liked to sleep with the lights on but it drove her crazy.

I took comfort in the fact that there was still some light leaking into our room from a light in the hallway before I turned on my stomach and fell asleep in my bed next to the wall.

It seemed like I had been asleep only a short time, when I snapped awake. My feet were freezing! Why were they so cold? I started to roll over to get up, but when I tried I could not move. There was something on my back, a dead weight.

Someone was on top of me!

My mind was jolted from sleepiness to a wild panic. Was it Brenda's boyfriend, Burt, whom I called Black Boy, playing a trick on me? He was like another brother, always teasing and wrestling with me. It must be. "Okay, Black Boy, you've gone too far . . ." I said, praying that it was him.

A rough hand hit me in the mouth and clamped down over it. "Don't scream," said a chilling voice.

This was not Burt.

I have no recollection at all of how I came to be turned over on my back, suddenly looking up into the hungry eyes of a dark-skinned stranger. I saw him, yet I didn't see him.

"Are you going to scream?" he taunted.

My mouth was still compressed under his hand. I could feel my teeth against my lips. The taste of blood heightened my panic.

He kept asking that question. I shook my head no.

I could not get my thoughts collected. I was terrified, yet I was in such a familiar setting: my own bed, my own room, my own house, my brothers and sister just a few steps away. My brain was racing beyond thought. My heart pounded against my chest.

Then another question came: "You gonna fight, or you gonna give it up?"

I felt him tearing at the sheets that were wrapped around me like a death cloak, pinning my arms and legs. "You gonna scream? You gonna fight? You gonna give it up?"

He tore at the covers, and I felt one side come loose. He was at my gown, trying to lift it up. "Give it up. C'mon, give it up."

The adrenaline finally hit my brain, clearing it, and the message went out: Kick. KICK!

I jammed my knee up into his groin with all the leverage I could get off the mattress. It was enough. The air went out of his lungs, he doubled over on top of me, his hand slipped off my mouth, and I screamed with all of the lung power I could summon.

"BUBBA! BUBBA! HELP ME! HELP!"

My attacker shot back up and punched me with a rocklike fist smack in the nose. I snapped.

I went wild, kicking and clawing and biting and scratching. Through the rage, I sensed Brenda's presence in the doorway.

"DON'T COME IN! GET BUBBA!"

I feared that my attacker might have a knife or a gun. Brenda was pregnant. I didn't want him to hurt her too.

She let loose screaming, "BUBBA! A man has Gladys!"

Her cries forced the attacker to pull back. He turned and looked at her, then at me. His predator's mind was at work, calculating the risks, the odds, the ways this might unfold.

When he turned back to me, I got my first clear look at him but my memory is only of a long and dark face that I did not recognize. His eyes were in the shadows.

Suddenly, he sprang off me just as Bubba and Robert ran in. Before they could get to him, he dived out my bedroom window, which he had jimmied open.

The guys leapt out after him and gave chase, but lost sight of him after a few blocks.

Bubba called Momma at work and drove to get her while the others tended to me. By the time they got home, I was no longer sobbing, but I could not control the shakes that had set in. They all comforted me and held me and helped me see that I had been blessed to escape with nothing more than a swollen lip.

Four days later, Bubba was bringing Momma home from work when they saw a figure hiding behind our honeysuckle tree in the front yard. When they walked toward the tree, a man jumped out from behind it and ran. Bubba said it looked like the same guy who had attacked me. About a week later, Brenda's best friend, who lived just down the street, was raped in her bed. This time, the man had a knife.

As far as I know, the police never caught that criminal. I carried a mistrust of other men in general for a long time. I was jumpy if anyone entered my room and I demanded that even Momma knock before coming in. I still sleep with a light on and I double check every window and door lock each and every night. But eventually, I realized that I couldn't live in fear and so I learned to put my faith in God and in something I learned about myself that night as a fifteen-year-old. My time had come to cross over from innocence and it had come at the rough hand of a dark-skinned intruder whose words still come to me in troubled times and in sleepless nights: *"You gonna fight or give it up?"*

That night, I fought, and God willing, I will never have to face a situation like that again because you never know how to respond.

My recovery from the emotional trauma of that night was surprisingly swift, at least on the surface. One major contributing factor was the fact that by then I had a boyfriend, and when he learned of what had happened, he did not run or blame me as some men do in the face of this sort of thing.

Instead, my Jimmy leaned down and kissed me sweetly right on my swelled-up lips. Such a charmer. The next morning, he took me out on the porch and sat with me for the longest time, just talking softly, keeping me company, holding my hand, and making me feel safe and secure. He was so gentle that day, and I loved him for it.

Jimmy was three years older than I and he played the saxophone in Mr. Terry's jazz band. He drove a pink Ford with glass-pack mufflers that rattled the windows when he cruised by our house, which he did a lot since he lived just around the corner. I'd had a crush on him for years and I was not alone. He had a butterscotch complexion, wavy hair, and a gorgeous smile. Did I mention that he was a sax player with a hot pink car too?

When we first moved into the neighborhood, I got to know Jimmy's mother, Miss Bobbie, who died a few years later. She had followed my singing since the Ted Mack days and whenever I walked by she would wave me to come up on the porch steps. "Hey, girl, what have you been up to lately? Come on up here and tell me."

Sometimes her daughter Pat, who was older than Jimmy, would sit with us too. She was a beauty with a reputation for being a little wild. She was always running off to New York and other places, where it was said she'd gotten into trouble. She always had great stories to tell of her adventures.

At first, I was too young to see Jimmy as anything other than a nice guy who was about my brother's age, but it wasn't long before I joined the other neighborhood girls in his thrall. It was quite a bonus when I discovered that he was in Mr. Terry's jazz band too. We began spending a lot of time together then. The music became our first bond. Jimmy played alto sax and today Kenny G gets Grammys for doing things with that horn that Jimmy had mastered way back then. He could play that sax. He was ahead of his time with his sound. His goal was to study music at Florida A&M University and then to become a professional musician.

We were very formal with each other when I first joined the band. Most of the other members were older and we wanted to maintain a serious decorum. We were drawn together, though, by our ages and our common interests. After a while, it seemed silly for Mr. Terry to drive all the way across town to pick me up and then take me home after rehearsals and performances. Jimmy lived so close. We talked to Mr. Terry about it and he had to agree, but he wanted to live up to his promise so he and I talked to Momma and she agreed to let Jimmy drive me instead.

He had girlfriends, though, and for quite a while, I was just the girl down the block and one in the band. But when his mother died from a heart attack, he lost the one person who most shared his dreams and believed in him the most and soon we began spending more and more time together.

Miss Bobbie had always told him that he could do whatever he put his mind to. His father was an alcoholic and Jimmy could not stand to watch him slowly kill himself. His sister also had self-destructive tendencies. He did have a very supportive grandmother, but her age kept her from stepping in to fill the role that his mother had occupied.

The more we were together, the more he began to confide in me. He was a gentle soul who felt things deeply. I listened, even when he wanted to tell me about his troubles with other girls. He'd gotten a girlfriend pregnant, a majorette at school who was very popular, but quiet and naive like me. Jimmy had loved her and she loved him, but he was torn about marrying her because of his dream of going to college for his music degree. I told him he should have thought about that before he got the girl pregnant.

We were straight with each other, and he did decide to marry the girl even though Mr. Terry advised him against it. I was torn, too, since by that time I had feelings beyond friendship for him, but for reasons that I don't know, the marriage never took place. The child was born and his mom named him Jimmy, which was appropriate since he looked as though his father had spit him out. He was a beautiful child—and to this day I consider him my son too. Ironically, he's a singer. Jimmy helped support them financially, but they never lived together.

Our relationship grew into love gradually. I remember a night after a performance when instead of just dropping me off, he came up on the porch to talk and he just reached out and held my hand. Then on another night, on that same porch under similar circumstances, he kissed me; for what, I don't remember. Soon, he was coming by not to take me anywhere but just to talk. Instead of driving by and waving, he began to stop every time. One day I found myself listening for the sound of his car and I knew I was hooked. And soon, he was hooked too.

By the time we started dating, he was into his senior year and I was fearful of letting him know how much I loved him because I was sure he would meet a girl in college and forget all about me back in high school. But it was impossible to hide my feelings. One night, Jimmy and I went on a double date with my friend Mary Swain and her boyfriend Willie. We went to the drive-in to eat and then Willie drove us to a wooded area that was just starting to be developed for housing. Willie and Mary grabbed a blanket and went for a walk. Jimmy and I stayed in the car. He put his arm around me and pulled me close and we began smooching. I felt his hand moving up my thigh and under my skirt and I pushed him away.

It was widely known at Archer High School that Gladys Knight was determined to be the last virgin in the Greater Atlanta Metropolitan Area. My Momma has done her job well in teaching that I should save myself for the man I intended to marry. "If you carry yourself like you know what's right, you shouldn't have a problem," she'd said many, many times.

Then again, there was also The Word as expressed more colorfully by my uncle Clarence: "If you goin', go first class or not at all. Never lay down with anyone you wouldn't marry."

Sex was not a major goal to me then. I'd hear my girlfriends discussing their escapades and it just didn't do much for me. "What's the big deal?" I'd ask. They'd look at me, shake their heads, and warn me that one day my hormones would kick in too.

Something was definitely kicking in the car with Jimmy. He was not giving up his gentle groping, and The Word as expressed by Momma and Uncle Clarence was coming to me in a new light.

But this is the man I want to marry.

Momma never knew how serious we were getting—at least she never let on or interfered. Jimmy was my first love, and in a sense, my purest love. We had known each other since elementary school and there was never any thought in my mind that he had been attracted to me because I was a celebrity. He knew me just as Little Gladys Knight from the neighborhood, and he loved me for who I truly was.

We shared so much, our backgrounds and our love of music in particular. We believed in each other's dreams and so when Jimmy was admitted to Florida A&M's music program, I was happy for him, and sad, too, because that meant he would be moving far away. I wasn't worried about our relationship, though. We had already talked about marrying after he finished school or sooner if the timing seemed right.

It has been true of nearly all of my relationships that I have had to spend a great deal of time away from the people I love. In this case it was Jimmy's going off to college, in others it was the demands of different careers. I believe that loneliness is not a matter of being away from your loved ones. It is a matter of not feeling loved. I've been lonely when surrounded by people if I didn't feel loved. I wasn't really lonely when Jimmy left. I certainly missed him. But I knew that he loved me, so that joy filled my heart.

It was Jimmy who had a hard time being apart. He called me every day. "I miss you," he'd say sadly, over and over again.

He was having trouble fitting in and making friends at college. Part of the problem was that Jimmy had already worked a lot as a professional musician and he was impatient with class work on music theory. He wanted to play. And he wanted to be with me, I was glad to hear. I tried to encourage him to stick with it because he had worked so hard to get the grades that it took to get into the program at A&M, which had one of the finest band and music departments in the country.

He tried for a while, but after only the first semester, he left A&M and transferred to Clark University in Atlanta. I was glad to have him home again, but I soon discovered that one of his problems at A&M had nothing to do with loneliness or frustration. He had begun smoking pot so much that it was interfering with his studies.

We had both been exposed to marijuana through our contact with other musicians. Jimmy had gotten into it through some of the guys in Mr. Terry's band. I remember the night he first tried it. I never went out roaming with the guys during intermission. I stayed near the bandstand, drinking a soda and talking to people in the audience or to friends. Jimmy wanted to be one of the guys so he joined them in the parking lot. He wasn't with them when they came back in. "Where's Jimmy?" I asked. The other members of the band started laughing. In a few minutes, he sauntered in. His eyes were bright and droopy. I knew that look.

I had seen it a lot on the tour bus. The first time I smelled the sweet, sharp scent of marijuana smoke, I jumped up and announced that we had to pull over because it smelled like something was burning, some rags or something.

Once again, Bubba was embarrassed by his baby sister. "Sit down and shut up," he said, grabbing me as the others on the bus had a good laugh. "Just put your head out the window and you won't smell a thing."

I learned to hold my tongue on the bus after that, although neither Bubba nor I approved of smoking pot. I didn't hold my tongue that night when Jimmy first tried it.

"You know better than that," I said.

"I know what I'm doing; it's okay," he replied.

"No, you don't. And I'm not going to sit here and see you do that to yourself."

It was our first fight over his drug use. It would not be the last. I loved Jimmy, but he couldn't find comfort and joy in the music the way that I could. He came to rely on other means.

CHAPTER 7

*W*hen Jimmy had gone off to college, I began my senior year in high school. I was only sixteen because I had started my schooling a year early. I had jumped right into life and into school. The Pips, who were all older than me, used to kid that it seemed like I was going to be in school forever. They were anxious to tour year-round, but I had other plans. I wanted to go to college, too, and once I hooked up with Jimmy, I thought I would get married right after college graduation. My dreams weren't of gold records or Grammys. I wanted a house and a family. The whole white-picket-fence package.

As it turned out, my sixteenth year was packed full of surprises, and my dreams of getting a college degree were not to be fulfilled.

Along with playing in Mr. Terry's jazz band, I was still singing around town on weekends with The Pips during the school year. It was a busy and incredible year in my life in many, many ways. On some nights, we would play two sets at two different clubs, running back and forth between them all night long.

One night, after we finished the second show at the Builders

Club, a popular dance joint where I had appeared with both The Pips and the jazz band, the house bandleader, Cleveland Lyons, asked me and the guys if we would hang around for a while. His friend Fats Hunter, the club owner, had purchased some new recording equipment and he wanted to try it out. Cleveland asked if we had any original material that we'd like Fats to put on tape. We jumped at the chance, since we had been working on some new songs, including one we really liked called "Every Beat of My Heart," which was written by Johnny Otis, a Detroit bandleader and renowned talent scout.

That night in the Builders Club, we ran through the song a couple times with the house band and then Fats laid it down on his new recorder. We thought we had something pretty special on that tape, and I guess Fats did too. We left that night and didn't think about the recording for a while because we had so much else going on. But a couple of weeks later, I was walking through the halls at school and people kept stopping me to say how much they liked our record.

"What record?" I asked.

"The one on the radio, 'Every Beat of My Heart.' "

I couldn't wait for school to get out so I could get myself to a radio. I didn't have to go home. Bubba picked me up after school and we heard it was blasting from the loudspeakers outside a record shop as we drove past on the way home. We parked and ran into the record shop and called Momma from there.

"Momma, you aren't going to believe this. They have our record here. It's playing on the radio."

"How could that be?" she asked.

It didn't take long to trace the mystery to one fat hustler named Fats Hunter. After recording our song at the Builders Club, he had recorded it as a record for his label called HunTom. It didn't seem to matter to Fats that he didn't have a contract with us to do that. He had no conscience, and he proved it when he took his thievery a step further. When he found out we were hot on his trail, Fats sold the master to a bigger record company, Vee Jay Records in Chicago, a major label.

Being scammed was nothing new to us. We had been ripped off

on the road by promoters plenty of times. In fact, not long before Fats weighed in, we had had a promoter in Paducah, Kentucky, refuse to pay us after we had done two sold-out shows for him. "We didn't do too good at the gate; I don't have anything to give you," he said. I was in charge of collecting the money on that trip, and this guy was making me look bad.

"Do you think we're blind and crazy?" I said. "We just did two sold-out shows! We want our money."

Then things got really ugly.

The promoter, a big black guy with the look of a street brawler, pulled a handgun out of a drawer and slammed it down on his desk.

"I said, I don't have no money for you," he said.

I went out to the car and talked to the guys, who wanted to rip the promoter apart at first, but the fact that there was a gun on the table made us all decide that we were a long way from home and we had better be getting back on the road. So, in as dignified a manner as possible, we turned tail and got out of pistol range.

We had learned early that rip-offs were inevitable in the music business. Fats, however, was the first to burn us in the record business. Rest assured there would be others.

Vee Jay sold the heck out of that record and it made the R&B Top Ten, but we never saw a penny from their revenues, so when the company folded a few years later, we weren't among the mourners. There seemed to be justice, too, in the fact that while Vee Jay had managed to become the first U.S. record company to sign the Beatles, a bigger company, Capitol, pounced in and took them away. Served them right.

We didn't make any money off Vee Jay's bootlegged record, but it did get our name out there to an even greater audience, including a talent scout for Fury Records in New York, Marshall Seahorn, who just happened to be passing through Atlanta. Marshall wanted to meet us so he contacted Zenas "Daddy" Sears, a powerful radio deejay in the South who was a big fan of ours. There were many deejays over the years who helped our careers. The Magnificent Montague in New

York, Jocko Henderson in New York and Philadelphia, and all the Poppa Stoppas, Hound Dogs, Moon Dogs, Woo-Woos, and Dr. Jives around the country were great supporters and benefactors.

In our hometown, Jack "The Rapper" Gibson had been a fan from the get-go. He even helped raise money to pay my family's travel expenses during the Ted Mack competition and he also hosted some of our shows at the Apollo. Pat "Alley Pat" Patrick was another big booster and so was one of the few early female rock-and-roll deejays, Zilla Mays, who was known as the dream girl at WAOK in Atlanta.

Zenas, though, stands out the most in my memory, in part because he was anything but your typical R&B deejay. Once described by his own son as looking more like a "lost paleontologist" than a rhythm-and-blues radio deejay, Zenas was a bookish white guy who had once been part of a television and radio comedy team. He learned about black music while working as an armed-services radio announcer in Burma during WWII. Since 85 percent of the troops there were black, he made an effort to find records that they liked. After the war, Zenas became a connoisseur of "race music" and a promoter of black culture through his radio stations. He boosted the careers of Little Richard, Ray Charles, Jerry "Iceman" Butler, and a lot of other black artists by playing their music on WGST in Atlanta and hooking new artists up with record companies. Aretha Franklin was one of the few performers who had a problem with Zenas—at least real early in her career. He was hosting one of her father's big gospel shows and Zenas introduced all of the performers except Aretha, who was then only five years old. She retaliated by walking onstage and kicking him in the shins, then walking off. With that reminder, the deejay did introduce little Aretha, who came out, took a bow, kicked him again, and left.

Zenas also took a lot of shots from racists who hated the growing popularity of black music among white teenagers. In the early 1960s when many white-owned stations refused to promote rhythm and blues, his advocacy was so strong that the Ku Klux Klan burned a cross in front of his radio station in the early 1960s.

When Marshall Seahorn called and said he wanted to recommend The Pips to Fury Records in New York, Zenas called my mother and hooked them up. Momma was wary of big-city recording-industry people by then but she agreed to see Marshall on Zenas's recommendation. It burned her more than us that our song was all over the radio and everyone but us was cashing in. Marshall charmed her. He was the biggest white man I had ever seen up to that point in my life, and he wore a big white cowboy hat that made him look even bigger. He smoked huge cigars and was as country as they come. This record man was so obviously good-hearted that instead of throwing him out, Momma invited him in for dinner. You had to be some special person to be allowed to put your feet under her table. Momma negotiated with Marshall over one of her famous country dinners and this time, we were going to have a contract.

There was one minor holdup. I had a track meet to prepare for.

I was definitely more committed to track practice than to band rehearsals in those days. You didn't mess with me once I got out there and went to work. Especially since my best event was the javelin toss. Stand back, Jack.

When Bubba and the guys came driving up to the practice field honking the car horn I ignored them. This was one of the biggest meets of the year. Finally, they got out of the car and walked up to the chain-link fence surrounding the field and started yelling so loud I thought those pickle heads were going to get me in trouble with the coach.

"Gladys, c'mon girl, we got to go to New York City. We've got a record contract! We've got to leave tonight!"

"I'm not going to New York. I'm going to Fort Valley for our meet," I said back, without taking my eyes off my javelin target.

"Momma said you better bring your butt home because we are supposed to leave in a few hours," Bubba said, invoking higher authority.

I ran and told the track coach, hoping she would overrule Momma, but she obviously recognized the importance of this deal more than I did. Either that, or her assessment of my javelin-tossing skills was something less than mine.

"Of course you have to go," she said.

So off I went to New York and our first real record instead of Fort Valley and the Javelin Tossing Hall of Fame. Fate is something, isn't it?

I was so sleepy after going home and packing and rushing to the airport that I fell asleep as soon as the plane took off. Later, the guys told me that I had managed to sleep through what may very well have been the worst plane trip of our lives. A short time after takeoff, the plane hit turbulence and it dropped nearly 100 feet, scaring the you-know-what out of The Pips and Momma while I kept right on dreaming. I think my subconscious must have registered the turbulence, though, because from that day on I have been a fanatic about checking weather and flying conditions before getting on a plane. I think I have a more demanding preflight systems check than any pilot out there. When people ask me about the weather, I give them a full report, believe me: barometric pressure, cold fronts, warm fronts. You name it, I've got it on my weather maps.

Bobby Robinson, the head of Fury Records, met us at the airport in New York with his partner Fats Lewis. They had two cars and Bobby wanted me to ride with him in his two-seater sports car. Momma, who was still getting over her near-death experience in the plane, was having none of that. Bobby was a too-cool-for-school little guy from New York City who was dressed to the nines. He had processed hair and long fingernails. Momma had liked his man in Atlanta, but her shyster alarms were going off all over the place on Bobby.

When he explained that we had to take two cars, Momma gave in a little and said I could ride with him but she laid down the law: "I need to know where we're going. I need to know what we're doing. I need to know."

Once she had laid down her need-to-know list, we formed a caravan into town. Bobby Robinson lived up to his word and behaved like a perfect gentleman.

We checked into the Theresa Hotel in Harlem, right across the street from the Apollo Theater. At the time, it was where all the famous performers stayed when they played the Apollo, but it was a bit of a dump. My country bumpkin brother and cousins, Bubba and little David, nearly fell over backward craning their necks to check out the tall buildings in the Big Apple. They walked down the street back-to-back because our cousin William had told them, "People up here just come and jump you from behind. So you cover my back, man, and I'll cover yours."

They acted like rubes who didn't know their behinds from a hole in the ground. We may not have been city slick, but by the time we left town, we had a record deal with Fury, and a plan to come back in a few weeks to cut our first record on that label.

We had to return to New York immediately after my graduation ceremonies at Archer High School. Fury wanted us to cut a new version of "Every Beat of My Heart" for them. They had reserved studio time for the wee hours of the morning on the day after my graduation and senior prom. So, needless to say, by the time we arrived at the studio, I could barely cut walking and breathing at the same time. As I mentioned earlier, my sixteenth year was a major one. All sorts of firsts occurred: my first record, my first song on the charts, my first romance, and my first hangover, which was one first I really could have done without.

High school graduation marked a rite of passage and we also had our senior prom the same night, so there were parties going on all over the city. I had really enjoyed high school and I decided that I was really going to enjoy my graduation and prom night too. I was determined to hit every party and every nightclub. I really hadn't planned on hitting the wall, but I did that too.

Jimmy picked me up after the graduation ceremony to take me to the prom. We danced and partied there for a few hours before he asked if we wanted to go to some clubs around town. On graduation and prom night, club managers turned the other way to let underage people see a little of what the future held for them in the way of entertainment. Although I didn't normally drink at all, I did have a couple glasses of brandy along the way to celebrate the big night. I was feeling special. We had been club hopping for a while when Jimmy said he wanted to stop by a little party at the house of Johnnie Lee, the drummer for Mr. Terry's band. I was worried about staying out much later since we were flying to New York on the red-eye that night to cut our first record for Fury, but Jimmy said he would get me home on time.

The little party at our drummer's house turned out to be a big surprise party for me. All the guys in the band were there with their wives and girlfriends. "You're finally a big girl now, so you can have a drink with us," they said.

The next thing this no-drinkin' fool of a big girl knew, she was chasing brandy with glasses of champagne. I cried at all the nice things they said about me, and hugged everybody and laughed and drank some more of that sweet-tasting champagne. I remember Jimmy being the responsible boyfriend and telling me we had to go, even though I was fighting him to stay. I was having a real good time by then.

Somehow or other, he managed to get me into the car and we headed for home, but I requested a sudden stop en route. I was so sick, I had to barf on the side of the road. Jimmy thought it was hilarious. "Girl, you can't hold your liquor."

I was sick, but I was starving too. My diet had been strictly a liquid one all that night. I was hoping that if I ate something, the red-eye flight to New York would not be as unbearable as I was imagining it would be.

When we pulled up to our house, I could see all the lights were on and Momma and Bubba and all the others were running around in a frenzy of packing and preparing to go to the airport for our midnight flight. I stumbled into the house and immediately caught the odor of freshly cooked collard greens. My momma and grandma had made up a batch that they said was the best they'd ever cooked.

"I made you up a plate, child, but there is no time now, so I'll wrap it up and you can eat it on the plane," said Momma.

I really thought it would be better if I just ate it up right then and there, so when she left the kitchen, I gobbled up the entire plate load. After that feast, there was not even enough time to change, so I wore my fancy lavender graduation and prom dress onto the plane. The plane took off, and, let me tell you, so did those collard greens. I fought and fought and fought with my mutinous digestive system, but somewhere over Arkansas, I had to bolt to the restroom. I got a standing ovation from the cast and crew upon my return.

In spite of my bleary eyes and pounding headache, we made it to the New York studio on time to work with Bobby on a new recording of "Every Beat of My Heart" for Fury. This one had an organ accompaniment instead of the piano backup on the Vee Jay version, but he wanted to make certain that people would know the difference. Since I was the featured lead singer on the song, Robinson suggested that we use the name "Gladys Knight & The Pips" on the label. We agreed and the group's new name must have been a good omen because the new record was very well received.

That was back in 1961, and we made music history that year when both versions of that beautiful slow ballad made it to the charts, landing as number two and number three at the same time. That had never been done before and it got us a lot of attention. It didn't get us any additional money, though. Bobby claimed that they had put out so much money to record and promote the record that there was nothing left to pay us.

He was turning out to be a real gem of a guy. A few months after we signed with Fury, he set up a meeting for us with a talent management company in New York. For some reason, I decided not to go into the meeting. Instead I sat in the waiting room while Bubba and the other guys went in to talk business. As I waited, I began to hear a lot of shouting and screaming coming from inside the room where they were meeting. It got louder and louder, and then things started crashing against the walls. I heard people scuffling, and then suddenly The Pips came bursting through the door. Bubba grabbed my arm.

"We're outta here. Let's go!" he said.

"Where are y'all going?"

"Just come with us. Now!" Bubba commanded.

This must have been some meeting, I thought.

Once we were outside the building, Bubba explained to me what had happened. It seemed that Bobby wanted this company to manage us because he was trying to work a deal with them to invest in his record label, which was having some problems with the Internal Revenue Service. The head of the company told Bubba and the guys that he wasn't all that interested in investing in Fury Records, but there was something that might get him to manage our group.

"We can make this deal, if I can have Gladys," he'd said.

Bubba said that's what had made them so upset. But I didn't get it. Of course he could have me; if he managed the group, he managed me too.

"We're a group. I don't go nowhere without y'all," I said.

I was clueless until Bubba clued me in.

"No, Dumbo. It wasn't about the group. It wasn't about managing. He wanted you, fool. He wanted to take you to bed. Get it?"

You could have driven a complete Barnum & Bailey circus train into my mouth as I stood there with it dropped wide open in shock and disbelief. I don't think I said another word until we'd taken a cab to the airport and flown all the way back home. It never had occurred to me that business was done that way. I may have just graduated from high school but I was still learning. Good Lord, I was so naive!

In spite of his unscrupulous business associates, Bobby did come through with a gig at the Apollo Theater for us. It was the first of what would be many there, and, once again, we proved that we were still rookies. Originally an Irish hoochie-coochie joint known as Hurtig & Seamon's Burlesque Hall, the Apollo became the first of all the old theaters on Harlem's 125th Street to offer live entertainment for African-Americans. That was in 1934, after the mayor had shut down all the strip joints in town two years earlier.

By the time we arrived, the Apollo was a legendary showcase for black talent and the place had a lot of traditions that we were totally unaware of. We were accustomed to doing one, maybe two shows a night on our regular Chit'lin' Circuit stops, and so after we did our second performance at the Apollo, we packed up to go home to Atlanta. We were headed for the front door when the stage manager spotted us.

"Hey, where y'all think you're going?" he said gruffly.

"Man, we're going home. We did our gig," said Bubba.

"Y'all crazy. You better get your black asses backstage. You've got three more shows to do," came the reply.

At least we scored as a comedy act with all the people lined up waiting for the next show. They were roaring after hearing that exchange and then watching us drag our suitcases and our sorry butts back up the stairs to our dressing rooms.

Getting that kind of a laugh, or any kind of audience approval, was no easy task at the Apollo. The audiences there were used to seeing the cream of the crop—Nat King Cole, Ella Fitzgerald, Sarah Vaughan, Count Basie, Charlie Parker, Miles Davis, all of the greats. So, when a new act was introduced, it had better meet the high level of expectations because the Apollo crowd came to make some noise and they could boo just as loudly and enthusiastically as they could cheer. It's been said that a lot of famous folks, as well as regular Harlem residents, came to the Apollo just for the opportunity to scream and yell and vent a lot of pent-up emotions. The actress Joan Crawford once said she went to the Apollo to practice her screaming techniques because there she could scream her head off without disturbing anyone.

Believe me, this was the toughest house in show business, particularly on Wednesday when they held amateur nights. The cheap seats in the second balcony were known as the buzzard's roost because if your act didn't go over, they picked you apart down to the bone, and if you failed to take the hint, a real hook was used to haul your carcass offstage. The Apollo crowds were so notoriously tenacious that the only way they could clear the house between shows was to run a thirty-minute film showing nothing but flowing water. It's been said that only the very hardiest could hold it through that water torture.

We were lucky. Even though we mistakenly tried to cut out early, the audiences at the Apollo adopted us. We never got booed there in the many times we headlined. I think it was because the infamous Peaches liked us, and when Peaches was on your side, things were sweet for you at the Apollo.

Peaches was the leader of a group of drag queens who had their own box just to the right of the Apollo stage. When he and his "girls" were in the house, the entire audience took its cue from them. If Peaches didn't like you, he would turn his back to the stage and talk in a loud voice, ignoring the show. You knew the hook was coming if you saw Peaches's backside pointed in your direction.

But if Peaches gave you his full frontal view, then you could count on hanging around. Peaches absolutely adored us. He would throw flowers onstage during our performances, and afterward he'd come by my dressing room to consult on wardrobe matters. "Oh girl, I like that outfit. I want one," he'd say.

Peaches and his "gal-pals" always came to the Apollo dressed to kill and I made sure I dressed to please them. Once I wore a backless yellow satin jumpsuit with a halter neckline and a hood attached to it. I came out with that hood on, vamping to the drag queens in their box, and when I reached a dramatic point in the song, I threw the hood off.

Peaches and company swooned in envy and nearly fell into the seats below at that move.

CHAPTER 8

$\mathcal{T}$he pull between my professional and personal life became even greater once I got out of high school, making the choices I faced all the more difficult. There was so much I wanted to do with my singing career, yet I dreamed too of having some sort of normal, structured life outside of show business. In yearning for both, it seemed like I was unable to capture either.

Suddenly, my life took on a pace and went off in directions that were out of my control. Just prior to graduation, I began to worry that I was pregnant. I was late, but I kept it to myself. I was afraid to tell Momma. I did tell Jimmy, who said he wanted to get married right away. I wasn't so sure.

Knowing that one of his former girlfriends had pressured him to get married when she got pregnant, I didn't want to make the same mistake. I'd seen how terrified and trapped he felt. I didn't want him thinking I was setting the same snare. I loved him but I didn't want to be married to him unless he loved me too. I put him off, saying I would "take care of it, one way or the other." I was bluffing, of course. I had no idea what I was going to do.

Jimmy, bless him, kept insisting that he wanted to marry me no matter what. "It's not because you are pregnant. We have been talking about getting married for a long time."

Just a few weeks earlier, my options had seemed unlimited. Our records were at the top of the charts and we were in increasing demand across the country. Now this. The path was narrowing. I was feeling panicky. This wasn't supposed to happen to a good girl like me.

I was afraid of what Momma might say. Afraid that I might hurt her because she had dreamed so big for me and worked so hard to see that my talents were developed. But I had to tell her. I had always shared everything with her sooner or later.

I was ironing in the kitchen when she came in. I took a deep breath and blurted it out. "I'm pregnant." She kept moving around as was her way. But, nevertheless, I saw her flinch. She didn't yell at me, but her disappointment came through. She was deeply introspective. I had fallen into a trap that she had seen so many others slip into, then struggle for the rest of their lives to overcome.

She sat me down at the kitchen table and talked to me, again, about teen pregnancy, about life after babies, taking responsibility for your children. Even how children can affect relationships. There was never any question about having the baby. Abortion was not an option in our family. We accepted our responsibilities and we shared in doing what needed to be done. We drew together in these times. Brenda had gotten pregnant a few years earlier and Momma had stepped in to care for her son, Chetley, while she returned to classes at Morris Brown College. Mind you, my mother only steps in if she truly believes that you are trying to do something productive with your life.

I know Momma had enough faith in me that she knew I would still pursue my goals in life, but I also know she feared that the quality of my life would be greatly affected by this early pregnancy. I had graduated from high school and I had a singing career, but I was still only sixteen years old.

I told her I would do whatever it took to raise my child properly, even if it meant working as a waitress. I didn't have to be a singer. In truth, I was more drawn to a life of raising children than to one of constant travel. It had always been that way with me, so I saw it as no burden. Although I had long talked about going to college, Mr. Terry had convinced me that my music career was already so far developed that a formal education would be redundant. I still longed for the experience of living on a campus and making friends in that setting, but I had decided he was right. I hadn't even applied.

Jimmy, meanwhile, had given up arguing with me about his desire to get married. He called Momma and asked to come talk to her about it. I decided I had better be there for this meeting. He made a persuasive pitch. He told Momma that he loved me and he asked her for my hand in marriage. She was naturally worried that we were too young and she asked if we were really ready for all of the responsibilities of marriage. To my surprise, she made no mention of the impact marriage and a child might have on my singing career.

Jimmy remained firm throughout her discussion of the hardships that we might face, so she said she would think about it for a couple days. She knew we needed her permission for a marriage license since we were still minors in the eyes of the law.

After a few days of contemplation, and without much discussion with either me or Jimmy, Momma said she would support our decision to marry. The wedding was a very informal affair, with the air of yet another postgraduation party. Daddy, who had grown more and more distant and was living in his own apartment, did not respond to my invitation, so Bubba gave me away. I invited to our no-frills wedding all the girls in the neighborhood who had been in love with Jimmy just like me. It wasn't exactly an engraved invitation.

"Ya'll want to come over to my house?" I'd yell when I spotted one of them on the street or on a porch. "Jimmy and I are getting married."

Some of them actually showed up. Mr. Terry and the guys in the jazz band were there, along with most of my immediate and greatly extended family. We were known for having so many cousins, aunts, and uncles that it was impossible to figure out who was related to whom and how. We were just glad to have their love and approval. Well, most of them gave us their love and approval. There is always one relative who likes to throw a firecracker into the campfire. Aunt Rosalee cried through the whole ceremony and on into the evening. "That's my baby girl," she sobbed. "You don't know what you are doing."

I did my best to prove her right by fumbling and stumbling my way through the big day.

Everybody was gathered downstairs in the living room, waiting for me to come down in my bridal dress, but I was late as usual. I have had a lifelong battle with being on time. I managed to be unavoidably late for my wedding, even though it was just downstairs, and I hope to be even later for my funeral.

I fussed around upstairs, with Brenda getting me moving, and at first I was on time. I just needed to get my hands moist, and I would be okay. Without even thinking about it, I picked up the lotion and hit the pump with my fist. A big glob of lotion squirted all over the front of my white satin wedding dress.

I panicked. I cried in frustration.

"Look at my dress! Look at my dress! Brenda, I can't go down like this."

There was no time to get the stain out of my dress, but Brenda came up with a divine inspiration. She grabbed the Bible that was decorated with orchids and streamers. I had planned to carry it down the aisle instead of a bridal bouquet. Brenda had fallen back on the old last-minute stain motto: If you can't get it out, cover it up.

"Take the Bible and hold it like this when you go downstairs," she said, placing it strategically over the lotion spot. "The streamers will cover up the stain."

"You can't see it?"

"Naw, go, girl!"

The Bible-toting teenage bride descended the stairs, and the wedding ceremony was conducted without any further spots or stains. It all seemed so anticlimactic. There was no ring for Jimmy, who had given me his grandma's ring. No full gospel choir. No six-course banquet.

After the ceremony, we were at a loss as to what to do with ourselves. We couldn't exactly go to the drive-in, or take in a movie. We hadn't given any thought to a honeymoon. For a while, we watched television in Bubba's room. Nobody invited us to stay. They probably thought we'd made plans.

Finally, after we'd had enough television, Jimmy looked at me and popped the question: "What do you want to do, Baby?"

"Whatever you want to do," I said.

For lack of a better idea, we spent our honeymoon at his grandmother's house just around the corner. She gave us the pull-out bed in the living room, and our marriage began.

With my schooling out of the way, Jimmy and I rejoined Bubba, Edward Patten, Langston George, and William Guest as we hit the Chit'lin' Circuit hard and fast to try and make some money before the baby came. Jimmy took on the role of band director, leading the house band and playing the sax. Most of these house bands specialized in "catch-me" music. We'd start singing and hope they'd catch up.

We did as many as sixty-five one-nighters in a row, hitting the roadside joints and honky-tonks across the South. This was the lower tier of the circuit. No dressing rooms. Bathrooms only if you were lucky. Separate bathrooms were a real luxury. All the beer bottles and pool cues you could dodge. No menus. No kitchens. Just a grizzly old guy selling catfish nuggets, corn fritters, or pig ear sandwiches in a corner. If it rained, you had to dodge the leaks while you sang. But, The Pips picked up some good moves under those leaky tin honky-tonk roofs, I'm telling you that's true. In fact, once our dressing room was at the bottom of a bar's empty can chute, and we had to dodge cans!

Many times we'd drive all day, play a gig, and then sleep in the car on the way to the next gig. Most hotels and motels wouldn't have us, but there were usually black-owned boarding houses that catered to performers. If we were lucky, we'd have time to get a room and take a shower. Real luck, though, was having some money left over to sock away. Two-hundred-and-fifty dollars a night didn't go far when it was split five ways. The doodlebug got the biggest cut.

The little money we were able to save went into the Triple K Trust Company Bank. Bubba, Brenda, and I were the founding partners, which is where the "triple K" came from. We started our bank when we first started singing together. We had visions of making piles of money early on and then using it to bankroll our dreams as adults. We'd sit around the dining room table talking about the lives we envisioned. I didn't see myself performing as a singer. I thought about being an airline stewardess or a nurse because I wanted to serve people. I was getting A's in home economics. I figured that was a skill I could count on.

The Triple K Trust Company Bank grew out of one of those dining room table dream sessions. We started depositing our earnings in a mason jar, which we locked into my mother's china cabinet. We made up a sign for the Triple K Trust Company Bank and put it on the jar. If someone needed money, they could make a withdrawal if they left an I.O.U. in the jar. I think the last time I looked in that jar, the I.O.U.s were more than the deposits.

After several months doing the road houses, we moved to the upper tier of the circuit, the theaters: the Royal in Baltimore, the Howard in D.C., the Uptown in Philly, the Apollo in New York, and the Regal in Chicago. These were a lot nicer places to play, and the pay was maybe $500 a night, but to be honest, I think we fit in better in the dirt-floor honky-tonks back then. We were still pretty much country cornbread folks: young, poor, and naive. The more sophisticated performers liked to talk to us because they got a kick out of our down-home accents. Some took us under their wings.

I was still wearing bobby socks with my dresses when I met Tina

Turner for the first time at the Howard Theater. We had the luxury of dressing rooms at the Howard, though they were tiny. There were five of them lined up on one wall along a narrow hall. I was standing in the hall one day when I heard a voice that was both regal and rough.

"Gladys, come here, girl!"

Tina was hailing me from her dressing room, where we spent much of our time.

I walked in. She turned, gave me a quick appraisal, and offered sisterly advice to the rookie.

"You ought to let me make you up," she growled.

Except for a little lipstick, I hadn't worn makeup since the Old Gold Girls took me under their wings back on the Ted Mack show. I just felt awkward wearing it, like I was trying to be more sophisticated than I was. Makeup seemed so grown-up and I didn't feel grown-up yet.

"I don't wear makeup," I told Tina.

"You should wear a little bit for the stage," she insisted. "I'll tell you what. Let me make you up and if you don't like it, you can take it off."

I submitted and received my first Tina Turner rock-and-roll makeover. If you think Tina can put on a show, you ought to see her apply foundation, not to mention blush, eyeshadow, and mascara. She arched eyebrows I didn't know I had, and created cheekbones where there had only been cheek before. By the time she put down her eyeliner pencils, I didn't recognize myself.

Tina was five years older than me and even though her origins were far more country than mine—she grew up in Nut Bush, Tennessee—she had seen a lot more of the darker side of life. In recent years, she has told the story of her beatings and abuse with coat hangers, shoes, and lit cigarettes at the hands of Ike. I didn't witness any of these, but I heard the horror stories from those who had. There was one story going around even back then that Ike had tried to shove a coat hanger down Tina's throat. I didn't believe it at the time, and I still don't know if it was true, but after reading of similar incidents in her biography—there was one report of Ike sticking a lit cigarette up her nose—it certainly wasn't far from the truth. In light of the life she was living back then, I found her kindness to me all the more extraordinary.

I've always felt a camaraderie with Tina, and I came to be close to her sister Alline as well as several of the Ikettes, but it was difficult to get to know Tina very well back then. She and I talked, but it never went very deep. I could tell she was unhappy, troubled, and scared. I wanted to put my arm around her and comfort her, but I was afraid to say what she needed to hear—that she needed to get far away from Ike. He was an intimidating presence, although to be fair he was always pleasant to me and complimentary of our performances.

Overall, our relationships with other performers were quite fleeting. It was true then, and to some degree it remains true today. I've seen Tina recently at a couple of award shows and such, but we've never been able to just sit down and talk because we are both always so busy. It hasn't changed much from our early days when everyone was always rushing from gig to gig, from backstage to onstage, packing and unpacking and packing again. How ya' doin'. You're soundin' good. Great show. See ya next time. Even if we yearned to get to know each other better, or to reach out to each other, there just was no time. What time and energy the audience didn't get, the road ate up.

Remember, this was back before we hit the big time that would bring first-class accommodations. We were barely getting by financially and we were young and hungry, riding in a packed car for hours and hours, day after day. It was sure no way to go through a pregnancy. I was three months along and we were about halfway through our engagement working again with the Ike & Tina Turner Revue in D.C. when I began to feel completely wiped out. The exhaustion hit one night as we were walking the ten blocks back to our hotel after a show because we couldn't afford a cab.

It hit me so suddenly I had to sit down on a wall and rest. The guys stopped and waited for me, but didn't pay much attention, figuring I was just having "a spell." When the others grew tired of waiting for me, they headed on to the hotel. Jimmy helped me to my feet. "Let's try to make it to the room now, Baby, so you can lay down," he said.

We continued walking and when we passed a sandwich shop, he asked if I wanted something to eat. I did, but I didn't feel like stopping. I wanted to get into bed. I was so tired all of a sudden. Jimmy got me to the room and then went down for sandwiches. He brought them back and then he split to go hang out with the guys. I didn't object. I didn't have the energy to ask him to stay and watch over me.

I tried to sleep but I couldn't get comfortable. There was a dull pain in my abdomen when I first laid down, then it grew sharper. I sat up to alleviate the pressure and that seemed to help. I thought maybe it would go away altogether if I stood up and walked around a bit. The pain did subside, but then it came back stronger. Where was Jimmy?

It began to hurt so bad I was crying out loud. I could hardly breathe. Where's Jimmy? I didn't know what was happening to me. I'd never gone through this before.

I tried to talk myself out of my misery. I told myself to be strong, to get through this. Fight it. Then it stabbed me, something inside stabbed me and doubled me over. I spent hours alone, in pure agony.

Jimmy came home long after midnight. He got into bed beside me, oblivious to the fact that something was wrong. I didn't tell him.

At dawn, I stumbled to the bathroom where I miscarried our baby.

I didn't wake Jimmy. I'd gone through it on my own and I grieved on my own. The lost child. My lost child. I had been looking forward so much to staying home and building a normal life for this child. I knew I would be a good mommy. I cried until exhaustion provided relief in sleep.

In the morning, I tried to downplay what I'd gone through. Jimmy wanted me to skip the performance that day but I refused. I told him I would be okay. It had been my way to run myself ragged.

As it was, we were barely making it, and the guys had families too. There was no taking a day off even on that terribly sad and tragic day.

Jimmy, Bubba, and the guys were solicitous that day, as were the stagehands and other performers, who must have sensed that I was depressed. Most hadn't even realized I was pregnant. But Tina Turner, her sister Alline, and the Ikettes knew. They watched over me very carefully that day. They made sure I ate, they made me food, and made sure I rested between shows. They also talked to me about pain and loss. And you *know* Tina could talk! I made it through all four shows that day. It wasn't easy, but it was part of that life. I've had guys tell me over the years that I spent way too much time in the company of men. It's true, I have lived among that strange species more than most women. I know their ways. I've adapted to some and I've adopted others. I was never allowed the luxury of falling back on my femininity if I felt sick or tired. I gutted it out with their encouragement. I also benefited from their support and their caring, but believe me, they didn't pamper me. The Pips made me carry my own bags once so that I'd learn not to overpack. They let me deal with racist gas station owners and crooked promoters so that I'd understand the dark side of the business and be tough enough to deal with it.

I learned to have a breadwinner's mentality and, to some degree, that has made it difficult for some men to deal with me. If a man needed a woman who relied on him for everything, I was not a good fit. If a man set out to break my spirit, he generally wore himself out trying. I don't know of many weak women, or weak men, who have endured in show business.

I've seen performers go on stage so sick they could hardly walk to the curtain, but when they stepped into the lights, you'd have thought they'd never been ill a day in their lives. Usually, the audience doesn't have a clue to what is going on in a performer's personal life, and that's the way it should be. They pay to be entertained. Sometimes, though, you just can't hide the fact that beneath the stage makeup, there's a person who is every bit as vulnerable, troubled, and even klutzy as everyone else.

Years ago, we were performing at the Latin Casino in Cherry Hill, New Jersey, when a sophisticated and slick female singer (whose photograph is on the cover of this very book) busted a front tooth while chewing gum right before a performance. Don't ask how that happened. It was Sunday and there was less than an hour to show time. We didn't think to put out a call on the public address system broadcast: "Is there a dentist in the house?"

I just did what I had to do. I went out on stage looking like the black Minnie Pearl. When I started to hear comments in the audience, I decided to go public about my dental dilemma. I told them what had happened and said that rather than canceling the show, I was going to lisp-synch.

"I don't think you paid to see my teeth. You paid to hear me sing," I said.

"You got that right, baby," agreed a drunk at a front table. "You can sing to me with no teeth!" He then proceeded to fall out of the chair, and that set the fun-loving pace for the show and everything went great after that.

So, I sang, and I sprayed, and the show went on.

CHAPTER 9

*I*n 1962, we recorded our first album on Fury Records and two of the songs on it, "Guess Who" and "Letter Full of Tears" made the Top Five on the charts. We were getting a lot of air play, but we couldn't buy food with air play. Fury was in financial turmoil, and our harmony as a group was limited to what was playing on the radio.

The scrambling to scrape by was wearing on all of us and our weakest link was breaking away. Bubba, Edward, William, and I all had a strong family bond and we were tight, even if we did have our occasional disagreements. Edward, whom I had once despised because I thought he was conceited and arrogant, had become my biggest backer and guardian, next to Bubba, of course.

I had learned that Edward's "too-cool" attitude was really just a protective cover. A dedicated family man with a wife and children at home, he turned out to be the most responsible member of the group, so much so that we took to calling him Daddy Patten. He was the one who was always watching the clock, trying to keep us on time and in line. It was amazing how our relationship had warmed. Not to say that he wasn't still a snappy dresser, and probably the biggest trash talker on the Chit'lin' Circuit. Coming off stage after a hot show, he'd find a member of the next act, whether it was The Temptations or The Dells and challenge them to: "Match that!"

Getting along with William was more of a challenge. He was like a spoiled child, very spoiled. He'd grown up that way, and it seemed like there was always a pretty woman ready to fall all over him and take care of him. He had a beautiful voice, probably the best in the group, but he never wanted to step forward and take the lead. He wasn't driven in any way, except to find the easy way.

Langston was his own story. He had been the last to join The Pips, and he had kept a measure of independence. A gifted performer who usually had been a lead singer or solo singer, he found it difficult to take a back seat when I fell into the role of lead vocalist.

When we came off our extended road trip for a few months in 1962, Langston began taking gigs as a lead singer with other groups around town, and we heard that he was doing well. The other guys and I still thought our future was in singing as a group, but if Langston wanted to go solo, we weren't going to stop him. We just needed to know where his loyalties were. We called a meeting in our four-wheeled office, picked up Langston, and parked just down the block from our house on Chestnut Street.

We explained that we were looking at another big tour and we needed to know if we could count on him. Was he staying with us, or was he going off on his own? He went ballistic. The pent-up frustrations and resentment rocked the doodlebug as Langston let fly.

"You're all a bunch of losers," he said. "You ain't going nowhere. I'm going to do my own thing."

With that unqualified resignation, our group was back down to the family of four, but one of us was singing a duet all by herself. Shortly after my miscarriage, I'd become pregnant again. This time, I told the guys that I was not going to tough it out. I'd made up my mind that I'd work only as long as it did not endanger the pregnancy.

"When I get to five months, I'm out of here," I told them, because we always planned ahead, and after the first miscarriage we talked about my being more careful next time.

They accepted my declaration without saying much, mostly because I don't think they believed I would do it. Things were happening out there. It was an incredibly exciting time to be a performer. The music scene was shifting and expanding. Jackie and JFK were doing the Twist in the White House. Smokey Robinson and the Miracles were tuning up their night moves in Detroit and Little Eva was doing the Locomotion on *American Bandstand*.

The baby boomers had hit the marketplace in full force and they were buying more radios, record players, records, and concert tickets than any previous generation. They were also making music like mad. It seemed like there were more groups performing than people listening. Boy groups that sounded like girl groups that sounded like black groups that sounded like white groups. It was anybody's game and everybody's game. There were no more rules other than it had to have a good beat, a good hook, and be easy to dance to. Ray Charles turned out a country album, The Beatles sang Delta blues, and a young Jewish couple in New York, Gerry Goffin and Carole King, was writing one hit after another for both black and white artists.

It was a wide open field out there, but I was shutting it down to have this baby properly. I went on the road for a few more months, but I took care of myself this time. I slept more, watched what I ate, and stayed in touch with my doctor back home. Jimmy and Bubba brought my meals to me in my room so I could stay off my feet when I wasn't performing. William and Edward managed to keep occupied without my assistance, but they were also very attentive.

During a show at the Uptown Theater in Philadelphia, some of the guys became entranced with the members of a new girl group out of Philadelphia called the Blue-Belles. They were all pretty ladies, and single, and they could sing, especially their lead singer, Patti LaBelle, whose version of "Somewhere over the Rainbow" was something else. That girl could sing her buns off. I knew she was going to go places, but as was so often the case, we were all so busy going places, we never had much of a chance to get to know each other.

Everyone in our group got along with the Blue-Belles, but it was tough to get through the protective barrier and rigorous schedule that their managers, Mr. and Mrs. Montague, enforced. They had to be out of their dressing rooms, in their dressing rooms, at dinner, and in bed according to the schedule set by the Montagues, who also functioned as chaperones. They were highly disciplined, which may have been good for their careers, but it made it difficult to get close to them. It wasn't until a little down the road that Patti and I had the opportunity to spend a lot of time together and to discover how much we have in common. As with Tina, we were often just two groups of performers passing in the night. Over time, though, Patti became one of my good friends.

Meanwhile, as my pregnancy progressed, we added another big piece of equipment to our traveling gear—a rocking chair that the guys gave me so I could sing while giving my legs and back a break. I didn't see any sense in trying to hide my pregnancy from the audience, and when I started performing in maternity clothes it gave me leave to sit down. After all, President Kennedy was sitting on a rocking chair and getting a lot of good press, so why shouldn't I?

I was more comfortable in this pregnancy because I wasn't pushing myself so hard, and Jimmy seemed to be more attentive this time around too. He stayed by my side most nights rather than going off with the guys in search of adventure. When I was five months pregnant, I kept my word and Jimmy and I moved back to Atlanta. Bubba, William, and Edward moved to New York to try and get in on the booming music scene there as performers and studio backup singers without me. They had a tough go of it, but they understood that I was trying to be a good mother.

We found a nice little two-bedroom apartment in a brand new complex in Adams Park. I still remember the apartment number, I-J, and the rent, which was $62.50 a month. Jimmy rejoined Mr. Terry's jazz band for a while, but they broke up so he found work with other bands around town. I kept busy decorating our first apartment. There wasn't much money for fancy things but my daddy was still working at Rich's Department Store then, so I could use his discount.

I think I took more pleasure in decorating our first little nest than I got out of two weeks on the road singing. Not that I didn't love singing, it was just all the fuss around it that wore me down. I had always craved having a place of my own and taking care of it and my family. I was a good cook and a good housekeeper. I was so grateful for the chance to experience that normal life for a while. I'd talk to my momma on the telephone for hours and hours, doing the ironing and washing and cleaning as we talked. It was such a peaceful time for me to be in one place, near friends and family.

On Sunday afternoons, I'd put on my best maternity outfit and go to hear Jimmy play at the matinee performances. I was so proud of him and I wanted so badly for him to receive the attention he deserved as a musician. He had studied the work of Cannonball Adderly, John Coltrane, and Charlie "Bird" Parker, and I had the confidence that he could reach their level. I only wish he had believed it too. Jimmy placed more limits on himself than anyone else did. He just didn't believe that he deserved success, even as he pursued it. I could tell it was eating him up even then. Many nights, I'd wait up until three A.M. for him to return home from a performance, but he wouldn't have anything to say. He just went to bed, keeping his troubled thoughts and self-doubts to himself.

One of the most pleasurable parts of being home was that Momma and I revived the tradition of the Knight family Sunday dinner feast. We would cook up a huge meal for Brenda and David and a whole lot of other family and friends who came by. I was basking in this domesticity one Sunday as I sat at our kitchen table, wearing my house slippers, taking a break from cooking, when Momma asked me what was wrong.

"Nothing," I replied.

She began doing her motherly nosing around thing, checking out my handiwork around the apartment and then came back.

"You in labor?" she asked.

"No."

She fiddled around some more, keeping an eye on me while I kept an eye on her. This was starting to make me crazy.

"It won't be long, Baby," she offered.

How could she possibly know what was happening before I did? This was making me mad.

She must have seen the steam rising out of my ears because she headed for the door, but not before asking Jimmy what time he'd be getting home that night, and assuring him that "I'll be around if Gladys needs me tonight."

My momma read me well. She had hardly gotten out the door and down the street before I felt the pressure building in my belly and parts south. They were light labor pains but there was no mistake that it was time to put down the cake pans and head for the hospital. Jimmy called Momma and told her to meet us at the hospital. I was surprised she wasn't already there, given her extrasensory perception of my pregnancy. Once he got me checked in, Jimmy went on to work because the doctors said it could be a while. The doctors had it right. Jimmy played two shows and made it back to the hospital to find me trying to walk the baby on out. I must have walked from Atlanta to Miami and back that night.

Finally, the doctors decided to give the baby a little help. Whatever they did, it worked. And it hurt. It hurt so bad that when the doctor said it was too late to give me anything for the pain, I hauled off and punched him.

"Keep that up and we'll strap you down," he warned me.

I must have been really hurting to sucker punch my own doctor.

It must have been my motherly survival instincts at work. They'd been pretty powerful during this pregnancy. Not only had I been nesting like a mother robin, spending hours getting the baby's room just right, I had also had really strong cravings for some very unusual things—especially dirt. Not just any dirt, mind you, it had to be premium Georgia Red. I know it sounds crazy but it is something I did as a child too, and so did a lot of other country women. My doctor said that it's the same kind of craving that drives pregnant women to eat a lot of starchy foods. Something that the baby needs isn't there, so your body sends out a signal. It wasn't that my baby wanted dirt, it was the minerals and nutrients in it. Georgia's red soil is full of minerals, iron in particular, and eating it satisfies the baby's need, as well as the cravings. Of course, a couple teaspoons of Geritol will do the trick too, but there was something about eating nice moist dirt that fulfilled a psychological need also, some primitive link to nature maybe. It's strange, but fascinating.

Naturally, I didn't just go out in the back yard, find a bare patch, and start shoveling it in. I ordered up my dirt special from my uncle in the mountains of North Georgia. He would go out to a place high up on a mountainside and dig me out some pure red clay and he would send it to me all boxed up. I liked it best after it had been sitting out in the rain for a while, then you could smell the forest and the clean earth scent in it.

When the baby finally came, the doctor joked that he was covered in mud because I'd eaten so much of it. It must have been good for Little Jimmy because when he entered the world on August 13, 1962, he was gorgeous, with a full head of thick, beautiful hair.

I had really enjoyed being home and preparing for him, and having him to take care of and the time to do it right was pure bliss for me. Little Jimmy was the cleanest baby you ever did see. His diapers were always snow white (well, maybe not *always*), and I had him on a regular schedule that was like clockwork. He was the best smelling, best fed, happiest baby in the world. And his momma was pretty happy too.

I kept thinking that this is what life was really all about, but my contentment was tempered by the knowledge that Jimmy Sr. was really struggling to support us and the pressure was wearing on him and on our relationship. One day I handed him a list of baby things that we needed, including essentials like milk and baby food, and he started muttering about how we couldn't afford all this. It was a lot of pressure, particularly if you remember that my husband was barely twenty years old, a time when most males are still footloose and fancy free.

The pressure didn't ease up any when I became pregnant again a little over five months after Little Jimmy was born. I didn't think that blacks could have "Irish twins," but once again, my momma made the call.

I had just cooked up another big Sunday dinner, given Little Jimmy a bath and put him to sleep, and Momma and I were sitting around the kitchen table talking.

She gave me one of those looks.

"You aren't feeling good are you?"

"I feel fine, maybe a little tired," I said.

"Seems to me you been draggin' around quite a bit," she said.

"I'm fine, really," I insisted.

It can be aggravating when somebody knows you that well.

She kept silent until she was about to leave. Then she gave me another quick appraisal and passed sentence.

"You ain't nothin' but pregnant," came her expert diagnosis.

"What did you say, Momma?"

"You heard me, girl," she said. Her knowing laughter trailed her out the door.

I didn't want to believe it, but Momma had been proven right the first time, so I hauled my butt into the doctor's the next day.

"Maybe I've got a tumor or something," I joked. "It couldn't be a baby so soon after the last one."

He gave me a pregnancy test and told me that my "tumor" looked to be due around November of '63.

"Jesus Lord," I said.

Once again, I was faced with the dilemma that has been part of my life, the inner conflict between my desire to be a traditional woman and mother working in the home, and my equally powerful need to fulfill the promise of my musical gift. I took great joy in caring for my family. I took great joy in using my voice to reach out to people. I have never needed fame or glamour or the trappings of wealth. But I have never wanted to bury my talents either, and when I saw how hard it was for Jimmy to support us, I felt like I was being selfish because I was not using a talent that could greatly ease his burden. I think I could have been happy staying home and being a mom and a wife and maybe doing something to make money that used my lesser talents, but it was not to be and I guess that is the way God wanted it.

I thought about it for a day or two and then one night when Jimmy came home from performing, we talked about my decision. "You know, I'm sitting on this skill and it's not that I want to go back, let me be straight with you on that, I'm happy and I appreciate how hard you work, but if you think it would be beneficial to us and our family, I would go back to singing."

It was a difficult thing for both of us. On the one hand, I wanted to be supportive and offer to help. On the other, I did not want him to feel that he had failed us, or that I didn't have faith in his ability to support us himself. Jimmy was so sensitive. I tried to phrase it so that it would be his decision to make.

"Well, of course it would help, I wouldn't lie," he said. "But it's really up to you if you want to go."

We talked it over for a long time that night and into the morning. In the end, we decided that I would go back to singing and Jimmy would work as my manager.

In my prayers that night, I apologized to God for ever asking Him to take my voice away. I had grown up and matured, and now it made me ashamed and not a little nervous to think of how much I had taken His gift for granted. It wasn't about seeking glory, or fame, or wealth. He had given me something that I could use to help my family and to ease my husband's burden. I think it was His plan, and now he was telling me it was time to get back on track.

CHAPTER 10

CHAPTER 10

*J*immy and I decided that if I was going to get back into show business, then I should resume my career at an even higher level than before. That meant we had to move to New York, where the next generation of hot young songwriters were being hailed as "the new Tin Pan Alley." Folk, gospel, rock, blues, country, all those influences were channeling into the Brill Building on Broadway just off Times Square.

The Pips were already there, living out of the President Hotel in Harlem, struggling, but surviving, although sometimes on twenty-five-cent hot dogs. They'd had some success with a song called "Darling" on the Fire label, but again the label's financial problems kept it from getting the promotional push it deserved. Before I'd left them to have Little Jimmy, we had made a pact that if I ever decided to come back and they were doing well, then I would make my own way as a solo artist if I chose to.

I didn't want to be so bold as to suggest that they weren't doing well, particularly when they had a record out there that was getting some attention, so Jimmy and I decided that I would go after my own club and theater bookings as a solo act.

I had been ready to give up singing professionally all together, and packing up and leaving our little apartment was one of the saddest things I'd had to do, but I have to admit that once I got back onstage, the thrill was definitely not gone. It may have been even more enjoyable than before. Motherhood had agreed with me. I felt more mature and confident. I felt comfortable up there singing lyrics that by now I had lived. It did take a while to get used to not having the guys up there with me, though. I missed the richness of their harmonies.

Jimmy helped me get back into the flow and then we decided that to get to the next level I needed a manager with more New York connections, so I signed with Irv Nahan, the manager of Jerry "Iceman" Butler, who had left the Impressions a few years earlier and was moving from rhythm and blues ("He Will Break Your Heart") to pop music ("Moon River").

My timing was good because Jerry had been making appearances with a duet partner, Betty Everett, who had had a hit with "It's in His Kiss" ("The Shoop Shoop Song"), but she had decided to go solo. I stepped in and did a lot of shows around town with Jerry as well as picking up a lot of gigs on my own.

When we first got to New York, our little family packed into the rooms that The Pips were renting at the President, but Jimmy had been scouting apartments for us. We weren't having a lot of luck until William suggested that we go see Marghuerite Mays, whom he had met while dating her niece, Little Marghuerite. When she and William hit it off, Marghuerite began managing The Pips, and she'd told them that she would like to meet me someday too. Jimmy and I called and set up an appointment to drive out to her home on Long Island.

Marghuerite, we discovered, was the ex-wife of baseball great Willie Mays, and she lived in a mansion. It had three floors, a swimming pool, a billiard room and a huge winding staircase perfectly suited to her patented grand entrances. She certainly made one on the day we met. While Jimmy and I stood in the hallway as her audience, she appeared at the top of the stairs and sashayed down like an elegant queen. Even though she wore only a white terry cloth robe, slippers, and very little makeup, she cut a dramatic and striking figure. That woman knew how to work a room!

In her sophistication, she made me feel like a little girl, and it seemed to me that she was looking at me in much the same way Tina Turner had. I envisioned her thinking, "I've got to make this one over."

We had come to meet her because William said she had a lot of rental properties, but Marghuerite offered to rent us a two-room flat off the billiard room of her own house. The flat was not in the most elegant section of Marghuerite's castle, but it wasn't exactly the dungeon either. We accepted her invitation.

Marghuerite was a fascinating woman with ties to all types of people and all strata of society. She had attained a high quality of life during her marriage to Willie Mays and after their divorce, she had done whatever it took to see that she maintained that life-style. She was a wheeler and a dealer and a masterful manipulator who made no bones about the fact that if you didn't have money or a way of making some for her, she wasn't interested.

I'm sure that is one of the reasons I frustrated her, but intrigued her too. She could see that Jimmy and I had doodley-squat in our barebones two-room flat, but she could also see that we had a bond of love and respect. It intrigued her that I deferred to Jimmy even though she thought of me as the biggest breadwinner in the family. I could tell she thought I was a bit of a fool in that regard, but that there was also something in our relationship that she envied or missed. One day we were riding together in her car and I started talking about love and what it is supposed to mean. She cut me off. "Well shit, honey, you can't eat love."

She said it, and that is how she lived, but she also talked frequently of Willie and I could tell that he had been the love of her life. She had never filled the void he left, although she had many male suitors from the ranks of the rich and powerful. I may not have agreed with her on many points, particularly on moral and money issues, but I admired Marghuerite's powerful spirit. She had chutzpah and incredible style.

I never stopped marveling at her ability to dominate a room. She'd appear as a vision of perfection. Her hair perfectly in place, her makeup applied skillfully, in black leather or camel hair, always with matching shoes and purse. She was in her early forties at that point, but she turned heads every where she went.

It was Marghuerite who took us to the next level in our careers. As I noted, she was a masterful manipulator, but we benefited greatly from her manipulations on our behalf. Although when Jimmy and I came to her I was performing as a solo act or with Jerry Butler, she believed that The Pips and I were stronger together than apart, and like a chess master, she moved us into position.

Jimmy and I and our son Little Jimmy had been living in her house only a short while before Bubba, William, and Edward appeared one day with all of their things.

"We're moving into the basement," they announced.

It was actually a wonderful thing to be living together again with Bubba, William, and Edward. Our extended family included several of the other boarders on Marghuerite's estate and her nearby properties. There were other singers and performers among them, as well as rhythm and blues songwriter Luther Dixon, author of the classic teen anthem "Tonight's the Night."

Within this family atmosphere, I revived the Knight family Sunday feast and invited Marghuerite and her family too. She had a daughter, Billy, who was around our age and who lived in a second floor wing and played princess to her mother's queen. Billy had a black Thunderbird and all the other amenities, but was really very sweet, shy, and introverted. Marghuerite also had a four-year-old son, Michael, who had the run of an entire floor of the house. He had a nanny, but he was out of control, spoiled rotten and temperamental. He was a lonely child and soon after we moved in, he was at our door every morning wanting to play with Little Jimmy. Michael adopted us and is a friend to this day who works as our stage engineer. At meal times he'd stand and watch us eat until I'd tell him to ask his mother if he could join us. Sometimes, particularly on Sundays, she would come too.

I think we gave Marghuerite a renewed sense of family, and in return, she served as our mentor, showing us how to be "stars." First, however, she put us back together again. She was already managing The Pips when we arrived in New York, and once we were living in her domain, she made it a point to give Jimmy and me regular updates on how *their* career was moving along.

"The guys are going to do the *Tonight Show*," she'd announced. "They've got a good gig going this week in L.A."

I was happy for The Pips and I refused to give in to her manipulations at first when she began dropping the one-ton hints: "Have you all ever thought about getting back together?"

I would fend her off, but she always got back to it. As it happened, we were doing a little nudging and negotiating ourselves. I felt that I would break out eventually as a solo performer, but I liked the way we sounded together. I had a real comfort level with the guys and we all agreed that there were still mountains we could climb together. Whether it came about because of Marghuerite's prodding or in spite of it, shortly after we came under the same roof—her roof—we came back together as Gladys Knight & The Pips.

Not surprisingly, our reconstituted group also featured Marghuerite as the manager. She had us right where she wanted us, and we didn't mind a bit. She saw us as diamonds in the rough and we had to agree with her assessment. Once again, it was time for a makeover.

When I reflect back on that time, I think of us as little ducklings toddling behind Marghuerite as mother duck. She taught us how to swim and survive in the big pond. When she set up a gig for us, Marghuerite waded in first and made sure everything was up to her standards. We were still all in our twenties and we needed a manager who stood up for us. If our dressing rooms weren't clean or big enough, she raised hell. And if the money wasn't ready when she went to collect our pay, Marghuerite cashed out.

Soon after we got back together, she accompanied us to a show that hadn't been very well promoted and before we went out on stage, she went to check on the gate receipts. She confronted the promoter whose attitude hinted that we weren't going to get paid that night. Marghuerite summoned us as she floated across the dance floor and proclaimed for all to hear: "C'mon babies," she said as she whirled and turned her back on the promoter. "He ain't gonna pay so it's time to *blind 'em with ass!*

Mother Marghuerite and her ducklings turned tail and walked out.

Jerry Butler who was also performing in the show that night had observed this scene while standing in the doorway. He was impressed.

"Damn," the Iceman said, "can I go too?"

While Marghuerite demanded that we get the star treatment, she also saw to it that we brought our act up to the highest standards. She revamped our wardrobes from top to bottom. She chose our hairstyles. She taught us how to carry ourselves like stars, and, in what may have been her greatest gift to us, she brought us together with Mr. Cholly Atkins.

Cholly had been performing on Broadway with his tap-dance partner Charles "Honi" Coles since before I was born. Coles & Atkins were a famous dance team and one of the longtime, all-time class acts in the business. They stopped performing together in 1960 when Honi became manager of the Apollo. Pops, as he was known to us, had become a freelance dance coach, passing on his skills and knowledge to the next generation by working with groups like the Cadillacs. He was known for taking self-taught street dancers and honing their moves to a professional edge. We had already incorporated interpretive dance moves into our stage act, but Marghuerite decided that Cholly's touch was needed. She brought us together and it was a brilliant move.

Like Maurice King, who refined our voices, Pops sharpened our stage presentation and made Gladys Knight & The Pips the standard for excellence by pushing us harder than we had ever been made to work. We came to apply that standard to everything we did and it is reflected in our corporate motto "Perfection in performance."

Pops was tenacious and no detail, no gesture, no toe wiggle escaped his attention. He ran us through about forty-five minutes of floor exercises and stretching before we even got to the real work. It was the dance slipper version of boot camp. You didn't just stick your foot out with Pops on duty, you placed it at a precise angle. You might describe the style he taught as "precision dance acrobatics." He would take the guys through every routine step-by-step, and then he made each of them perform it individually. They had to be able to hit each move on the dime and if Cholly demanded it they'd better come up with five cents change too: Doo-wop. Boogie, boogie, boggie. Doo-wop. Boogie, boogie, boogie.

Sometimes it was hard for me not to stop singing and just watch the guys do the glide and stride. Bubba remembers that after working with Cholly, he felt like an athlete. Putting on his Pips clothes was like suiting up for a game: "Show me the mike, show me the lights, I'm ready to rock."

As a woman and the lead singer, I was a little more limited in what I could do onstage, but I was a quick study and often Cholly would invite me to try a routine too after telling the guys, "Bet you Gladys won't mess up." Pops didn't want me dancing during the performance, but he worked on my presence, teaching me to strut the stage like a proud lady, while singing my butt off.

Pops was more than a dance coach for us, he taught us a far greater level of discipline and dedication to our art. His wife Mae whom we called Momma, critiqued our performances and any television or radio interviews we did. She'd tell me straight up if a dress made me look too heavy, or if my pronunciation was off, or if our diction needed to be cleaned up.

After hours and hours of drilling under Cholly's command, Bubba, William, and Edward were pirouetting, sliding, and freeze-framing in synchronized routines that were to become our trademark and the envy of the industry. Word got around swiftly that we had been "Cholly-a-graphed," and at performances we'd spot members of the Temptations and other groups packed backstage studying our routines. He did work with other groups, but Cholly was always our Pops.

Even as we refined our stage presence with Cholly and Momma, we continued our life-style lessons under Marghuerite's equally demanding eye. One of her credos was that if you weren't going to go first-class, don't go at all. One night all the guys were heading out the door for a little R&R when she ordered them to halt.

"Where ya'll going?" she inquired icily.

"Oh, we're just going up to Harlem for a while," said William.

"Not looking like *that* you ain't," came the critique.

Marghuerite ordered them back to their closets and dictated what she believed to be more appropriate attire.

They returned dressed to her specifications but she wasn't done with them.

"How are you going to get there?"

"We'll just get a cab," said Bubba.

"Oh no, you won't. Take the Black Cloud," she said, referring to her spotless Lincoln Continental.

Before finally allowing them to go out into the world, she padded their pockets with extra cash. "They don't have to know how much you got, but never go anywhere without money in your pockets," she instructed.

When it came to me, Marghuerite opened her own closet, granting me permission to wear some of her most beautiful and expensive gowns. For performances, she would sent her valet, Bernard, to help me get dressed properly. Like her car and many of her other prized possessions, Marghuerite had names for her dresses. One of my favorites was the Peacock. It was a black sequined dress with a multicolored train of purple, turquoise, red, and yellow. That dress was so tight on me, I could only take baby steps in it, and you could forget about sitting down. It was Marghuerite's dress, which meant that its intended use was for posing, and posing only.

The Peacock was wonderful, but even it took a back seat to the Ostrich. It was a peach one-piece lace jumpsuit with a v-cut in the back and a train made of ostrich feathers. Bernard would hold the train for me like a bridesmaid until it was time for me to go on. Then, just as I would hit the stage, he would throw it out so that the feathers would float behind me as I made my entrance.

It was too much, especially for Bernard, who was himself a slave to fashion. He would sometimes weep at the sight of me in that outfit because it reminded him of his personal heroine, Josephine Baker: "Ooooooooooo, Gladys you look like Josephine tonight, yes you do, girl!"

Marghuerite had no problems ruling on everything from what shoes I should wear to what women the guys should be dating. She ruled over us as if we'd been born into her kingdom. Being called to her bedroom for a meeting was like being summoned before the queen. Wearing one of her many regal negligees, she would hold court from her bed made up in red velvet. It too had a title. She called her pillowed throne the Red Cloud.

We called her "Sister" but "Your Highness" would have been more appropriate. She was one of a kind. She opened many doors for us, as well as her home and heart. It was Marghuerite who introduced us to Sammy Davis, Jr., who became a big supporter and part of our family.

Marghuerite and Sammy had traveled in the same social circles for years and she always held him up as a role model. "When Sammy does anything, he does it first-class," she'd say. "I want you to watch him and study him."

In his act, Sammy wore a black tuxedo with a velvet collar and red lining. Marghuerite liked it so much she had a tailor make three of them for Bubba, William, and Edward. Those flashy tuxedos became a trademark for the guys when they incorporated them into the act. When we got to a dramatic point in a song, "Givin' Up," they would pop the middle button holding their jackets closed and then flash the red lining. That always got a big reaction from the audience and it became one of their signature moves.

Marghuerite brought Sammy to one of our shows at the Audubon Ballroom in New York and introduced us to him afterward but it wasn't until the 1970s that we worked with him.

I credit Sammy with teaching me how to properly sing a ballad. We were performing one night in Vegas for an older, mostly white audience that didn't seem to be familiar with our music. They just didn't seem very attentive, particularly during ballads such as "Help Me Make It Through the Night" or "The Way We Were," which were usually favorites with my audiences. I could hear them talking and laughing through much of the performance.

Sammy would sometimes come to our shows and sit on the side of the stage and afterward give us encouragement and tips. On this night, he came back and offered a little gem of wisdom about dealing with unresponsive audiences.

"Let me tell you what to do in a situation like that," he said, being fatherly. "People instinctively want to hear what others have to say, so when you get a crowd like that, let the audience take care of it themselves. The next time you go on and people are talking, just sing softer and keep getting softer and softer until they almost can't hear you. Somebody will eventually tell the people around to be quiet so they can hear, and soon, they will stop talking because of pressure from people around them."

It worked like a charm. Sammy was good for tips like that. Whenever we played together he would share his show biz savvy. It was like he had adopted us on Marghuerite's recommendation. If we didn't check in with him when we were in the same town, we'd get a call, "Oh, so now we too big to see Sammy," he'd tease.

There wasn't any chance of that happening, believe me. He was one of my many heroes.

CHAPTER 11

*M*y second child, Kenya, entered the world in a time of uncertainty and tumult, and while she has given me great joy, her birth did seem to be followed by no little upheaval in my life too.

She was born on November 25, 1963, the day a stunned nation said farewell to its assassinated president, John F. Kennedy, whom we had gotten to know through his sister Eunice Kennedy. She was a fan of our music and had invited us to play at fund-raisers as well as at the White House on a couple of occasions. Like most people, I was shocked by JFK's murder in Dallas two days earlier and I'd been glued to the television whenever I wasn't performing. I had intended to watch news broadcasts about the funeral, but my baby had other plans.

I had originally vowed to get more rest during this pregnancy, but it had not worked out that way. The night before Kenya was born, we did three shows in Westchester, New York, and then drove back down to Long Island, arriving at three A.M. We had been working all week and the guys were afraid I might have the baby on stage—I was so huge!

I fell asleep for three hours but then woke up and instead of going to bed and tackling the pile of laundry in the morning, something drove me to wade into it right then and there. That always happens before labor.

Jimmy got up and started breakfast and our son decided to help him flour the meat. He looked like little Casper the Friendly Ghost by the time they finished.

We laughed and looked at each other.

"Why are you watching me like that?" I said.

"Just why are you so busy, missy?" he asked slyly.

I hate it when everyone knows my business before I do. I was nesting big time, and we both knew what that meant.

The first labor pain hit about two seconds later but I tried to hold out. I didn't want Jimmy to get too smug, but part of it was that I wanted to watch the news coverage of JFK's funeral. It wasn't to be.

Because we didn't have health insurance, Bubba and Jimmy drove me to Flushing General Hospital—the closest public hospital—arriving only after they'd gotten lost two or three times. I had to go through a public welfare interview earlier before they would admit me. I was in so much pain, I don't even remember the delivery room. I just remember waking up in a big room with eight other women bedded beside me.

Jimmy and Bubba were standing there.

"What took you so long to get back?"

"Gladys, you've been out for five and a half hours," Bubba said.

I had no idea. I didn't even know whether I'd had a boy or girl until the nurse brought her in. Then I wasn't sure she was mine because she was so fair skinned I thought she was a white baby. The nurse had to assure me that they had not mixed the babies up, and she nearly had me convinced until the baby's eyes opened and they were light gray.

"Where did she get those from?" I asked Jimmy.

He said he thought some of his family had eyes of that shade.

"Well, whose ever baby she was, she's mine now," I said.

Jimmy and I were still deliberating on what to name our baby girl, when Marghuerite the queen mother made a royal appearance at bedside.

"Where is the baby? I want to see her right this minute," she ordered.

I explained that they only brought her in a feeding times.

"No, I want to see her now."

She probably would have had the nurse beheaded if it hadn't happened to be time for a feeding anyway. When our baby was brought to me, Marghuerite issued another proclamation.

"This child is mine, and her name will be Nelca."

Jimmy and I found that a bit bold, but we smiled. We knew Sister. She would bulldoze right over you if you let her. This time, we just decided to step aside for a while and let her think she was having her way. That was just fine with her.

She took the baby in her arms and set to claiming her.

"Hi, Nelca. Oh, you are just the prettiest little thing. And look at those beautiful eyes. My Nelca. She's going to be Miss America one day."

Having given us her royal blessing, Marghuerite handed *her* baby back to me, and left in a whirlwind of expensive scents and fine fabric.

"Well, what do *we* want to name her?" asked Jimmy.

We threw a few names back and forth—Nelca was not a contender—before I dozed off for a few minutes. Jimmy started reading a newspaper and I awoke to find him saying, "Now *that* would be a beautiful name for our baby!"

He showed me the front page, which had a story headlined "Conflict in Kenya."

As it turned out, the entire headline was appropriate. Although it had little to do with this beautiful baby girl, I was headed into tumultuous times in my private life. While the guys and I had been so focused on refining our performing skills, Jimmy had drifted off. Instead of taking a cue from Marguherite's work with us and getting his own act together, Jimmy seemed to have given up on himself.

He was getting deeper and deeper into drugs. He'd increased his pot smoking from maybe one joint a day to six or seven. He didn't do it in front of me or the kids but the impact on him was obvious. His clothes reeked of it, and he had lost all ambition for his career. I begged him to quit but that didn't work. I flushed his stash down the toilet, which angered him, but he always found more, even when there didn't seem to be money for anything else.

Like many women in these situations, I began to blame myself for his decline. I knew it hurt him to stand by as I became the family provider. I thought that maybe I could have helped him overcome his frustration over the fact that his own talents had not been widely recognized. I even wondered if my lack of sexual experience was responsible for his turning to drugs. Maybe if I was more assertive in the bedroom. . . . So many women do this to themselves. They take responsibility for their man's failings. They think if only they did something different he would change. The truth is something I came to realize later. It wasn't my love that Jimmy needed to save him. What he really needed was to learn to love himself as much as I did.

I was scared for Jimmy. My parents had instilled us with the message that if you did drugs, you would die. As adults, we understood that that was not necessarily true, but the association of drugs and death stayed with us. The first time I witnessed hard drugs and their impact on someone was at the Howard Theater in Washington, D.C. We were working with one of the great women blues singers and one of the sweetest women I knew, Etta James. I'd heard that she was using heroin and one night I walked into the little box of a dressing room we shared and found her lying on the floor under a table. A couple of her band members were already there trying to help her. I remember one of them talking about her needing "a fix." I stayed back. Poor Etta was twitching and squirming and there was fluid coming out of her nose and eyes. Etta eventually overcame her addiction, in fact, I saw her perform recently at the Hollywood Bowl and she was phenomenal. But watching her suffering from withdrawal pains that night years ago was frightening, particularly since I feared it was where Jimmy was headed one day.

I loved him, but I was not willing to follow him there, especially with two young children. I wanted to have a traditional marriage but I was not about to defer to a husband on this track. I'd long feared this part of Jimmy's character. I knew it was there from when we first started dating. After his mother died at such a young age, he would often say that he would die young too. I feared that he had said that so often that he intended to take his own life, in one way or another. I had hoped that his talent would win out, that he would take pride and joy in developing it and abandon those dark thoughts, but it wasn't to be. He had lost what faith he had in himself, and no matter what I did it seemed he couldn't see any other way out.

My sympathy and concern for him were tempered by my instincts to protect our children from what he was becoming. The bonds of our marriage were being strained to the breaking point, and they snapped after a confrontation aboard a show bus in Columbia, South Carolina, as part of a touring group of performers. When it was decided that I had to go back to work, I had called Momma and she flew to New York and took the kids back to Atlanta while we were on the road. My sister, Brenda, and brother David were helping her take care of them.

I missed my children dearly, particularly since I was having so much difficulty with their father. I had confided in my friend and fellow performer Mitty Collier, who had a hit with "The Love of My Man." In truth, we were both having trouble with the men we loved. She and I got on the bus to talk privately about our shared problems between shows. We'd just boarded when Jimmy called to me angrily from a seat in the back.

"Gladys, I want to talk to you."

Mitty gave me a look of concern, but I gestured that I could handle it. She got off the bus, leaving us alone. For a couple of minutes, I stood in the aisle at the front of the bus as he sat in the back berating me for some imagined slight. I didn't back down. It was obvious that he was sky high.

The argument grew more heated and Jimmy got up from his seat and moved toward me menacingly. There had never been any physical abuse in our relationship, but I feared it was coming at that point. We began yelling face-to-face, and he exploded. He grabbed me and we began wrestling in the front of the bus parked in front of the concert hall. People who had been leaving stopped and stared through the front windshield. Jimmy and I were too caught up in our anger and frustration to pay them any head, but a crowd started to gather.

Bubba appeared suddenly on the steps of the bus.

"Look, I don't want to get into your business, Jimmy, but that's my sister and I don't like to see you treating her that way. She is your wife and it is embarrassing for all of us to have you fighting in front of all these people," he said. "You should take it home."

Jimmy responded by taking a swing at Bubba. They began fighting and wrestling and soon they fell out the door of the bus onto the ground. The show's master of ceremony, Bill Murray, broke through the crowd that had gathered and he and some of our road crew pulled my husband and my brother apart.

Mitty led me away to a car that took us to our hotel. I sat up crying all night in her room. I'd never been in a fight like that before. I was a mess all night and into the morning. The bus ride to the next show was a quiet one, filled with tension. Jimmy kept his distance until we stopped for lunch. He came over to me then and said that when the bus reached New Orleans, he intended to leave it. I tried to convince him that leaving was not the answer, that we needed to talk and work things out, but he would have none of it. The anger was mostly gone from him, now I could tell he was embarrassed and ashamed not only over the fight but also because he felt he had failed as a father and husband.

After the show in New Orleans the next night, I really expected Jimmy to be on the bus even though he had said he was leaving. I hadn't given up, and I had hoped he wouldn't either. He wasn't there.

Staring out the window as we pulled away toward our next destination, my numbness gave away to the realization that I'd lost my husband. He had not said that he wouldn't be back, but my heart told me he was gone. The children were safe back in Atlanta with my momma, and I knew I had to keep working to feed them. I had harbored dreams of returning to the role of full-time mother but it didn't appear to be in the cards.

I didn't talk to Jimmy for many weeks. I picked up a few reports on his activities from other show business people as we traveled across the south. I'd heard that he was working in Jerry Butler's band for a while. Then Tina Turner's sister Alline called to tell me that he had joined a house band in the Central Forest Club in Houston, Texas. She'd gone to see him and she was worried.

"He's in trouble," she said. "He's doing hard stuff now."

My darkest fears for this sensitive but troubled man were coming true. Shortly after I heard that news, I learned that we'd been booked into that club. I actually looked forward to seeing him, and I hoped that I might be able to help him. I didn't know what else to expect.

We saw each other when I reached Houston, but I almost didn't recognize him. His boyish handsomeness had weathered into a rugged look that aged him ten years. His face was puffy, I guess from the drugs, and he looked so worn out. The intimacy that we had shared since our early teens was gone. He danced around any attempt I made to break through the polite front he was putting up. I could tell he didn't want to be there, that it was painful for him. We talked about our children, but it was like I was describing their progress and their activities to someone I'd just met. We traded phone numbers. We hugged but it was bittersweet when we parted that day. Two years would pass before I'd see him again. He came to Detroit, where we'd moved, because he was playing with Jerry Butler again and they had a gig at the famous nightclub, the Twenty Grand. I invited him to stay at the house with Momma and me and the kids so that he could spend time with them. He agreed. But after only two days, he said he had to go.

"I can't be with you all like this," he said. "I start craving it. I start wanting my family back."

He had decided to answer what was apparently the far more powerful craving for self-destruction. When he left that day, all my lingering hopes and dreams for him—and for us—went too.

I was only twenty years old, with two young children, and only my own earnings from performing to keep us afloat. Jimmy hadn't contributed anything since his departure in New Orleans. I hadn't pushed for it because I was used to going it alone by that time. Fortunately, my mother was there to care for the kids when I was on the road, but it was still painful for me to overcome my own powerful maternal instincts.

The guys on the bus knew to leave me alone for the first few days of any trip that pulled me away from my kids. Many times I left the house in tears with the sounds of their young voices burning my ears, "Mommy, don't go. When are you coming back?"

Why is it that the men didn't cry when they left their children behind? I knew. They usually left their children in the care of their wives. Leaving their families was expected of them as men and heads of their households. They often looked forward to it as an adventure and a way of fulfilling their obligations. For me, it was a matter of survival.

This conflict within me made me increasingly aware that I was at a disadvantage as a woman in a man's world, and that I had better toughen up. There was little sympathy for my tears and my misgivings about leaving the children. They expected me to accept the man's role and the woman's role in the lives of my children. Deep down, I resented having to play those dual roles. But I went onstage and I sang.

Occasionally, I brought the kids along on the road. I wanted to be with them, but I also hoped that they would come to understand what I did and why I did it so that they wouldn't grow up resenting me. Mostly though, I left them with my mother, who stepped into the role willingly even after having worked so hard to raise her own brood. She became their surrogate mother as well as their grand-mother. Her role in my life has been so great it nearly defies descrip-tion. Although today she is nearly blind, her vision for her children has never lost its clarity. She has been our champion and our guiding spirit. In the early days when we were on the road, Momma would send us notes to keep us going. She once sent a necklace with a mus-tard seed on it to symbolize the passage in the Bible that says you need only as much faith as would fit on a grain of mustard seed in order to move mountains. The necklace was my momma's way to reminding us that if we had faith in God and in our talents, we would persevere.

A spiritual woman, Momma also taught us how to do a prayer chain and it became a part of our regular routine just prior to perform-ing. We would join hands and say a prayer backstage in order to use our gifts to carry out God's wishes. Some of the less spiritual people we encountered on the road thought this odd but others who shared our churchgoing background—the Temptations and the O'Jays in par-ticular—picked up on it too. I was once explaining to a reporter how much Jesus Christ was part of our lives and just before we went on camera she stopped and said, "Do you mind not saying Jesus Christ on the air?"

"Yes I mind," I said. "If I deny Him, He will deny me."

Oh, Momma and her spiritual teachings stayed with us. There is no denying that fact. When we were kids, she had always insisted we say a prayer before every trip and we took that habit on the road with us too. It was a good thing too. We may well have been one of the most accident-prone but blessed groups of all time.

One of our closest calls came on a trip from Atlanta to New York. My younger brother David and I were with William and some friends in their car. William, my baby brother, David, and I were going to New York to join the other Pips for a show at the Apollo. We were taking turns driving and sleeping and during the night, somewhere in North Carolina, the teenage nephew of one of our friends, Luella McClenden, got behind the wheel. We didn't know that he hadn't had much driving experience and when it began raining it became obvious that he didn't belong in the driver's seat, especially on a two-lane highway. He had trouble even pulling onto the highway after taking the wheel. He was about to drive past our exit, when Luella yelled that he was about to miss his turn; he swerved and lost control of the car. It hit a pole, spun around and fell into a ravine. Just as the car started to plunge down, I heard David say "Get down G. (my nickname)," and I felt him push my head toward my lap.

When the car stopped falling, we could hardly see where we were because of all the smoke coming from the engine. We were so far down into this deep ravine that we couldn't see the tops of the pine trees surrounding us. Fortunately, no one was seriously injured, probably because we had been packed in so tightly. There hadn't been much traffic on the road and we doubted if anyone had seen us take the plunge so we knew we had to get out of there on our own. We formed another kind of chain, a human chain, to help each other up the ravine. Once we'd reached the highway, we flagged down a car and got to a service station. A wrecker pulled the car out of the ravine and amazingly, it was still roadworthy. We drove all night, without giving the nephew a turn, and made it to New York in time for the first show. I was so sore I could hardly move, so I was not what you would call a real animated singer that day. The Pips had to move in double time to make up for the Gladys statue onstage with them.

Although she didn't seem to have much in the way of a spiritual life, Marghuerite too benefited from Momma's teachings when she accompanied us on a trip through Kentucky—a trip that none of us will ever forget. We were in a two-car caravan with The Pips and some other performers. We had done a prayer chain before starting out and along the way we'd been entertaining each other singing gospel songs. Momma's spirit must have been with us because around two A.M. an eerie feeling swept through both Bubba and me in our car. William, who was driving the car in front of us must have felt it, too, because right then, he pulled over into a service station parking lot.

"You feel something strange?" Bubba said.

"Yeah," William replied. "What's up with that?"

It was a little scary that we'd all felt it, like a sudden chill, but it was warm outside, but it was more, like a sense that something was about to happen, though we couldn't tell whether it was good or bad.

William was shaken up so much he suggested we say a prayer together. We grabbed hands right there in the parking lot. Even Marghuerite joined in this time. We did a prayer chain and then got back in our cars. The guys were driving carefully because they were both still a little shaken up and there was a light fog. As we came across a bridge over a small creek, the fog suddenly turned red and got thicker so that we could hardly see beyond the front of the car. Then there was a bend in the road and in the middle of our lane, there was a car, or what had been a car before it was wrecked. It was badly mangled. We pulled over to the side and got out to see if we could help but we couldn't find any people either in the car or on the roadside. Now we were really shaken up. We searched some more but didn't find anyone so we returned to our cars, to go back and alert the people at the service station about the wreck. But we didn't leave without saying yet another prayer. This was one of thanks. If not for the grace of God, and the protective love and guidance of our Momma, we might have been part of that mangled mess on the highway. She was with us then, and always.

CHAPTER 12

CHAPTER 12

*B*y 1964, we were covering nearly 80,000 miles a year and getting nowhere fast. At least that's how it felt. We were popular with the fans, but still cash-poor. Marghuerite and Cholly had prepared us to make the move to the next level as entertainers, now we needed a blockbuster record to move us into the strat-o-sphere, as the deejays of those days would say.

She had hooked us up with Larry Maxwell of Maxx Records and we did a song with him entitled "Giving Up Is Hard to Do," which did well thanks to the deejays who picked up on it, particularly Magnificent Montague in New York, who invited us to his station one night to publicize the record. While we were there he locked the door to his studio so no one could get in and then he played it almost all night long over and over. We talked to callers and promoted the record and all of our upcoming concert dates. I don't know about the listening audience, but we talked so much we put ourselves to sleep. Ol' Magnificent Montague had to wake us up when he finally unlocked the door to go home.

The radio deejays were a big help to us in our careers, but to really break out, we needed something more. Maxwell's record company was a small one, and like us, he itched to move up, so in 1965 when he was offered a job promoting records for Motown in Detroit, he asked if we wanted to go with him. He said Motown's founder and chairman, Berry Gordy, was prepared to offer us a contract. We'd already heard a lot about Motown and not all of it was good as far as I was concerned. Many of the other performers we'd appeared with and traveled with on concert tours were from Motown. They had a huge load of talent with Smokey Robinson, the Temptations, the Four Tops, Stevie Wonder, Martha and the Vandellas, and the Supremes, to name a few.

That truckload of talent was part of the problem in my view. They were all totally dependent on Berry and the company.

After Maxwell made his pitch to me and The Pips, we called a meeting in our new, improved office. Yes, from the doodlebug, we'd moved to a somewhat roomier Oldsmobile station wagon and then to a somewhat less dilapidated silver Cadillac. We parked on the street and proceeded to meet. From the start, I was a minority, which seemed to be my standard place in life. The guys were ready to jump to Hitsville, which was Motown's nickname because of all the big records they'd been turning out. In 1964, Motown had charted five Top Ten singles. They would have twice as many in 1965.

Motown's artists were all over the radio and television. Their Motown Revue promotional road tours were drawing huge crowds across the country. But I wasn't so sure Motown was right for Gladys Knight & The Pips. Motown had developed nearly all of its talent from within. It was known for taking young talent from Detroit's housing projects, street corners, and honky-tonks and refining rough-edged, rhythm-and-blues singers into pop performers. Some critics griped that Motown was taking the soul out of the Detroit sound in order to cross over into the white market. But nobody was arguing with Gordy's success. He ran Motown like a star factory. His groups were put on salary even if they were selling millions of dollars worth of records. In other words, the royalties all poured into someone else's pocket.

The question was, did we need them? We were already a successful group. Would promoting us be a priority within the star factory or would we be a stepchild in that environment? What could they do for us that we couldn't do for ourselves?

Berry was charismatic, which is characteristic of successful entrepreneurs. He was the son of a Detroit plastering contractor, who had worked as a chrome trimmer on the Ford assembly line while hustling talent and producing records on the side. Frustrated after being ripped off by bigger players and going through bankruptcy with his first record company, Berry began Motown in 1960 with an initial investment of $700 borrowed from his father, a former Georgia cotton farmer.

Seven years later, Berry's new record company was worth $30 million. Along with having an eye for talented performers, most of whom had been around Detroit for years, Berry had recruited a top-notch house band, and a team of talented songwriters, including Smokey Robinson, who fed him a high-profit diet of chart-busters, and the record production team of Holland-Dozier-Holland that in a span of three years produced twenty-eight Top Twenty hits (twelve of them number one).

That's what Berry could give us, the guys argued.

"We already know how to take care of ourselves. We have our own system. All we need from them is a record," said William.

I had to admit that William was right. As a group we were ahead of our time in many ways. We had already formed our own corporation with a pension and profit-sharing plan. We had done our own booking and money management off and on for years. We were known as one of the most reliable and professional acts in the business.

It was something of a joke among our group's members and other entertainers that Berry had modeled Motown on Gladys Knight & The Pips, Inc. But the joke was not far from the truth. Over the previous few years, everyone we'd hired to help us refine our act had been recruited to work for Motown. Our vocal coach, Maurice King, was there now. So was Cholly Atkins.

Berry had hired them to head Motown's Artist Development Department, where they trained performers in voice, dance, and stage presence just as they had trained us. Berry had even hired his own version of Marghuerite Mays—a woman who was an expert in etiquette, posture, makeup, and fashion. This lady ran what became known as Motown's charm school where all of its great girl groups were tutored in everything from how to walk and speak, to which fork to use for the salad and which sleeping positions were best for preserving their bouffant hairdos while on the road.

Since Mr. King and Pops had both had it written into their Motown contracts that they could still work with us, we didn't need to sign on with Gordy to get their services. Did we really want to be part of an outfit that had its own company song (written by Smokey) about how neat, clean, united, and *swinging* its employees were?

Still, the guys argued, we definitely could use some of Hitsville's hit-making powers. The one missing handhold in our climb to the upper levels was a steady string of hit records. As usual we put it to a vote with each of us having equal voting power. It was 3–1. I was outvoted, which was nothing unusual.

In a few days, we were motoring to Motown and a new chapter in our career as a group. We signed a seven-year contract with Motown, which was longer than anything we had signed with the five other record companies that had represented us to that point. We were put on salary like everybody else, but unlike everybody else, we kept close track of every penny. There has been a great deal written over the years about artists who felt they were ripped off by Motown, but our experience was fairly unique. As a veteran group, we knew a thing or two about the financial end of the business, and what we didn't know, we hired our own lawyers and accountants to tell us.

Motown was run like the old company store in cotton country. You got a salary but they docked you for expenses. For young artists, many of whom came from extreme poverty, the system seemed like a dream. Motown bought its artists their cars, their houses, and often their groceries, but those expenses were usually charged against future earnings.

If you didn't keep close track of what your expenses were and how much you were being docked, your salary paycheck might come printed in red ink. We kept track.

Initially, Berry and his managers tried to entice us by telling us they were going to buy us cars and houses, but we told them no thanks, we could take care of that ourselves, just give us our money. Anytime they tried to bill us for an expense or to "give" us something, we demanded to know what the real cost was going to be to us. Our caution paid off. Once we noticed a deduction in our paychecks for some ridiculous amount for "musical arrangements." Now, those arrangements were nothing more than a few notes scrawled on a piece of paper by Motown's famed musicians. It was up to us to take those scrawls and make music out of them. When they billed us for that, we demanded that they give us the piece of paper the arrangements had been written on. After all, we said, if we are going to pay for them, we want to have them. They couldn't come up with the goods, so the charge came off our tab at the company store. It wouldn't be the last time we questioned their accounting procedures.

We quickly earned a reputation for being more independent than most of Motown's groups, which was fine with us. Berry kept telling us how much he loved our group and our sound and how much he respected what we had accomplished on our own. We said we wanted his input and his full attention to promoting us and our records. There was no doubt that he was a star maker, if he focused on you and your career as he had with Diana Ross and the Supremes and the Temptations, you got the songs, you got the records, you got the press, and the tours and the money.

On the flip side of that, if Berry wasn't personally behind you, nobody else at Motown had the power to pick you up and carry you to the top. Berry was Motown. He built it and he ran it with an iron hand.

From the start, it was apparent that we were not going to be one of the boss's priority groups. He was honest about that and I loved him for it. We were relegated to the lower tier of Motown acts with the Monitors and the Spinners. Some of their members had to do odd jobs around Hitsville in order to keep their paychecks coming. They doubled as chauffeurs and gofers until they scored on a song and went on tour, even then they never became part of the cliquish inner circle.

We didn't become anybody's coat handler, but our status was made clear in other ways early on. We'd hear about parties at Berry's house and company picnics *after* they happened, which is usually a clear sign that we weren't on the A-list.

We got a glimpse of life on the A-list at Motown when we were sent out on tour with the Supremes. They were the headliners, we were their opening act. If it was intended as a lesson in humility, it failed. We showed the Supremes a few things on that tour, and we were also exposed to a whole new audience thanks to their drawing power.

Not that we thought we were better than them. We loved their music and their style and we were in awe at their ability to captivate an audience that was comprised of more whites than blacks. The Supremes didn't really have any elaborate choreography, but in their mohair sheath shirts or long tight satin dresses, they had an aura of class that made them more of a lady group than a girl group.

Off stage, it was a bit of a different story. We had known the Supremes for a few years. The first time we performed with them, we weren't with Motown and they weren't headliners. Back then, they were just three little city girls, Diana, Mary Wilson, and Florence Ballard, from Detroit's Brewster housing project who were struggling to get into "the club" that Motown represented in Detroit. On that pre-Motown tour, I shared a dressing room with the three of them and I could see how Florence and Mary were very close and caring of each other while it seemed that Diana already considered herself to be above them as a performer.

Diana's attitude had earned her the nickname Miss Cute on the tour. She may not have been the most talented of the trio or, for that matter, the cutest, but she was certainly the most driven, and when a performance did not click one night, I heard her fussing at Florence and Mary, telling them that they were to blame. Minutes later, though, they emerged as the Supremes and Diana was back in character, poking her head out of the sunroof of their car, giving the star wave, showing that famous "stretch-limo" smile.

By the time we met again on the Motown tour, their name had changed to Diana Ross and the Supremes and they were one of the hottest acts in the country, but Diana was still as competitive and driven as ever. During one of our performances at a theater-in-the-round on the tour, The Pips and I were cooking on stage and getting a great response when I noticed Diana standing in a doorway watching us. She only stood there a short time, but there was something in the look on her face that told me trouble was brewing.

After the show, she didn't say anything, but the next day, the word came down from Motown. The road manager informed us that "Berry" wanted us to come back to Detroit pronto. We were yanked off the tour without explanation. We didn't need one. We figured Diana had seen the enemy and it was us. As the headliner, she wasn't about to have an opening act outshine her. When we returned to Motown, Berry didn't try to hide the truth.

"I hear you were giving my act a hard time," he said with a chuckle.

We weren't really happy about being pulled off the tour where we had been getting great exposure, but everyone in the business knew what had happened. It was something of an honor, really. It showed that we were headliners too, even if we hadn't yet had the hit records that Diana, Florence, and Mary were putting out.

We decided from then on to make our own breaks without Berry Gordy's blessed deliverance. We didn't hide our disenchantment, and before long, we had formed a little club of our own with some of the other malcontents including Martha Reeves, Marvin Gaye, and Ivory Joe Hunter. One night we were all meeting at our house in Detroit when we got word that someone from Motown's management was coming over to talk to us. Word had gotten around about the Hitsville mutineers. We scattered like a bunch of spooked chicks but as far as I know, nobody from management showed up.

Being one of Berry's outcasts eventually paid off with our first hit. The malcontents were still a very talented bunch and we stuck together. One of our nonperforming sympathizers was Norman Whitfield, a producer who was also struggling to get into the inner circle. He had been working with us since the spring of 1967 and had given us a Top Forty hit with "Everybody Needs Love," which was a hand-me-down song from the Temptations, who had a minor hit with it before we did.

Motown did a lot of that. One group would take a song to a certain point and then, after a brief period, the management would have another group record it to see if they could do anything with it. It was a hit-and-miss business at Hitsville. Still, we were eager to have a blockbuster record that we could call our own, and Norman was just as hungry for a breakthrough as we were. One day when we were about to leave the studio, he stopped us in the hallway. Norman was a blustery guy, but I'd never seen him that hyped up.

"I've got something I want you to hear," he said. "Follow me."

He was being very mysterious.

We followed him to his office, a cramped cubbyhole that you couldn't turn a page in. Waiting for us outside it was Barrett Strong, one of Motown's first performers who had become a house songwriter.

Grinning like the cats who'd recorded the canary, Barrett and Norman handed us a tape.

"This is it," they said gleefully.

"It" was a tune called "I Heard It through the Grapevine." They played it for us.

"Why don't you see what you can do with it," Norman said.

I wish I could say that we knew immediately that this song would be a great hit for us.

Okay, I will say it, because it's true.

We knew this was a great song, and that we could make it even better. We had a great feeling about it as soon as we heard it, and we felt that once we added some background vocals, it would be even better.

We treated that demo tape as if it was the Hope diamond. It certainly was our hope for the future of our career.

We "borrowed" a big reel-to-reel tape recorder from a Motown studio and took our treasure home. We set the recorder up in a hall and started messing around with different phrasing, adding little licks and grooves. We lived that song for about a month, getting to know it and playing with ways to make it our own. We listened to it over breakfast, during lunch and dinner, and in between. We played it in our sleep.

When we agreed that we had a version of "Grapevine" that was ripe for recording, we ran to Motown in search of Norman.

"Oh man, you've got to hear this," we said, unable to control our enthusiasm.

He put the tape of the music on and we began singing.

> *Mmmmmmmmmm, I bet you wonderin' how I knew*
> *Baby, baby, baby 'bout your plans to make me blue*
> *With some other girl you knew before*
> *Oooo-ooo-Ooo-Oooo*
> *Between the two of us girls, you know I love you more . . .*

Norman was kicked back listening and trying not to smile, but we could tell we had him. When the guys got to: "Just about, just about, just about to lose my mind" we knew Norman had made up his. We had a hit and he knew it. He could hold it no longer. He shot out of his chair.

"We've got to get a studio right now."

He called to find out if Studio A was available because it was the most intimate of the three at Motown. It was also considered a lucky place because a lot of the biggest hits had been recorded there. He found out that Smokey was using Studio A, so he called down there and begged him to let us use some of his time. Smokey, whom we'd known for years, made a joke of saying no, but gave it to us anyway.

True to our position low on the Motown totem pole, we had to lobby hard to get our recording of "Grapevine" some playing time. It sat around for a while but eventually, and appropriately, word of it began to get around the office and the business. People kept hearing that it was a great song through the magic of interpersonal communication. Finally, that fall, Motown released it.

That was all they did. They released it and then stood back. No full-page ads. No television or concert appearances. The Motown promotional machine apparently had blown a gasket.

But this song was not to be denied. We had our own connections out there beyond Hitsville, and we did all we could to get records to the deejays who had supported us over the years. They responded by making "I Heard It through the Grapevine" the blockbuster that we had been dreaming of. It locked onto the number one spot on the R& B charts for six weeks and stayed at number two for another three weeks.

At the end of 1967, the biggest selling record of the year for Motown belonged to the bottom of the totem pole gang. Thank you very much.

It wasn't just a record for us. It was a work permit, and work came flowing our way. We moved right on up to the plum spots with chairs in the dressing rooms instead of stools or boxes: the Latin Casino in Cherry Hill, New Jersey, the Flamingo Hotel in Las Vegas, and the Copacabana in New York.

Making it to the Copa, in particular, had been a major goal for us. To headline there was to know that your music had reached across all boundaries. The audiences there ranged in age from twenty-year-old rock and rollers to sixty-year-old serious music lovers. All the great pop and jazz singers played there; Sinatra, Sammy Davis, Jr., and Mel Torme were regulars. We were beyond the record as an act. We really began to feel like successful insiders when the Copa's owner, Jules Podell, adopted us. He was a man of few words but waiters would jump when he merely tapped his ring on his table. He was an imposing guy and I was a little intimidated by him, but everywhere we went after playing his club, we were greeted by a telegram from him wishing us luck. I don't want to know how he knew our schedule, but what he wanted to know, he found out.

The success of *Grapevine* helped us reach a new level of popularity across the country and around the world, but back at Hitsville, U.S.A., it seemed we were regarded as second-team players who got lucky and scored big. This lingering attitude struck home about a year after our breakthrough song was introduced. The guys and I were relaxing in the lounge at the Flamingo Hotel in Las Vegas when we heard the familiar music for our song being played over the sound system, but it wasn't *our* voices singing it.

It was Marvin Gaye, our friend and fellow Motown outsider. He had recorded *our* hit song. Or so we had thought. Marvin made it his hit song too. His version did even better than ours. In 1968 and 1969, it sold more than four million copies. Marvin broke through with it too. He sang it on the *Hollywood Palace,* on the *Joey Bishop Show* and on the *Tonight Show. Billboard* magazine named him one of the country's most popular male vocalists, right up there with Elvis and Glen Campbell.

It burned us a bit that Berry Gordy couldn't give us at least a couple of years to bask in our success with that song, but we didn't begrudge Marvin a hit. He deserved it, though we did tease him some about stealing our song. We even performed it with him in the mid-seventies on a Dick Clark special called "Salute," featuring the story of Gladys Knight & The Pips. Marvin was a special guest and we had a great time singing with him, which was a gift because it turned out to be one of his last television appearances before he was shot and killed.

It was true, too, that by covering "Grapevine" so soon after we had a hit with it, Marvin stripped away some of our identity as performers. To this day, people still debate who did it first. Now you know.

There is one more bit of Motown era trivia I might as well clear up while I'm on the topic. In 1969, we were headlining at the Regal Theater in Chicago when we first saw a young group out of Gary, Indiana, the Jackson 5. Their father, Joe, had brought them to the theater hoping they could audition for a spot in the Regal's talent show the next day. Bubba, William, and Edward knew Joe from his days playing with a Detroit rhythm-and-blues band, the Falcons. Joe had quit playing in order to support his wife and nine children by working in the steel mills in Gary. He still loved to play, he told The Pips, but now he was focusing on managing a new act—his sons. He said he had put his guitar in storage and left it there for more than ten years but one day his second son, Tito, found it and began secretly teaching himself to play it. When Joe caught Tito banging away on his beloved old guitar a couple months later, he gave him a whipping. Then he said, "Okay, now let's see how well you can play it."

Joe said it soon became apparent that all of his children were talented musicians and five of his sons formed a group with five-year-old Michael, a pint-sized James Brown clone, taking the lead-singer role. He promised to bring them by and he did later as we were talking with the Rev. Jesse Jackson outside our dressing room. Joe introduced us to Tito, Randy, Jermaine, Marlon, and little Michael and I thought they were a cute bunch of kids, and very well disciplined. They were polite, quiet-mannered, and hungry, apparently, because they were all carrying identical brown-paper lunch bags.

I invited them to sit in my dressing room while they waited for their audition. Michael's little legs dangled over the couch, unable to reach the floor.

"I hear you guys sing," I said to him.

A typical publicity shot of Edward, William, Bubba, and me during our early Motown days. *(Courtesy of the author.)*

Gladys Knight & The Pips on *The Ed Sullivan Show* in 1971 when I sang "If I Were Your Woman." *(Courtesy of the author.)*

I was blessed to have been coached early on by the famous Detroit Flame Show Bar and Fox Theater music director Maurice King, who helped me define my singing and stage style. *(Courtesy of the author.)*

Equally important to the career of Gladys Knight & The Pips is the legendary choreographer, and our "Pops," Cholly Atkins, seen here with his wife, Mae. *(Courtesy of the*

This photo was taken in Puerto Rico when "I Heard It through the Grapevine" was climbing the charts. *(Courtesy of the author.)*

That's me and Bubba in the studio, probably recording a commercial. *(Courtesy of the author.)*

A classic 1968 pic of me and my Pips. *(Courtesy of the author.)*

Here's another publicity shot taken in the 1970s, when I was good and skinny! *(Courtesy of the author.)*

Gladys Knight And The Pips

I remember this picture of me and the guys well. It was taken when we were taping a national commercial for Coca-Cola's "Memories" campaign. *(Courtesy of the author.)*

Here we are during our "Neither One of Us" days. *(Courtesy of the author.)*

Me and the guys feeling on top of the world in Las Vegas. *(Courtesy of the author.)*

That's me and my
second husband,
Barry Hankerson,
in 1975. *(Courtesy
of the author.)*

My youngest
child, Shanga Ali
Hankerson, when
he was just a baby.
(Courtesy of the author.)

I don't know where or when this photograph of me was taken, but it is one of my all-time favorites. (*Courtesy of the author.*)

Major magazine publisher John H. Johnson and I in what must have been 1980, since I have on the white mink coat I wore back then. (*Courtesy of the author.*)

My kids, Kenya, Shanga, and Jimmy, in 1982 at Momma's house in Las Vegas right after we got Shanga back. (*Courtesy of the author.*)

Me and The Pips hanging out in Atlanta in the early 1980s with writer Wes Smith, who ended up helping me write this book. Watch out for the pedal pushers! *(Courtesy of Wes Smith.)*

Here I am singing solo in New York City. *(Photo by Lloyd Terry.)*

My daughter Kenya and I are huge tennis fans, and here we are with our hero Martina Navratilova at a celebrity tournament where I hit a few shots with my favorite pro. *(Courtesy of the author.)*

Here I am surrounded by my old Chit'lin' Circuit pals The Dells. *(Courtesy of the author.)*

That's me and Bubba surrounded by The Emotions, who sang at my daughter Kenya's wedding. *(Courtesy of the author.)*

I love this shot of me and my poker-playing buddy Leslie Uggams taken a couple of years ago in New York. *(Photo by Lloyd Terry.)*

Me and the innovative actor-director Robert Townsend. *(Courtesy of the author.)*

Nancy Wilson, me, and former New York City mayor David Dinkins. *(Photo by Lloyd Terry.)*

A proud moment for me, this picture was taken when I received an honorary doctorate degree from Morris Brown College in Atlanta. *(Courtesy of the author.)*

Two proud moms with their handsome sons: Shanga, me, Patti LaBelle and her Zuri. *(Courtesy of the author.)*

Patti LaBelle, Dionne Warwick, and me doing our thing on the "Sisters in the Name of Love" HBO special I produced in 1989. *(Courtesy of the author.)*

Whitney Houston and me at an AIDS benefit in New York. (*Photo by Lloyd Terry.*)

Me and Bill Cosby at a charity event he hosted. (*Photo by Lloyd Terry.*)

Me and my former costar Flip Wilson from our sitcom "Charlie and Company." (*Courtesy of the author.*)

Me and my girls, Dionne, Patti, and Cyndi Lauper.
(Photo by Lloyd Terry.)

California congress-
woman Maxine
Waters, me, and the
incomparable Nancy
Wilson. I hated my
dress. I'm too fat!
*(Courtesy of the
author.)*

My son Jimmy Newman, all grown up with his beautiful family: Rishawn, Michelene, Jimmy, Nastasia, little Sterling, and laughing Stephan. *(Courtesy of the author.)*

Me and my pretty sister, Brenda. *(Courtesy of the author.)*

My daughter Kenya Jackson and her handsome brood (Braves fans all!). Clockwise from top: Jim, Jontiel, Jimmy, little Aaron, Kenya, giggling Aria, and Julian. *(Courtesy of the author.)*

My momma (or Gram, as we all call her now) gives Shanga a big hug and kiss at his high school graduation in 1993. *(Courtesy of the author.)*

Les Brown and me in happier days; this portrait was taken on our first wedding anniversary. *(Photo courtesy of the author.)*

My ever-loving big brother, Bubba, taking care of business as usual. *(Photo by Lloyd Terry.)*

Two of my spiritual mentors; left, Bishop Blake of the West Angeles Church of God and Christ in Los Angeles; and right, the beautiful Rev. Colemon of Christ Universal Temple in Chicago. *(Courtesy of the author.)*

Me and "Uncle" B.B. King earlier this year in Atlanta. *(Courtesy of the author.)*

"Yeah, we sing," he replied in a voice that was barely a whisper.

"Is it something you've wanted to do a long time?" I asked.

They shyly nodded yes.

Their father wasn't so shy. Joe asked if we could get someone from Motown to come and check out their act. He reminded me of my momma, who never missed a chance to promote our talents. I hadn't heard them perform at that point, but I told him that I'd see what I could do for them.

Then his sons went down to the stage and started practicing.

"Oh, look at this," I said. They were obviously something special. They'd only been performing about three years, but they were already as polished as many of the Motown acts. They obviously had been studying the Temptations and The Pips too.

I got on the phone to our manager at Motown.

"Look, I know I don't have a lot of clout with you all, but someone should come down and see Joe Jackson's kids here at the Regal. Berry should see them for himself. They're called the Jackson 5."

Our manager, Taylor Cox, listened and he said he would get back to me, but he didn't. When I called later, he again said he'd get back to me. Again, he didn't call. Nobody from Motown showed up in response to my calls on behalf of Joe Jackson and his talented sons.

And so, they were never heard from again.

Just kidding. Actually, it was another Motown artist, and another of its outsiders who finally got Berry to pay attention to the Jacksons. Bobby Taylor, a member of the Vancouvers, caught the Jackson 5 a few months later, after they had become a regular featured act at the Regal. He arranged for them to audition for Berry who promptly signed them to a contract.

Berry sent them out to Los Angeles for prerecording rehearsals at Motown West's studios there. They did so well it was decided to give them a song that had been written for another Motown group—ours. It was entitled "I Want You Back," and Berry had actually been considering giving it to Diana Ross because it had turned out to be such a good song. Instead, though, he let the Jackson 5 record it, and it became their first hit.

To add insult to injury, when it became apparent that the Jackson 5 were going to be superstars, Berry decided that their discovery should be credited to another one of his superstars. So, not only did we not get credit for first spotting them, neither did Bobby Taylor.

For years after that, Motown's press releases said that the Jackson 5 had been discovered by none other than Miss Cute, Diana Ross.

CHAPTER 13

CHAPTER 13

*I*t was the mid-sixties, a time of social rebellion and civil unrest. There were antiwar demonstrations on campuses and racial riots across the country, including Detroit, where the riots erupted in 1967 only a few blocks from our home. We watched the looting and the fires on television in amazement since we had just returned home from Motown's studios by way of 12th St., which is where the riots began just shortly after we had driven past that area. Once again, my guardian angel must have been sitting on my shoulder. These were turbulent times when young people, black and white, were rebelling against injustice, but also against tradition. They were scary times in some ways, but also a time when people were less inhibited—even little Miss Goody Two Shoes.

It was during this period, that we defied Motown's traditions and also cut loose a bit from our button-down, churchgoing upbringing. Believe it or not, we even earned a reputation around town as a partying bunch.

Blame it on the Rat Pack, or at least on one of the Pack's more potent poisons. I'm talking about Mr. Harvey Wallbanger.

Let me back it up a bit. When we moved to Detroit we left Marghuerite's mansion, and Marghuerite's management, but I guess we learned a little bit from her about having a good time. She had done a lot for us and we were appreciative, but not so much that we were willing to fulfill her demand for an equal share in our group's lifetime earnings. We didn't need a fifth Pip, and so we parted company with that great lady. But I guess some of her zest for life rubbed off on us.

Thanks to the long-term Motown contract, which guaranteed us a salary, Bubba and I decided to buy a big old two-flat house and to make that house a home, Momma and Brenda and her family moved to Detroit with us and our families. We lived on LaSalle Street, which became famous as the place where all the Motown stars lived. We didn't live on the fanciest part of LaSalle with all of the huge turn-of-the-century mansions, though. We and our Motown friends lived in a more normal neighborhood of nice regular homes. Martha and the Vandellas lived with singer and songwriter Ivory Joe Hunter just down the street from us, so did Jackie Wilson and the Temptations. It was one big, mostly happy, and occasionally delirious family.

We weren't the favorite children at Motown, but we kept ourselves entertained, sometimes with a little help from Mr. Wallbanger. We were introduced to this delectable but potent cocktail by Sammy Davis, Jr., when we did a few shows with him in Las Vegas. Being a host with the most, and a certified member of the Rat Pack with Frank Sinatra, Dean Martin, Joey Bishop, Peter Lawford, and assorted others, Sammy had not only a valet and a chauffeur, he also had his own private bartender—in his dressing room.

When we'd stop by to visit, Sammy would have his bartender make up the drink of the moment for us, and at that point in history Harvey Wallbangers were the only way to fly. Since I had never been much of a drinker (do I have to remind you of my graduation night?), Harvey Wallbangers appealed to me because they tasted like orange juice with an attitude. They were refreshing and sweet going down.

Kind of Harvey-ish at that point. It took a few minutes for the wall-banging part to kick in, but when it did, things got hopping.

Harvey Wallbangers became the official drink of the parties we had on LaSalle Street with our Motown friends and neighbors and visitors. Our place in particular became sort of halfway house for band members and other performers passing through. The parties just seemed to be a natural response to having a lot of crazy people packed in one neighborhood. Though we hardly ever planned them in advance, we would cook up all sorts of food, get a bartender, and put out the call to everyone at Motown. It was an open invitation but of course the "chosen ones" rarely graced us with an appearance. We didn't miss them. How could we with a house full of Marvellettes, Miracles, Temptations, Vandellas, assorted Staples, and sometimes one, two, three, even four Tops?

Aretha, bless her, would call sometimes to check out the action, but I can't recall that she ever showed up.

"Gladys! Aretha's on the phone."

"Hi Re! Come join the party."

"Well, who's there?"

"I'm not telling you. You have to come and find out."

She missed some great parties. I suppose by some entertainer's standards, our gatherings were pretty tame stuff, but for me it was about as naughty as I got. We must have played a couple thousand rounds of the drinking game Bullshit.

"Who shit?"

"You shit?"

"I shit?"

"You shit?"

"She shit?"

"Who shit? He shit?"

Oh, you get the idea. Somewhere in there you had to chug a Harvey Wallbanger. It seemed to make perfect sense at the time.

We did a lot of dancing at those parties, too, and usually everybody's shoes came off in honor of one of our favorite party songs:

"Barefootin'." That's how our little get-togethers got to be known as barefootin' parties. They became so well-known by that name that when people showed up at the front door of our house they automatically took their shoes off. Sometimes we'd have shoes stacked halfway up the wall.

Those parties were our nightlife, but we had what we called "day life" parties too. We would gather up all our kids and all the Motown kids and have picnics in Kensington Park on a lake about an hour outside Detroit. We'd have big ice tubs full of sodas and the women would cook hamburgers and the men would catch fish and we'd grill those too. There'd be football games and baseball games. The Pips and I would pick up a team and play a team picked by the Temptations and the losers would have to sing. There would be times when we'd be yelling and screaming and singing so much at those picnics that if I had a concert that night or the next day I didn't have a voice.

I miss that sort of camaraderie with other performers. These days it seems like the business is so competitive, especially for young performers, and everyone is so isolated. We used to share stories and songs and dreams together in those days. Back then it wasn't about competing—although there certainly was plenty of competition—it was more about cheering each other on and taking pride in each other's accomplishments. We got to know each other in more relaxed settings and we cared about each other.

We got to be particularly close with the members of the Temptations because we had a lot in common, especially Cholly Atkins. They had asked Pops to work with them after they opened for us in a show in Ohio in 1961. After they saw the moves he'd taught The Pips, they decided they'd better get with Pop's program. It was through the Tempts that Pops went to Motown and that had helped lure us too.

Melvin Franklin, the Tempts' incredible bass singer, had probably the most interesting living quarters of any of the Motown crew. Along with having a rare basso profundo voice, Melvin thought he was Batman. He called his house the bat cave and he had a Batman outfit and a batmobile car. He even wore his Batman outfit to parties sometimes. Come to think of it, that voice of his probably was powerful enough to work like a bat's sonar.

Both of our groups recorded "I Wish It Would Rain" when we were at Motown, and David Ruffin, the Tempts' lead singer, liked to show up during our performances when we did that song. We were playing Vertigo West in Detroit one night when I spotted David in the audience so I invited him to come up and sing that song with us that night, I just stepped back and let him have the stage. I didn't realize just *how* strong his voice was, though. He got about halfway through the song and it started raining *on the stage* and we were indoors. Later we were told that it had been pouring so hard outside that the theater roof had sprung a leak and the water was falling onto the stage. I prefer to think it was David's doing. Isn't that the sort of thing you would expect from a guy born in a cabin in Whynot, Mississippi?

We shared a lot of good times with the Tempts and some hard times too. When we were with Motown, David was involved with Tammi Terrell, who was to have some huge hits with Marvin Gaye singing love songs such as "Ain't No Mountain High Enough" and "Ain't Nothin' Like the Real Thing."

She and David were one of those bad-boy, good-girl matches. They were a beautiful couple and both highly talented, but it was a troubled relationship and it ended in tragedy. Tammi toured a lot with us and she and I became very close friends. She told me that she and David were having problems but she never went into specifics. Tammi called me one day in 1966 and asked me to meet her at the Motown office because she had something to tell me. When I arrived, she said that she was "so scared." She'd found out that she had a brain tumor. She said she'd hit her head, but she didn't elaborate. I tried to calm her and hold her. We prayed over her health and I think I helped her overcome some of her fears. She was only twenty-one years old.

She and David broke up just as she and Marvin were taking off as a singing duo, but about the time they really hit the charts, Tammi began having health problems. She started having seizures. She collapsed in Marvin's arms just as they finished "Your Precious Love" during a college performance in Virginia in 1967. At the hospital, she told doctors she had been taking handfuls of aspirin because of her severe headaches. She started having trouble walking. She couldn't remember lyrics, and she lost nearly forty pounds even though she was already slender.

She had eight operations but she died in 1970 of complications caused by the brain tumor. Marvin was so shaken by her death that he refused to perform live for several years. He always said that there was more to Tammi's death than anyone knew. I'd heard rumors too, which were mostly about her volatile relationship with David Rufkin, but Tammi always kept that all to herself and she never told me what had happened.

As performers, we certainly were not protected from life's ups and downs, but at Motown, we shared both, and we comforted each other in the hard times. One of life's ups for me during that time was a wild and crazy young man who had been baptized as Steveland Morris. But he was really a wonder. I watched Little "Tevie" grow up at Motown. He was ten years old when he signed with Berry who renamed him Little Stevie Wonder. I'm told that for a long time, Berry paid him like Little Stevie, something like $2.50 a week even when he was traveling Europe with the Motown Revue. But when Stevie got big, he got his big payday. After winning ten Grammys in two years, he negotiated the biggest contract Motown had ever given and what was then the most ever awarded in the business—$13 million over seven years. Nobody called him Little Stevie after that.

When Stevie's mother first brought him to Berry, she had to get past scores of other mothers at the door. They all claimed their children were musical geniuses. A mother with a child who she said was a musical genius and also blind was a new twist, but Berry was prepared to be unimpressed. He took Stevie into a studio filled with the instruments of Motown's house band, and then watched in astonishment as he felt his way around the room, playing every instrument he got his hands on: the piano, the organ, the drums, the horns.

"You're signed," the boss said.

I've been friends with Stevie for many years, working together and witnessing his amazing life. It's simply amazing that it's lasted this long considering his insistence on driving other people's cars all the time. He likes to have you get in the car on the passenger side with him behind the wheel. He would work the pedals and you would steer and tell him whether to use the brakes or the gas. He loved to hear about all the strange looks he'd get going down the street.

I think Stevie's insistence on driving all the time may be one of the reasons he is widely known for never being on time. We have that trait in common. I've paid a price over the years for being late to one thing or another, or another, and I've tried to mend my tardy ways, but that Stevie, he has me beat when it comes to showing up after the band has gone home, the floors swept and the glasses all put away.

When I recorded "That's What Friends Are For" with Stevie, Elton John, and Dionne Warwick to benefit AIDS research a few years ago, I got to the studio in Los Angeles at 5 A.M. to record my part. Elton arrived at the same time. Dionne, who put the whole thing together, had been there working since the previous morning. We all recorded our individual parts of the song, then we had to wait for Stevie to show up so he could record his part and we could get down our shared bits. We waited a day and a half. That evening, Elton actually got up, went to an all-night party and came back while Dionne and I slept on sofas and waited. Stevie was tied up at the airport. If you've ever seen the video of that song, which was done after Stevie finally showed up and we'd been waiting all that time, you'll notice that my eyes look a little red. Now you know why.

The Motown years were breakthrough years, I'll give Berry Gordy that. We came into full maturity as a group and as individuals. We also loosened up a lot. Bubba and the guys no longer felt like they had to protect me and, I became more like one of the guys. When we traveled, instead of staying in my room all the time, I went out with them, particularly in Las Vegas, where Harvey Wallbangers were not the only vice I learned.

The first time I gambled and really won any money, I was with Bubba and Berry's songwriter sister Gwen Gordy and her husband, Harvey Fuqua, a member of The Moonglows, along with a few other friends. We had just done a performance at the Flamingo Hotel and Gwen invited us to go to the Dunes casino. It was late and the gaming floor was nearly empty. We all wandered over to the craps table because there were a few people having a lively time there. I didn't know anything about this game so I just watched for a while trying to pick up on it. It looked like more fun than cranking the arms of a slot machine, and when the dice came around to Bubba, he picked them up.

I put a ten-dollar chip on the table. Bubba rolled and won. I liked this game. I put another bet down. Bubba rolled a winner again. We did it a third time and won that too. Now a crowd was starting to gather. Nothing like a hot hand on a slow night in Vegas.

Gwen, Harvey, and their friends wandered over too, and she started betting hundreds. Another guy placed a couple thousand down, looked at Bubba and said, "Keep rolling son, keep rolling."

Figuring dumb luck is as good as any, I kept betting too, but only in tens and twenties. I'd been with Bubba through thick and thin, if he was hot I thought I might as well be in on that too.

He found ways to win at craps that night that I don't think Vegas had ever seen before. The pit bosses kept talking about him winning "the hard way." All I knew was that we were all winning with him and it seemed easy enough to me.

Other gamblers were jumping up and down and screaming. The guy with the thousand-dollar chips was tossing Bubba a couple hundred dollars in chips every time he won. "Keep rolling son," was all he'd say.

After about forty-five minutes of incredible luck, Bubba sensed that he'd better take his winnings and cash out. He gave up the dice, bowed to the applause of the crowd, and we headed for home giddy with laughter.

It was around dawn when he and I gathered in our suite and

counted up our earnings. We'd won $3,000 and had a darn good time doing it. I'm sure some of the other people betting on Bubba had won a lot more, but we were overjoyed. That was a lot of money to us. We were beside ourselves at this good luck, so we decided to do what we always saw people do on television when they'd won a lot of money. We took all the cash, which we'd gotten in $100 bills, threw it up in the air and started jumping up and down and rolling in the dough.

The next morning, I went to a store down the street and splurged on a $400 white leather suit I'd been eyeing all week. I couldn't remember ever before spending that kind of money on myself. Or even just allowing myself to have that kind of reckless fun. It felt good, really good.

CHAPTER 14

*W*hen I'm singing a song, I live in the lyrics. Before I even go to the studio to cut a record, I study the words and the music to create a character in my mind based on the person in the song. I try to imagine how they got to the point emotionally of singing the words. Then, to stay in that emotional state and in character when I am in the studio, I often record in darkness.

I couldn't get into the character that I found in the song that Berry Gordy wanted me to record near the end of 1970. She was not someone I felt I could identify with. The song was "If I Were Your Woman." The lyrics are the words of a woman who is in love with a married man. She is a bold thing, singing, "If I were your woman and you were my man, you'd have no other woman, you'd be weak as a lamb."

I'd come a long way from the little church mouse of Mount Moriah, but I wasn't exactly joining the bra burners and the women's lib movement that was sweeping the country around that time. I always felt liberated. I didn't mind being a housewife, I didn't need to burn my bra. But I had never been that aggressive in going after a man. It just wasn't my style. I was taught that the man pursued the woman.

I thought the lyrics were too suggestive for my image, and for me personally. Cher maybe, but not Gladys. I wasn't even sure I wanted to be alone in a dark studio with this woman and her song.

Sometimes when I get a song that doesn't exactly match up to where I am or where I've been in life, I can make it fit by imagining the story in the song happening to me on down the road, but I didn't want to ever see myself as the sort of woman who would be chasing another woman's man.

It was given to me as just one song for an album to be released in 1971, and so I recorded it to be a good Motown soldier, but I was shocked when Berry said he wanted to make it the title song and release "If I Were Your Woman" as a single. He thought it could be a hit. I begged him to take another song instead.

"It's not me," I pleaded.

"But it's a hit," he said.

He even bet me that it would be a hit, and back then you didn't bet against Berry Gordy and win very often.

I lost. But my consolation prize was my second number-one hit at Motown. It was an odd feeling to have that much success with a song that I didn't like all that much. As I've gotten older, and a little more self-assertive, I've grown to like it and understand it more, but back then it bothered me to do it, even though Berry proved to be right.

I also still felt there was something inherently missing in our relationship with Motown. Imagine what we might be doing if we had constant input from Berry, we thought. As 1973, the last year of our seven-year contract with Motown, got nearer and nearer, we did a lot of deliberating over the positive and negative implications of either staying with them or jumping to another record company.

We may have been stepchildren at Motown, but we were definitely part of a family, and we had developed close personal and professional relationships with many of our soul stepbrothers and stepsisters. As a record company whose artists were almost entirely black performers, Motown fostered a unity that went beyond shared labels on our albums and singles. In many ways, it was a very comfortable place to work, but there was also a sense that perhaps management took advantage of that. We didn't want to be taken for granted, or cheated, by anybody. Our Chitlin' Circuit days taught us that.

In the early 1970s many of Motown's top performers began rebelling at its rigid rules and regulations, and especially its accounting procedures. In 1971, Stevie Wonder demanded an audit and found that instead of getting a 50-50 split, which was standard, he had been getting only 2 percent of his record earnings, Motown was getting 98 percent.

That same year Motown's top writing team—Holland, Dozier and Holland—sued, claiming they were owed more than $22 million in back royalties. We were ahead of the pack in questioning Motown's books, but with so much of its talent in rebellion—and with Berry Gordy moving to Los Angeles to try and develop some Motown movie projects—a new company president tried to make us feel more appreciated. Ewart Abner had been the head of Vee Jay Records before coming to Motown. He claimed he wanted us to renew our contract. Even though Vee Jay was the company that had ripped us off years earlier by putting out a copy of "Every Beat of My Heart" without paying us a cent or having our permission, he'd been the one who tried to be straight with us about how we fit into Motown's plans. I suspect that maybe he was trying to make up for past wrongs because one day he called us into his office at Hitsville U.S.A. and presented us with a $2,000 check and a gold record for that song. It was a nice gesture, but we knew he probably owed us a lot more than $2,000 and a wall plaque.

Our next and final hit song for Motown, ironically, was "Neither One of Us" ("Wants to Be the First to Say Good-bye"). We received our first Grammy for it and it made our decision to leave Motown a bittersweet one. Around the time that we were going to have to make a decision on whether to leave or stay, we went to Motown's accounting department and asked to withdraw about $3,000 from road money we had not collected on our records. We needed it to pay our taxes. They said the money was not there. Motown claimed to have no record of it. We had made another mistake. We had started to trust them.

When we demanded our royalty money, they tried to leverage our tax instead. They said if we would sign another contract, they would pay our taxes for us. We weren't that desperate. We hired a lawyer and said our good-byes. We won that lawsuit and to my amazement, we are still getting checks from Motown because they are still selling our records.

Motown, meanwhile, had lost its focus just as rhythm and blues was enjoying a huge surge in crossover popularity. When Berry decided to get into the movie and television production business in the early 1970s, the rest of Motown's executives back in Detroit were lost. Some artists like Diana Ross and the Jackson 5 still were taken care of, but there was a mass exodus of other artists, writers, and producers around that time. We signed with an independent label, Buddah, and it turned out to be the best thing we ever did. Our career soared to new heights.

We were big fish in a small pond at Buddah where, for the first time, we got the respect and support we felt we deserved. We had a new team helping us to guide our careers: Sid Seidenberg and Floyd Leiberman. For a singing group or any other type of group to be successful, each member of the team must be doing all she or he can do to assist the overall effort. What a team we had. Sid and Floyd worked in close harmony with us. Neal Bogart, a record industry mogul who had worked with Donna Summer and Cher at Casablanca Records, also was a great help to us at Buddah as were promo men Milt Sincoff, Cecil Holmes, and Ron Weisner, who later became my manager as well as manager to Madonna and Michael Jackson. That sort of support is largely missing today in the record industry.

Buddah was totally supportive of our tours, our television projects, and our records. They even gave cars to each of us—no strings attached. Bubba and I each picked out Mercedes. William and Edward drove home Cadillacs. More importantly, Buddah gave us complete creative freedom. Bubba and I co-produced and wrote many of our songs, sometimes with the help of songwriter Sam Dees and William, too.

Before we left Motown, we had collected a batch of songs we liked. There were several from songwriter Jim Weatherly, a former All American quarterback at the University of Mississippi, who already had written many great songs for Motown. There was one song we liked a great deal, but the lyrics just weren't clicking for us. In the original version of the song, Jim's lyrics had a woman deliberating on whether to follow her man, a singer who was giving up on his dreams of stardom and taking a late plane flight out of L.A. back home to Houston and "a simpler place in time."

We liked the tune, but just as I had trouble fitting into the role of a brassy man-hunter in *If I Were Your Woman,* I couldn't identify with either flying in a plane or going home to Houston. I'd hated flying ever since that plane dropped one hundred feet on us on the way to New York. And I'd never been to Houston. I didn't even know anybody from Houston. It would be years before I'd even hear about *Whitney* Houston.

So, Bubba and I worked with Jim on rewriting the lyrics so I would be more comfortable with them. It actually worked out to be fairly easy. We changed the plane to my *favorite* mode of transportation, and dumped Houston for my home state. We then worked with arranger Tony Camilo to give the song a feel similar to Al Green's "Let's Stay Together," which we admired. I'll bet we redid the arrangement five times before we came up with one that we really loved.

Once we had it all together, we took it into the studio to record it. We had a unique way of working in the studio. We always went in with a tight arrangement, but we did a whole lot of improvising once we got the tape rolling. Bubba is especially good at coming up with phrasing that puts a great tag line on songs.

That night, we all worked some magic. While I stood in the glass recording booth, Bubba sat at the engineer's console. When I got to the end of the song, he began improvising lyrics. Everything he sang, I repeated.

> *My world*
> *My world*
> *His world*
> *His world*
> *My man*
> *My man*
> *His girl*
> *His girl*
> *I've got to go*

"Great," said Bubba. "Now, when you get to the 'I got to go. I got to go,' I want you to go way on up there with it."

He rewound the tape and played it back to that part of the song. Just as it reached that phrase, Bubba got out of his chair and pointed to the ceiling. I went up a note just as he indicated. Bubba loved it, and so did the rest of the guys in the studio. People were standing up and applauding. I came out of the booth and they were still high-fiving.

"What's with you all?" I asked.

"You've got to hear it, we've got it," Bubba said.

He was right. The rewritten and retitled song, *Midnight Train to Georgia* was packaged in an album that also included "Best Thing That Ever Happened to Me," and "Where Peaceful Waters Flow," which were also written by Jim, and "Imagination." The album went triple platinum and three of the singles from it went gold—"Midnight Train to Georgia," "Imagination," and "Best Thing That Ever Happened to Me," which is the song that includes the line that I chose for the title of this book.

"Midnight Train" was the first song in a long time that felt like it truly belonged to us. Our fans must have agreed, it is still selling. More importantly, it broke through all barriers and crossed over onto the pop charts, proving once and for all that we were nobody's step-child.

If there were any lingering doubts, we got another boost from an unexpected source. Motown packaged "Neither One of Us" into an album right after we left, and it too went gold.

We had worked all those years and released all those records for more than a half dozen record companies and while some of them did very, very well, none had brought us so much attention. All of a sudden we had two gold albums in one year. Nineteen seventy-three and 1974 were huge years. We sold 7.3 million albums and singles in 1973 and the following year we were nominated for four Grammy awards.

I was ecstatic about the impact of our decision to leave Motown and to join Buddah. Finally we had a record company that was behind us 100 percent. They promoted us and our music like nobody had before. We found ourselves on more television shows than Bob Hope. We did *In Concert*, *Midnight Special*, *Soul Train*, *American Bandstand*, *Johnny Carson*, and *Mike Douglas* in the United States, as well as two British shows: *The Old Grey Whistle Test* and *Top of the Pops*. Buddah also sent us on an extended promotional tour to the biggest venues in Boston, Chicago, New York, Las Vegas, and in Europe too.

Suddenly doors were opening to areas we never dreamed possible. We were asked to do the sound track to a movie, a television special, even a television series. The icing on the cake came at the 1974 Grammy awards. We were double winners, taking the R&B category with "Midnight Train to Georgia," and the pop category with "Neither One of Us."

It was the greatest feeling in the world to walk up there and receive those Grammys after so many years of sitting in the audience hoping and dreaming about the day we too would reap the fruits of our labors. All those nights on the road, sleeping in the car, eating hot dogs, or not eating at all. All the rehearsals and voice training with Mr. King. All the workouts and practice with Pops. All of the hours in the studio at Motown. All of the nights when we were opening for acts instead of headlining. All that time away from our children and other loved ones.

Was it worth it? I don't know how you balance that scale. It had taken a lot to reach that level as performers. We had put our hearts and souls into our singing careers, and it had certainly taken its toll on our personal lives. Our families, too, had made sacrifices. Nothing in this world comes without a price. This is one truth that I've sung and that I've lived.

CHAPTER 15

I've heard it said that when you close one door in your life, another always opens. When we closed the door on Motown, doors opened all *over* the place.

The call from a television producer in Detroit was particularly interesting primarily because it offered us a chance to do something locally and to make a real difference in the community. I didn't know the producer but I checked him out. Barry Hankerson was the president of Operation Get Down, a youth services program in Detroit, and more involved in city politics than show business.

Barry's idea was to produce a television show called *Times, Rhythms and Rhymes,* in which he profiled the careers of Gladys Knight & The Pips and our good friends, the Four Tops, Nipsy Russell, Freda Payne, and others. I returned his initial phone call and spoke with him, presented his idea to the guys, and we decided to do it. I had work to do and children to care for.

On the personal side, I'd seen a few men off and on, but nothing serious had developed and I had stopped looking. I'm a believer in

God's plan. Things happen for a reason, in my mind, and if there was someone else out there meant for me, I believed he would find me.

"Would you like to go to lunch today?"

We had just finished doing a rehearsal of *Times, Rhythms and Rhymes* in a Detroit television studio with Barry. I was on my way out the stage door, and he stopped me to talk about the project. The lunch invitation came out of the blue.

I had things to do.

"No, I don't think I can, thanks."

I didn't leave any doors open, not because I wasn't interested in him. I hadn't even given him a thought. He was part of the scenery rushing through my life at that very exciting time. A nice guy, a little younger than me, but he seemed to have his head on straight. He worked with kids. He seemed mannerly and there was an air of kindness about him. But I was busy, busy, busy.

It was tea time for Momma and the kids. She was trying to teach them table manners and how to interact politely with adults, so she'd created this daily ritual of having tea and cake with the kids. It became part of the family routine. The doorbell rang. Barry had come to return the family photos that he had borrowed for the show. In return, Momma invited him to tea. I'd just gotten home from an out of town performance and I was exhausted. I sent word down that I was resting and he could just leave the photographs with Momma.

She was having none of that. You didn't play the diva in her house, even if it was *my* house, especially when she was in her Miss Manners mode.

My messenger returned with the word from Momma.

"Grandma says you had better get on downstairs."

I resisted the urge to shoot the messenger. I ignored the message instead.

Then Momma Manners herself appeared in my doorway.

"This is impolite. The man came callin'. You get off your bed and come down."

This woman obviously had forgotten that I was a double Grammy winner and international recording star.

I got my butt up, but I didn't do it in any big hurry.

By the time I came down the stairs my momma and Mr. Come-a-Callin' were deeply engrossed in conversation. He was explaining to her all the good work he was doing with Operation Get Down. She was impressed.

I had to admit. He was looking sharp that day. I hadn't paid much attention before. He was obviously intelligent and serious-minded. There was a street-edge to his manner—he did seem to know all the politicians—but there was a shyness, too, even if he had come knocking on my door.

I joined the tea party and quickly found myself plunging into a conversation that spanned the music business, the plight of inner city children, and world affairs.

Momma slipped away. Barry and I continued to talk for a while. Then it was time for him to go.

"He seemed like a nice man," Momma said.

I didn't respond. The walls were still up around that part of my heart. I had work to do, opportunities to pursue. I was on the road constantly during that period, trying to get into as many of those newly opened doors as I could.

We had been offered a network variety show. It was a summer replacement show that could be picked up as a regular series if all went well. It was an unusual situation, but an intriguing one. They had to fill a prime time spot over the summer so they decided to try three different variety show pilots, alternating them each week. The Pips and I were the hosts of one. The second was hosted by the multi-talented actor, singer and dancer Ben Vereen. The third was hosted by the Captain and Tenille. The Captain had once been a piano player for the Beach Boys. Toni Tenille was a jazz singer who had turned to pop at that time. They'd had one hit song, a little ditty called "Love Will Keep Us Together," which won a Grammy in 1975. Later, they'd record one of the most unusual songs I'd ever heard, "Muskrat Love," and "Do That to Me One More Time."

The guys and I were flying back and forth to Los Angeles a lot to work on our pilot in the summer of 1974, and one night before we were about to take off again, Momma said she wanted to talk about something. She said that since Bubba and I were gone so much, she was concerned about her and the kids being left alone in the house. Detroit was going through some changes. Although at that point, we lived in a very nice neighborhood, Sherwood Forest, crime was finding its way there too. The decline of the auto industry in the 1970s was putting a lot of people out of work. In the absence of jobs and with city funds for special programs depleted, crime, drugs, and gangs were flourishing.

Momma's idea was to bring another adult, and added security to the house, by leasing out the fourth floor, which was set up like an apartment with its own living room, bed, and bath, and a giant recreation room. She even had a tenant in mind.

"Do you remember that little guy Barry who came over that time for tea?" she said. "He's looking for a place in the neighborhood. I was thinking that he might be a good tenant. What do you think?"

I hadn't thought anything about Barry Hankerson since that day he came calling. But if Momma was comfortable with him, and if she wanted someone else around. I had no problem with him renting out the top floor. What could it hurt?

When we returned home, Momma said she had contacted Barry and he was going to move in. Later, she told me he was moved in, but I hadn't seen him. He had his own outside entrance and Momma said he worked all the time. I was gone a lot, too, working long hours even when I was in town.

The kids seemed to like Barry. He seemed to be giving them a lot of attention. He was like a kid around them. The Pips and I had recorded a Christmas album that year and working on it had really psyched us up for the holidays. We went a little wild decorating the house, and Barry pitched in. As Christmas approached and we talked about what we were going to get the kids—this was going to be a big Christmas for them since we had finally started making some serious money—he suggested that we turn the rec room on the fourth floor into a playroom for the kids by putting all of their presents in there. He wasn't using the space, and he would help me decorate it, he said.

For the next few weeks, Barry and I worked to get the room ready while the kids kept trying to sneak in to see what we were doing. Kenya had asked for a train set and Chetley (Brenda's son) wanted a pellet gun and a target. Little Jimmy was dying for a racetrack. We had plenty of work to do getting all that ready. Barry and I were like a couple of kids ourselves as we set up the *baddest* train set and race-track ever assembled. We made mountains of papier-mâché and put real dirt on them. We built little houses that lit up and surrounded them with working streetlights, trees, benches, and toy people. We put a target range in the room for Chetley and his pellet gun too.

Santa's elves would have been proud. On Christmas Day, we took the kids upstairs and they couldn't believe their eyes. There was a whole miniature city in that room. They didn't come out until we called them down to dinner. It was one of their best Christmases ever, a time when they got even more than they asked for. I did too. At some point between the time the first toy track went down and the last papier-mâché mountain went up, our friendship grew into romance.

Momma was scandalized at first, which sort of surprised me since she had invited this man into our house in the first place.

"It's one man for me and I'll be a Knight until I die," was her motto.

Her point was that I was still legally married to Jimmy, even though we hadn't been together for nearly ten years at that time. I'd put that side of my life off in a corner until Barry had put me back in touch with it. Jimmy had abandoned me and the kids. I'd been alone, but now it looked like there was a possibility of having someone to share life with.

He filled a void in my life. It was like I'd shut the door to that part of me. More than that, I'd cut off the power, closed the vents and boarded the windows. He'd walked in and brought light, air, and heat back to it.

Before anything serious could happen, however, I had to find Jimmy, and get a divorce. The last I'd heard, he was working as a musician around Atlanta again. My only real line to him was through his grandmother, Momma Stamps. From time to time, she would call, ask about the kids, and fill me in on Jimmy. On a few rare occasions, he had called to talk with the kids himself. After those conversations, they always had more questions than I could answer. I had explained to them, once they were old enough to understand, that he was a fine saxophone player. They even had a photograph of him with his sax in their little scrapbook. I told them that he loved them and he loved me, but I was honest with them about his drug problems. I let them ask any questions they wanted to ask, and I tried to be straight with them. With the open-minds of children, they seemed to accept their father's absence and his situation. They seemed to have no anger about him leaving us. Somehow, they understood his struggle and the choices he had made without blaming him.

Still, they missed having a father. Kenya even went looking for him once when she was only about eight years old. We were visiting Atlanta and we had gone to my old elementary school on English Avenue. On the way there I pointed out Jimmy's family's house. While we were at the school, visiting with folks, Kenya slipped away and ran as fast as her little legs could take her down to her daddy's house, which was only six houses down from the school.

She knocked on the door and when it opened she announced:

"Hi, I'm Kenya."

Jimmy just happened to be there. He swept her up in his arms and hugged her, then he quizzed her about how she'd gotten there. He brought her to the school. We'd just discovered she was missing and we were frantic but when I saw them coming, I couldn't scold her. She was all smiles.

"This is my Dad," she told everyone.

As a person and a human being I cared deeply for him.

When I called and told him I needed a divorce, he was my friend.

"I would never stand in the way of your happiness," he said. "What's up?"

"I'm thinking about getting married," I told him.

"I've heard," he said.

"What?"

"You don't need to get married."

That he even offered an opinion on that topic surprised me.

"I'll give you your divorce, but I'm telling you, you don't need to get married. I just feel it. You don't need to get married." Looking back now, I still don't regret the decision to get married.

I had earned the right to that happiness, and I would always be reaching for it.

Barry too had been married before. He was divorced and his ex-wife had custody of their son, Jomo, whom I had fallen in love with the moment I laid eyes on him. He was three years old, wearing a little red raincoat and matching hat the day Barry brought him to Jimmy's swim meet. He had the sweetest, gentlest spirit about him. He became my son too on that day, and forever. So when he was dropped off on my wedding day wearing play clothes, I sighed, smiled and set about doing what I had to do.

I should have been getting my hair, nails, and makeup done to absolute perfection. Instead, I found myself in Saks Fifth Avenue shopping for a boy's suit. I hadn't even had a chance to try on my wedding dress yet, since it had just arrived the day before from Giorgio, custom made for me. The rest of my kids were going to be dressed to the nines, I didn't want Jomo looking like he'd just gotten out of the sandbox. Barry was getting ready at a friend's house so as not to jinx the wedding, so it was up to me to get young Jomo suited up.

At Saks, I ran into a guardian angel in the form of Esther Gordy Edwards, Berry Gordy's sister, who had been in charge of Motown's "charm school." Esther had been more interested and involved in our careers than her brother ever had been. She'd never missed one of our shows around town and she was always supportive. In fact, she was the only person from the Motown brass who came to the wedding.

"What are you doing here on your wedding day, Gladys, you should be home getting yourself ready," she said.

"I have a dilemma," I said, pointing to Jomo and his scruffy clothes. "I've got to get my son, Jomo, some clothes for the wedding because he sure can't come to the wedding dressed like this."

Once I had a suit for Jomo, I rushed back home with him to get the bride ready. Leaving Jomo with Momma, I grabbed my wedding dress still in the box and a few other essentials and started back out the door headed for the Mayor's mansion on the Detroit riverfront, where the wedding was to be held.

My sister Brenda was going to be my maid of honor and she was waiting for me, along with a whole crowd of people already there for the ceremony. I was running on G-time once again late as usual! Dashing up to a dressing room, I handed the dress box to Brenda.

She pulled the wedding dress out and helped me get into it. I was so frantic, my hair was a disaster, that I didn't notice anything strange with the wedding dress until I walked over to a mirror.

"Oh my Lord, it's four inches too short!"

"Nothing we can do about that now, girl," said Brenda. "Let's see what we can do about your hair."

She tried to hide my no-do hair do under the veil, but it wasn't fitting right either. So much for my custom-fitted wedding outfit.

Ready or not, I had to get down the aisle. We were already running two hours late. In her rush to get ahead of the tardy bride, Brenda hurried down the ornate staircase leading into the foyer where there were more than 150 people who were running out of patience. About a quarter of the way down, her heel caught on the back of one of the stairs and down she went. Standing at the top of the staircase, I could hear everyone gasp. Poor Brenda fell all the way to the bottom of the stairs. The ushers rushed over to help her. She was dazed, but nothing was broken other than the heel of her shoe.

Having witnessed my sister's plunge down the stairs, I wasn't looking forward to my descent. As I went down, very carefully, my mind was not exactly filled with pleasant and loving thoughts about the institution of marriage and the great life I hoped to embark upon. No, it was more like

What the hell went wrong with this stupid dress. My hair is a freaking disaster. This veil is absolutely worthless. What the hell am I doing? Can't we start over?

Barry looked so happy to see me I wanted to slap him!

But instead, I married him, although when the minister got to the "for better and for worse," part, it sure sounded like he put the emphasis on the "worse."

There was one other snafu:

"Repeat after me, I Barry Hankerson take thee, Gladys Maria Knight."

"I Barry Hankerson take thee, Maria Knight Gladys." Barry shook his head and took a deep breath. "I mean, Gladys Knight Maria."

Even I had to laugh at that. Barry was so nervous he never did say my name right. Was it an omen?

When the time came for Barry and me to leave, Kenya, Little Jimmy, Jomo, Chet, Valisia, and Little Bubba came running. "We want to go with ya'll," they screamed.

It was a natural thing, the kids were always with us.

I looked at Barry. He looked at me.

Our honeymoon destination was just the house we'd bought together down the street from our other place, where Momma was going to stay.

And so, the newlyweds and their newly formed family piled into the Just Married car and went home to kick back, cuddle and watch cartoons.

It was bliss, however short-lived it was to be.

CHAPTER 16

$\mathcal{F}$or a brief and shining moment, it seemed like my life was finally in balance. My career was still in high gear but I had it under control to the point that for the first time in a long, long time, I was getting to do all of those things that I'd been dreaming of ever since I was a little girl making magical mud pies in the backyard.

I was cooking. I was baking. I was doing laundry. I was carpooling, PTA-ing, Little-Leaguing, Girl-Scouting. I had become the lady in the household cleanser commercials, singing my way through the grit in the bathroom tiles. Life as an adult was never better for me.

Little Jimmy seemed to flourish in our new family environment. He thrived on Barry's attention and the male companionship that had been sorely lacking in his life. Kenya, however, seemed to have more difficulty adapting, and it didn't help that Barry and I were starting to have major disagreements. She had grown very close to Momma and if she perceived any tension between Barry and me, she made a beeline for Momma's house. I had to tell her that she couldn't always run over there. We had our own little family, and we had to work out our own problems.

Like many couples, we had some very challenging situations to deal with, which over time worked to pull us apart, such as in-law problems, basic parenting style conflicts, financial management fiascos, and the general mismanagement of my career by the group's representatives, Sydney A. Seidenberg, Inc. This caused major dissention between Barry and me. We had the same thoughts but different methods. Barry was correct in his assessment; there was no way the management should be making more than the artist.

Meanwhile, along with the building stress in the marriage, my own dreams of having a regular television variety show also collapsed. In the three-way competition between our show, Ben Vereen's, and that of the Captain and Tenille, the best ratings had gone to our show and that of the Captain. We had tied. We'd figured our chances of winning were pretty strong because at the time, Gladys Knight & The Pips were riding high with nine gold records, two platinum albums, and one triple platinum album. The Captain and Tennille had only one hit song to their credit. But they got the prime-time show, and we got the shaft.

As for the marriage, after about two years I was ready to call an end to it. Our conflicts were sucking all of the joy out of my life at a time when I should have been basking in my singing success and in the lives of my children. But just as I was preparing to make the break, I found out I was pregnant. Once the doctor gave me the news, I rejected the idea of leaving Barry. I couldn't bear the thought of bringing another child into the world without a father there, and I didn't want to fail at another marriage. We tried again.

Shanga Ali Hankerson was born on August 1, 1976. We got the name Shanga from some good friends who also had a son named Shanga, whom we had doted on. Ali came from one of our favorite people—and one of the world's too—Muhammad Ali, who has the heart and spirit of a child. I'd known Ali for years and had even been lucky enough to see him fight once in a match with Larry Holmes, which Ali lost, and I always felt it was my fault because we sang the national anthem that night and I was hoping it would bring him luck.

The great fighter lived in Cherry Hill, New Jersey, and we often visited him. Or I should say, our children took us to visit him. He'd spend hours entertaining us with his elaborate magic shows. He'd entertain us with tapes of his old fights, giving us his running commentary until he'd get tired and just curl up in the middle of the floor and go to sleep. We didn't know it then, but he was already exhibiting the early symptoms of Parkinson's Disease, which would slow his body, but not his agile mind, considerably over the years.

By the time Shanga came into the world, we were in a much better position to see that he was adequately cared for on the road and off the road. I had a husband close to home to help make decisions for the family. I didn't have much choice in the earlier years than to leave my other children with my mother after Jimmy left me. There was no way I could take them on the road, but with Shanga, I could afford to hire someone to watch him while I was rehearsing and performing. And we were no longer traveling in the doodlebug, or living in it either.

Shanga was the link that brought our family together.

Four months after Shanga was born, I took the kids down to Atlanta to see Jimmy's grandmother, who was gravely ill after having a stroke. She had always been so good to me and the kids. I didn't want her to pass away without seeing her great-grandchildren one last time. The morning before we went to see her, I called her house to let her know when we were coming. To my surprise, Jimmy answered the phone. He sounded good, even excited that we were there. I found myself feeling the same about seeing him, perhaps hoping that he had shaken his demons.

We made plans to visit him later that afternoon, but when we went over to the house, Jimmy was nowhere to be found and nobody seemed to know where he was. I feared the worst, that he had gone into his running mode, rather than staying to face his children. While we were at Jimmy's house, our old high school pal Grady stopped by. If anybody knew where Jimmy had run off to, it would be Grady.

"I know you know where he is," I said. "His kids are here to see him. Tell him I said he ought to get back here."

Grady pleaded ignorance at first, but finally he went to find Jimmy for me. He returned in less than half an hour with him. Immediately, I recognized the dull look in Jimmy's eyes. He had not rid himself of his demons. Worse, when he got closer, I could see that somebody had been beating him. There was a cut just above his nose. I felt my anger rising at him as much as at whoever had hurt him. How could this beautiful and talented man let himself sink so low that people were pounding on him?

Jimmy was jumpy and evasive when I asked him what was going on with him, but the kids were so thrilled to see their father that I stood back and let him bask in their attention. He needed to know he was loved. They had changed a lot since he last saw them. Little Jimmy was eleven and Kenya was ten. He took the two of them into the back bedroom, where they talked for a long time. When Jimmy came back out, he looked like he had been crying. "Could they spend the night with me sometime?" he asked.

"Sure, why not?"

We went into the living room and sat down. There, Jimmy confessed that he thought I resented him all these years for not paying child support. "How could I be resentful?" I replied. "I never asked you to help me."

The more we talked, the more guilt he unloaded about being a poor father. Trying to be kind to this fragile man, I told him that I understood that he'd done what he could.

"I want to see them," he said. "I want them to spend next summer with me. But I know you won't let them do it."

"Why not? They are your kids too."

I wasn't worried about Jimmy taking care of them. I was confident that they were old enough now to handle themselves in any environment. And I knew that he probably would not follow up on this request. He was caught up in the emotions of seeing them as young people who loved him unconditionally. I was glad that he was getting the opportunity to discover that. It seemed to bring him some illusion of peace, but we had been here before.

Around dusk, we prepared to leave. We stood on the porch to say our good-byes. I was carrying Shanga.

"And who is this little man?" Jimmy said, taking the baby from me and holding him up in the air. "You're a handsome little guy."

"You're my son too," he added.

I looked at Jimmy's swollen face, and for a moment I saw through the years and recalled the bright-eyed young dreamer who was my first love.

"You know it was really nice to see you," I said. "I hope whatever you want for your life, you're successful at it.

"Do me a favor, Jimmy," I added. "Don't stop dreaming."

As I walked down the porch stairs and to the car, Jimmy called after me playfully. "You still looking good, girl."

I stopped and turned around.

"Oh, *now* you want to flirt with me."

Grady, Jimmy, and some of their other friends who had come over fell to laughing so loud I could still hear them hooting and hollering as I started the car and drove away from the curb.

I had not taken Jimmy's offer to take the kids for the summer all that seriously, but the kids had. Right away, Little Jimmy and Kenya wanted to know if we would be back to Atlanta next summer.

"Are we coming next year?"

"Can we come, Momma?"

"Yeah," I said. "If you want to, sure you can."

That's how we left it. I didn't want to kill their dreams of getting to know their father better.

Two months later, I was at the beauty shop getting my hair done, when I got a phone call from Momma.

"You need to come home, sweetheart," she said softly. "They just found Jimmy dead. He died in his sleep. Come on home."

I was not surprised by the message. I was surprised, however, by the depth of the hurt and sorrow that swept over me, then . . . and even now.

For years, I had been preparing for just such a phone call. I just didn't think it would be this soon. It had occurred to me that Jimmy had been rushing toward death since the day his mother passed away. I'll never forget how he always said "I'm going to die young."

He was thirty-five when he died. I hoped that he'd finally found lasting peace.

His family said Jimmy had some kind of seizure in his sleep. The autopsy found that his spleen had ruptured. Whether drugs caused it, I still don't know, but I have no doubt that all those years of drug abuse had taken their toll.

When I told Kenya and Little Jimmy, they were sad, but they, too, seemed to have accepted that their father's self-destructive lifestyle would bring him to an early death. I think it's telling that to this day none of them have drug or alcohol problems, which is the one blessing out of Jimmy's tragic story.

Barry felt the kids and I should attend Jimmy's funeral, and sent us. There, we discovered that Jimmy had another little girl, this one with a woman whom he never married. The child was about nine or ten and looked very much like Kenya. She had the same light-colored eyes as Kenya, but was very quiet until our kids drew her out.

After the funeral, the kids and I went back to the hotel. I kept them up half the night listening to stories about how I met their father, and about his skill as a musician.

I'm grateful that Kenya and Little Jimmy were never bitter about their father's leaving them, or about his drug abuse. They always forgave him his tragic faults and held him dear to their hearts. They gave him the ultimate gift of unconditional love. I did, too, and I am grateful for the peace and laughter that we were able to bring into his troubled life during our visit just two months before he died.

CHAPTER 17

*M*y marriage to Barry had rapidly faded. I was backsliding from a confident and secure woman into one whose self-esteem was becoming far too dependent on someone else's evaluation.

In public and while performing, I put on a front. Women tend to do that. We suffer in silence for the sake of preserving a relationship that is deteriorating at its very foundation. We think that if we smile through it and stay busy, things will return to a bearable level. Being in denial, you can't even think clearly. It takes an amazing amount of strength just to figure out what your next step should be.

I turned for strength to my roots in the church. I'd never left the church. I still went regularly with Pat Carter, Zora "Blondie" Brown, my friend for thirty-five years and wardrobe assistant, or Ray Hall, my hair stylist and buddy. One Sunday, while we were at the apartment in Los Angeles, Ray called to see if I was going to church. From the tone of my voice, he could tell something was wrong.

"You all right, Lily?" he asked, using the pet name he called me.

"Yeah, I'm doing fine," I said, barely above a whisper. "We're going to church, aren't we?"

From the moment that Rev. James Cleveland began his sermon, it seemed that he was preaching directly to me. He spoke of the need to strengthen our faith in difficult times and about the importance of remembering that no matter what we're going through, God is there for us. I was in such pain, spiritually and emotionally, that my faith needed to be rejuvenated.

The reverend made his call to the altar, inviting those in need of renewal to go to the front of the pulpit and pray. Ray and I walked to the front of the church. As I knelt at the altar, I tried not to break down.

When we returned to our seats, I was filled with the sense that I needed to let these dammed up emotions flow out of me, but I'd been holding them back so long, I couldn't.

I went back to the altar and prayed again but I still wasn't ready to release the pain. Anxiety swept over me. Almost as soon as I sat down, I turned around and walked back to the front. This time, when I knelt down, the dam burst. Ray knelt beside me and held me while I shook and sobbed.

We stayed there until the end of the altar call, and then Ray helped me back to my seat. We were the last to leave the church that day. I was drained but relieved too. When I returned home, my circumstances had not changed, but my response to them had. My despair had been replaced by the courage to make a change.

Just prior to that day in church, it came to me that I needed to renew my faith. Now I was committed to taking action and my thoughts reinforced that:

I will not live like this anymore. I will not be threatened anymore. If this marriage is over, I am not going out with my back bent or my will broken. I have faith in God's plan for me and I know that plan is in His hands. As long as I do what I'm supposed to do to walk in His light, everything is going to be all right. Everything is going to be all right.

So I decided to make a move and to put our lives in the hands of God. Make that God and the divorce court!

The tragedy of many divorces is that the children, whom both sides still love, are the ones who suffer the most. As much as we both loved our son, there were many times during this period when I wondered if either of us was fit to be Shanga's guardian.

I couldn't see letting Barry have custody. It tore me apart. I'm sure he felt the same way about me then. But a mother's protective instincts are nothing to trifle with.

In the judge's final decision, it was ordered that Shanga would live with me at my new home in Las Vegas most of the year. I settled there because I could perform in the casino shows and still be home for Shanga during the months he spent with me.

While he was making a regular visit to Barry, who still lived in Detroit then, they disappeared. No one knew where they were, or at least, no one would tell me. It nearly drove me insane. I didn't know if they were gone for good. I had no idea. For two weeks I lived in torment. I couldn't sleep, eat, or think straight. Then they just re-appeared with Barry stating that Shanga kept asking for his mom and he couldn't take it so he brought him back.

It was as if they'd taken a walk around the block. It even seemed to have done Shanga some good, which didn't make *me* feel any better. He was full of energy and excitement, and he wanted to tell me everything about where he and his daddy had been.

"I went to Africa," he said.

"You went where?"

"We went to the jungle and rode the elephant."

Here was this child that I loved so deeply, just bursting with excitement about this incredible journey that his father had taken him on, and all I could think was what torture they had put me through while they were gone on their little adventure.

I tried to be happy for Shanga. I really was happy for him because he seemed to have had such a great time.

Now I was not only a stay-at-home wet blanket mother, I was

also the woman who was keeping Shanga from seeing his father, whom he clearly loved and enjoyed being with. If ever there is such a thing as a surefire lose-lose situation, it revolves around divorce and child custody matters. Shanga cried every night because he missed his daddy. I knew he loved me, too, but he was obviously a daddy's boy at heart. You can't control that, I'm afraid.

There is no denying that divorce can take a terrible toll on the children. Thanks to my decision to leave his father, Shanga was himself torn. After a while, he was no longer content to be with just one of us at a time. It was as though he was afraid the one who was not there was abandoning him. If I left him with Barry, or with Momma, Brenda, or his nanny, he would insist that I check in every half hour or so, just to give him comfort. It was the same with Barry if he was not around. Because of our differences, we had denied our son his right to a sense of security.

He began seeking that lost comfort and security elsewhere, as any human being could be expected to do. With Shanga, it became food. He ate and ate and ate to satisfy a hunger that was beyond his reach. While the food bloated his body, his spirit was undernourished.

Shanga had always been a strapping child. He weighed ten pounds when he was born. My father had said, "Look at that boy, he's grown already." By the age of two, the doctors said he was seriously overweight. Instead of giving him comfort, the weight he put on frustrated him and made him irritable. It got worse and worse, in spite of my efforts to put him on diets and to get him to lead a more active life. I tried a parade of diet specialists, doctors, psychiatrists, and health gurus. I sent him to weight-loss camps. Nothing worked. Whatever he lost, he immediately put back on.

At eleven years old, he weighed 320 pounds and I was afraid he would die of obesity. I feared my son was going to have a heart attack and die. Realizing that his problems were more emotional than physical in origin, I tried to find him mental challenges to help build his self-confidence and self-image. He was considered to be gifted intellectually, so I put him in the best school I could find. I praised him constantly.

Kenya took him under her wing and took him with her wherever she and her friends went, but he was so wounded emotionally at that point that it was difficult for anyone, particularly a teenage sister, to give him what he needed. It was so frustrating. At one point, during an argument with Shanga, I called him a "fat slob." I couldn't believe I'd said it. Shanga didn't react on the outside; the hurt was all within. If I could only cram those words back into my mouth. How could I hurt him that way?

School seemed to help him in some ways, but naturally, other kids teased him mercilessly about his weight. He was tough, and he seemed to have a cocky exterior, but I knew he was hurting, and it was only going to get worse if I did not take drastic measures. I found other parents of obese children with the same frustrations I had. The children were not allowed in the gym unless they were eighteen, most diet programs were not child sensitive, and the parents had no groups to help them cope. Richard Simmons helped us tremendously, and the Weight Watchers Camp we finally found was helpful also. But, it is absolutely imperative that there be a lifestyle change at home to gain success for and with your obese children. I found a residential weight-loss program in Texas when he was thirteen years old, and even though it cost nearly $20,000 a month, I was prepared to put him in it. I was getting desperate. I was even planning to move to Texas to be there for him.

By that time, Barry and I had begun to work together because of our mutual concern for Shanga. It was a fragile peace, but one we had worked out for our son. At first, he was scornful of the idea and the cost of my plan. He made the point that throwing money at a problem did not guarantee a solution. He was right. I was just at my wit's end. He noted, too, that when Shanga spent time with him, his weight always dropped noticeably. Barry had moved to Los Angeles by then. Jomo was living with him. They were involved in athletics and played a lot of basketball together. Whenever Shanga visited they always pushed him to participate and it made a difference in his weight when he was more active.

I was surprised when Barry said, "I don't see why you don't let him come live with us."

It was not easy to admit it, but I knew Barry was right. My home environment was obviously not conducive to Shanga's progress. Each child is unique and Shanga needed a male environment. He had always responded better to the guidance of men. It was time for me to show my love by stepping back and letting Shanga live with his father.

I bought a house in L.A. so that I could be near them if they needed me. I wanted to give Shanga as much comfort and security as I could. He was free to come and go as needed or as the three of us decided. Shanga lived with me during the week while in middle school and stayed with his father on weekends until high school, when he moved in with Barry and Jomo, visiting me on weekends. Almost immediately, the change in him was dramatic. His weight began to drop and I have to admit it was because Barry and Jomo ran it off him. They stayed on top of Shanga from the get-go. They began playing basketball with him every day. Initially, Shanga couldn't get down the court more than a couple times, but the guys just kept pushing him. Barry believed in tough love. He kept Shanga active and made him stick to a healthful diet consisting of Lean Cuisine and Healthy Choice meals that he hated but ate anyway. As a result of their care, he became quite an athlete, lettering in football and basketball. Later, in his sophomore year he made the varsity football team at the University of San Diego as an offensive tackle. He was also recruited and offered scholarships by several other schools, including the University of Pennsylvania, Columbia, and Oregon State.

Jomo became Shanga's biggest supporter. Even though he was six years older, Jomo treated Shanga like a best friend as well as a little brother. He even took him along when he had a date. Boys need men. Barry deserves as much credit as I do for making Shanga into a responsible, caring, and, yes, handsome young man. Through our shared love for Shanga, Barry and I have fashioned a relationship that is far better than I had ever imagined it could be. We have even worked together. He produced the one and only play I've done in my career, although my goal is to do more. It was called *Madame Lilly* and we did it in Los Angeles in 1990.

People who witnessed our marriage and divorce can hardly believe that we worked together, or that we are friends today. I'm proud that we were mature enough to put our differences behind us and rally around our son. We came a long way, through fear, bitterness, and distrust. It wasn't easy. But in the end, it was well worth it. Our willingness to work together may have even saved Shanga's life.

I know that sometimes it's just not possible to stay in a marriage, even though there are children involved who may be hurt. Take it from me, the parents have to get beyond their hurt and anger because although they may be leaving each other, their children still need both of them. Shanga grew to be an exceptional young man, as did Jimmy and Jomo. Shanga graduates from the University of San Diego next year, as did his big brother Jimmy and sister Kenya. Jomo graduated from Pepperdine University. Shanga has adopted the same entrepreneurial spirit of his brother and sister. As this book goes to press, all of us eagerly await the grand opening of his new restaurant: Gladys Knight and Ron Winan's Chicken and Waffles, in Atlanta. Go Shanga! I am proud of you and of all my children.

CHAPTER 18

$\mathcal{W}$ith the disintegration of my second marriage and the financial pressures that came with it, I guess it is no surprise that I unconsciously sought refuge from all of the uncertainty and stress in my life.

As strange as it may seem in light of my reputation for being a Miss Goody Two Shoes, from the late-seventies to the late-eighties, I found solace in an addiction.

I had gambled and played penny-ante poker, but never anything like Vegas. Bubba and I won $3,000 one night in 1977 in Vegas, and we had rolled in it on the hotel bed like a couple of people in a movie. It wasn't the winning or the money that hooked me. It was the losing; the losing of myself in the excitement of it all.

I was a board-game junkie and a video-game junkie long before I became a gambling junkie. I'd been a celebrity since I was four years old. I'd been fighting to be a normal kid, a normal teenager, a normal wife and mother all those years with very little success.

Once I got hooked, casinos became my private playground. I

could stay as long as I wanted to stay and I was always protected by the pit bosses and croupiers and security guards. They protected me from fans, drunks, IRS agents, and from fame.

It wasn't a sickness at first; it was something rare for me—one hell of a lot of fun, an extension of the card parties we used to have up at my buddy Myra Waters's house on Laurel Canyon Boulevard in Los Angeles. I met Myra back in the late-sixties in Sammy Davis's dressing room at the Sands. I walked in one night to say hello and Sammy gave me the sign to stay still and be quiet. There was this itty-bitty woman sitting on the floor with her back to the door and she hadn't seen me sneak in.

Sammy loved to play pranks on people.

"Now, Myra," he said. "Tell me again how you are a better singer than any woman in Vegas."

The woman on the floor took another drink of her cocktail. She still had no idea I was standing there.

"Shoot, Sammy, you know I can sing better than Aretha Franklin and Gladys Knight," she said. Then she began singing "Getting to Know You" from the musical *The King and I*, but in her enthusiasm, she also tried to do the instrumental and percussion accompaniment, to very comic effect.

"Getting to know you, getting to know all about you . . . PA-chow . . . PA-chow . . . Getting to know you . . . getting to know what to say . . . PA-chow . . . PA-chow."

Sammy and I cracked up, and Myra spent the rest of the night apologizing and telling me how much she loved my singing. From that point on, Sammy and I nicknamed her PA-chow, PA-chow. Myra was a singer and songwriter and producer and one of those people who just seemed to know everybody in the entertainment industry.

She hosted poker parties for her women pals. You never knew who was going to show up because Myra knew a wide range of people. Some of the other regulars included the great jazz and blues singer—and one of the most versatile cursers I've ever known—

Carmen McRae, the actress and singer Leslie Uggams, Dionne Warwick, and the queen of comedy, Lucille Ball of *I Love Lucy*.

It was a wild bunch, believe me. Usually we would start off with Carmen cursing out everyone who had not called or visited her since the last card game. She'd get to cussing folks out, telling us how we were all no damn good, and we'd have to let her go on for a while before she would finally run out of cuss words and names to call us.

"Okay, you bitches, let's play," she'd say, and then we'd be off and running.

Lucy was a big card player. Myra used to go to Palm Springs and play with her there too. She was serious about her cards so she wasn't "on" as far as being funny all the time, but she definitely got a kick out of us and she let us know when we weren't playing fast enough or if someone did something stupid. "You might as well take your money out of the pot right now because you sure as hell aren't going to win anything," she'd say, taking a long drag on a cigarette.

We'd have some big pots with serious money going, especially when we played Black Mariah, which is a killer game where the pot keeps building and building. It was usually a $5 or $10 ante to get in and we would usually have five or six players. The most I ever took home was about $3,000 or $4,000. Myra won $4,000 or $5,000 a couple times. She lost that a few times too.

Gambling became a great diversion; it was a life-style for me really. When the IRS came after me because of improper losses claimed on *Pipe Dream*, after my divorce from Barry, I took my gambling up a notch. I was worried about paying the IRS, and about paying for college for Jimmy and Kenya too. If one of them called needing money for something—books, another semester, clothes, whatever—I used it as an excuse to gamble. But in all honesty, I can't blame my gambling on debts or money problems. It ran deeper than that. It had more to do with escaping from the world for a while and getting lost in a game.

I got serious about gambling when I started playing baccarat. Initially, my favorite casino game was blackjack, but it got so I couldn't play that without being bothered by people. I switched to baccarat because those tables were roped off. I recognized the game from television and the movies. It was like something out of a James Bond film. It looked elegant, a rich person's game. At first, I stood outside the ropes and watched, trying to figure out how the game was played. After about three weeks of this, the pit boss came up to me. "Gladys," he said, "why don't you come on in?"

"Oh no," I said. "I don't want to play."

"Well, you can come in and watch."

I did, but I was still too scared to play.

Then, I went to one of Dionne's concerts at the Hilton in Vegas. After the show, she and her husband Bill invited me to hang out with them. "We'll get something to eat," Dionne said. To my surprise, they did their dining at the baccarat table, where food and drink were also available. There was even a hot buffet. Great, I could gain weight and lose money at the same time—the perfect vice.

I hung out and watched for a while but didn't get up the nerve to play until one night at the Aladdin with my hairstylist Ray Hall. We went into the casino and I showed him the baccarat table, telling him that I'd been wanting to play but had never worked up the nerve to do it.

He'd been thinking the same thing. We pooled our courage and went. It was a slow night. The croupiers had fun teaching us how to play. The minimum bet was $20, but the croupiers recognized a couple of nervous rookies. They let us open with $10. We won the first hand and we kept on winning. We were hooked. Every night after the show, we went back to the table and played for $10 a hand until one night when the table was full. The minimum had been raised to $20 but most players were betting much more. There was some very serious money moving that night, but Ray and I stayed with the minimum bet. We were having fun, but we weren't sucked into the gambling addict's mentality, yet.

Years later, whenever I would play with those same croupiers, they'd remind me of what a tight-fisted rookie I'd been. "Gladys, you have really grown up," one of them told me once. "I remember when you were scared to play twenty dollars."

That wasn't being scared, I realize now; it was being smart. It is part of the casino's game plan to make you feel better about yourself by risking more and more of your money. Of course, that is how casinos make *their* money. After I got the feel of the game, I raised the ante, and gambling became my traveling passion. I played all the casinos in Vegas as well as those across Europe, in the Bahamas, and in Puerto Rico. In San Juan, the Caribe Hilton was my lucky spot. I met a woman who claimed to be a professional gambler there. She played blackjack around the clock and I picked up some tips from her. In Reno, I would play the mini-baccarat tables and take home $40,000 and $50,000 a night.

I thought I was in control in the early going because once I got ahead, I never allowed myself to lose more than I'd won. If I started losing, I'd get out and take my winnings home.

In truth, I was quickly losing control. My inner dialogue was all about rationalizing the gambling. I told myself that I was playing for college money for the kids, or to pay off my debts. Part of the reason I got so sucked in was that I'd always been good at games and I was good at gambling too. For a long time, I made good money at it and my gambling earnings definitely helped pay the bills in those difficult times.

Before long, however, I really wasn't playing for anything other than the thrill of gambling. In the gambling world, at least, I became as well-known for my gambling as for my singing.

It was an empowering feeling, then, to know that I could walk into any casino and ask for cash up front and they would cover me. At first it would be limited to $2,500. Then it went up to five and ten grand. Eventually, I could ask for $20,000. I'd just ask for "five" and $5,000 would appear.

At first I could maneuver well enough to handle that much cash and pay it back, but then I started falling behind. I would get calls from the casinos gently reminding me of my unpaid balance. Contrary to the casino mob image, nobody ever threatened me. They were always gentlemanly, but I watch the movies, and the deeper I got into debt, all I could think of was that I was going to end up at the bottom of some lake wearing cement shoes.

Sometimes, I would have to go to Bubba and other family members and ask them to help me get out of the debts. They knew what I was doing and they didn't like it. Momma used to beg me not to play. But I kept going.

When I moved to Vegas, I started driving alone to the Strip. I liked playing alone, so I could concentrate. They took good care of me from the parking lot to the tables. I felt like royalty from the minute I arrived at the casino. I was attended to by the parking valets, security guards, pit bosses, croupiers, and casino management. I played behind red velvet ropes that protected me from autograph seekers, thieves, and scam artists. They brought food and drinks right to me, at no charge.

Inside the windowless casino and behind those regal ropes, I felt like I was with family. I knew all the croupiers by name. I knew about their families and their hopes for their lives. I'd watched many of them move up the career ladder within the casino, from dealer to manager to pit boss. I let myself believe that they cared about me beyond my capacity for losing money to them. I think they did, as I cared about them.

When I got brave enough to start placing higher bets, they seemed just as nervous about it as I was. They pulled for me to win. If the table got crowded, they always kept an eye on me, winking at me to let me know I was safe and secure. I realize now that I was like the child who sought shelter from the storm in the lions' den. I thought I was escaping my problems, but I was only making them much, much worse.

I had so much weighing on me at home, so many expectations, so many people depending on me, wanting things from me. When I was performing, it was the same thing. I had to be on all the time. When I gambled, I was a kid again in my private play space.

I didn't have to go to anyone and ask what they thought or wait for them to vote on it as I'd had to do for so many years with The Pips. I could do what I wanted to, when I wanted to do it, and nobody had anything to say about it.

In the end, that is why it became so addictive and dangerous for me. Gambling became a substitute for actually dealing with my life. By the mid-eighties, it got to the point where I'd stay out all night through to the next morning. I would miss taking Shanga to school so my mother would have to take him. At one or two in the afternoon, I would still be at the table, calling her on a cellular phone, asking her to pick Shanga up for me.

I was abandoning all my responsibilities to stay at the table to play. One night I was on a winning streak in Reno. I took a break and went to the ladies' room. When I came out of the stall, there was a woman standing there. She started talking and pleading with me. She wanted money so she could continue to play. She didn't appear to know who I was, or care. She was begging a stranger for gambling money.

She was pathetic, and I saw myself in her desperation. I told myself that I had not reached that point, but like her, I was living from stake to stake, game to game.

"You need to go home," I told her. "You need to quit. Tomorrow is another day."

The more I told her no, the more desperate she became. "Have my watch," she said, unsnapping it and handing it to me. From the looks of the watch, she could not afford to be playing.

"I can't take your watch," I said. "Keep it, come back tomorrow."

Even as I encouraged her to walk away, I knew that I couldn't.

When she and I walked out of the restroom, her husband was waiting. He gently put his arm around her and said, "We're going home."

She protested, but she let him lead her out. I felt sad for her, but

I kept telling myself I was not that bad, not at that point. I was still in control.

I went back to the table and played into the night, putting the woman out of my mind, but she stayed in my subconscious. Chip by chip, dollar by dollar, I began to understand the hold gambling had on me. It began to sink in that I was losing money just so I could keep playing. I wasn't thinking about the money I had won, only that I didn't want to stop.

That's how I came to lose $45,000 in one night.

Just a few months earlier, I'd written all of the Vegas casinos a letter asking them to stop fronting me money. But that night, I asked the croupier for $2,500 and he gave it to me. Deluded by my addiction, convinced that his loyalty was to me, his friend, and not to his casino bosses, I felt that I had "sweet-talked" him into it.

There were some croupiers who had been urging me to take my winnings and go home. With that $2,500, I had won $45,000. They recognized that I'd had a terrific streak of luck, but they knew that I should have cashed in and gone home. I knew it, too, but I could not walk away.

My brother-in-law Grady Clark, who often accompanied me, was also a heavy gambler. He tried to tell me too. He rarely interfered. I ignored him too. He gave up and went off to eat.

The croupiers who had advised me to go took a break and left me. I kept playing, and my losses mounted. *It only takes one good hand to get back in the groove.*

It never happened. I lost it all.

Nobody said it was all right. Nobody said I'd just hit a streak of bad luck. Nobody said it would be better tomorrow.

People turned away; even those that I knew would not look at me. To this day, I can still see their expressions of disapproval and concern.

I heard the pleas of the woman in the bathroom, only it was my voice pleading, my desperation echoing off the tiles.

I went straight from the table to the pay telephone booth. This was a move that I'd known was coming for a long time. After the last cent was gone, I became physically ill—cold sweat, shaky hands, sick in the pit of my stomach. I just lost it all. It had happened.

It was my first step toward getting well.

A woman answered after two rings.

"Gamblers Anonymous."

"I need help," I said without identifying myself.

Those were the words she needed to hear.

"Where are you?"

"I'm at the Golden Nugget."

"Okay, leave there right now and meet me on Oakey and Maryland Parkway."

I walked out and went to that intersection and as I waited for her, I felt like a deathly ill patient awaiting the arrival of her doctor. I felt like I was going to throw up out of shame and self-revulsion. I *was* sick. I was an *addict*.

Before I'd gone outside after hanging up with the woman from Gamblers Anonymous, I'd gone to find my brother-in-law sitting in the casino restaurant. I plopped down across from him at a table.

"You lost it all, didn't you?" he said.

He was looking directly at me, and it wasn't with approval or good humor.

"Yep," I said. "Every dime."

I took a drink of ice water.

"I just made a call," I said.

"I'm with you," he offered.

For the first time since I lost the money, and maybe for the first time in many years, I felt like I was getting my life back under control.

When the woman from GA arrived outside, we talked briefly and agreed to go to Brenda's house nearby. There, we talked for hours while sitting outside under a tree. Actually, I talked. She listened. "I've been where you've been," she said after I'd told her what I'd done that night and over the last ten years or so of my gambling addiction.

She then explained what I needed to do. Over the next several days and weeks, I did exactly as she instructed. First, I told my mother and my family. They knew I was in deep, but it was the first time I admitted it to them. Then I attended my first Gamblers Anonymous meeting. My longtime friend Preacher Wells accompanied me. He had been watching over me and protecting me from the beginning of my gambling addiction. He'd often shown up when I was playing. "How did you know I was here?" I'd ask him.

"I know," he'd say.

Preacher Wells knew a lot of people in the gambling industry and there were many times when I'd be way behind at the gaming tables only to discover that he had very quietly arranged for my credit to be cut off for the night. A casino employee would appear beside me and whisper, "The preacher says, 'No more.' " It is great to have friends like that, believe me.

I was nervous, worried about what people would think of me. Would they welcome me or make fun of me? Maybe they would get a kick out of seeing someone like me fall so low. Preacher Wells told me not to worry but I'd had a good-girl image for so long; now I'd blown it; I worried that I'd never be able to walk back up on stage without people laughing about my foolishness as a gambler.

"My name is Gladys Knight and I'm a compulsive gambler."

"Hi, Gladys."

"Welcome, Gladys."

There were no laughs, no cruel remarks.

After I'd told my story at that first meeting, everyone clapped. It was the first time in a long time that I had gotten applause for anything other than my singing.

I only went to one other meeting. I can't say I haven't craved gambling and the false feelings of security and control it gave me. I have even played some since then. But I believe I have reestablished control over the compulsiveness that had overcome me. When I walk through a casino now, it doesn't have the same allure for me. The ringing of the machines and all the noise no longer excites me. It's like quitting smoking, which I also have accomplished. You wonder how you ever tolerated that smell in your hair and on your clothes. I wonder now how I had ever deluded myself into thinking that casinos were a safe place to escape my troubles and my cares.

When I looked at people gambling in the casino I said to myself, "I know they are having fun, but they'd better be careful."

Instead of escaping into the baccarat table, I learned to confront head-on those things that had been troubling me, and to go after those that I had been searching for. I started demanding my own space. I started telling people no.

Most important, I learned to take responsibility for my own happiness, and to take joys in whatever dosage is available every moment of every day.

CHAPTER 19

wo years after I acknowledged my gambling addiction and walked away from the baccarat table, I also ended my dependency on three men whom I loved a great deal. When I launched my new act without The Pips, I was forty-five years old, and finally, I felt in control of my life.

I had come through childhood as a performer guided by adults. I had struggled and fought and followed the wishes of The Pips in establishing our career as a group. I had experienced both the rewards and the burdens of our shared success. Then, I decided I wanted to learn how to do it all over again, on my own, I waited a long time for my coming out party, and I guess you could say I came out with a vengeance.

The solo debut in Las Vegas followed my first HBO television special, *Sisters in the Name of Love*. I produced it with the help of Bob Henry, who had produced our summer replacement show and also *Charlie and Company*, a short-lived sitcom I starred in with Flip Wilson in 1985. The critics said our comedy was too much like *The Cosby*

Show, though there were other family shows at that time, I guess because black folks all look alike.

I had performed in a handful of acting roles in films, television, and theater, but rather than wait for something to come to me, I wanted to create my own projects. *Sisters* appealed to me as way of showcasing the talents of African-American women performers. Of course, I had a long list of candidates for the show; among them were my first makeup consultant, Tina Turner, along with Aretha Franklin, Patti LaBelle, Dionne Warwick, and Roberta Flack. I could never track some of them down, or get others to commit because of scheduling conflicts. Aretha, bless her, committed, then backed out, but my two closest friends in show business, Dionne and Patti, signed on to perform with me.

With the help of Bob as well as Bubba, my son Jimmy, daughter Kenya, my momma, and many others, we pulled the special together in just two weeks. We rented the Aquarius Theater in Los Angeles for the show. We filmed over two nights and even though we sold tickets in advance, there were long lines of people trying to get in. We had only three days to rehearse, but things were going great. Magic was in the air. Patti's manager came to one rehearsal, bringing songwriters Burt Bacharach and Carol Bayer Sager. I think they wanted to see if we were going to pull it off. We sang such a soulful version of "A Place for Us," that they were close to tears. We had it going on and we were all three enthused about doing the show.

The show itself was a rousing success and I was proud of our accomplishments and even more proud of my sisters who supported me. We as a people are not known for that kind of love, unity, and support. I thank them for being there. Of course, like real sisters, we had our little spats during those intense few days of preparation and performing. After the first show, Dionne asked me and Patti to meet with her. She was concerned because she felt Patti was not taking the *Sisters* format to heart. In her view, Patty was singing as a soloist even when the three of us were supposed to be harmonizing. Patti is such an emotional singer that she tends to lose herself while performing, which is fine when she is singing solo, but it can cause problems in a group-singing situation.

I was there when Dionne asked Patti in a very pleasant but firm manner to "stay on her note." Dionne didn't jump all over her or tell her she was being hoggish or even try to dim her light, as Patti has put it since then. I'm not interested in taking sides or hurting either Patti or Dionne, but since Patti discussed this incident in her book, I'd like to set the record straight. I heard Dionne simply tell Patti that she could do whatever she wanted during her solo parts, but when we were singing together, we needed her to say on her note for the sake of harmony.

I wanted Patti to be herself and to sing with all of her great passion, but I agreed with Dionne that she needed to bring it in a little in order for us to harmonize. Dionne was particularly upset that Patti jumped in and sang my part in "That's What Friends Are For," since I'd done it on a best-selling record and it was something of a signature piece for me. From my point of view, Dionne went about it tactfully and politely enough: "In the next show, when we come to Gladys's part in 'That's What Friends Are For,' would you please let her sing it?" she said.

Patty responded, "Oh yeah, right. I just got carried away, girl."

She seemed to understand and for the second show, we sounded terrific. Somehow that minor behind-the-scenes incident became overblown. But, what happened on camera was terrific. We did *Sisters* proud. We ended the show with "There's a Place for Us," and let me tell you, we were sobbing like nobody's business. Patti was crying so much she couldn't sing her part. She could hardly stand up. I was trying to give her a shoulder to lean on while Dionne squeezed my hand. The audience went wild and gave us a standing ovation and it was a night to remember, for the good things, which kept on coming.

The show won three Cable ACE awards, and for her controlled but dynamic performance, Patti was named Entertainer of the Year. I could not have been more proud to have been the producer of a show that helped her win that honor.

Sadly, in spite of all the awards the show won, when I tried to do a second Sisters show, nobody would give me the financing. But I don't give it up. I fight. I decided to bring Patti and Dionne together again to record "Superwoman" with me. Once again, the two of them had a little tension going, even during the recording session, but they are both professionals and, when all is said and done, they have a great amount of love and respect for each other. They understand, as I do, that all people, but blacks in particular, have to learn to put our differences aside and work together for our mutual benefit.

It seems to me that there is far less cooperation and mutual support among black artists today than when I was starting out, and that concerns me. We had friendly rivalries with the other groups. As we came offstage, we'd challenge the Temptations to "follow that" and it would inspire them to work even harder. It was a healthy competition, and it was reinforced by long hours of working together to help each other get better.

We believed that there was enough success out there for everybody, but I don't see much of that mentality today. The mood out there now seems to be that there is only so much success and if you can't get it, you'd better block others from grabbing it away. Most frightening is the violent gang mentality that has penetrated our business. That is intolerable, and it has already resulted in the loss of some highly talented young performers.

We need to be supportive of each other in this industry. There are enough barriers in our way as it is. The racism and segregation today is not the in-your-face WHITES ONLY sign on a water fountain, or the front door marked NO NIGGERS on a restaurant wall or hotel. It is every bit as insidious but it is far more subtle. It exists on the radio, on television, and in the boardrooms of the entertainment industry.

It is most obvious when you consider that most of the time music performed by blacks is automatically classified as "rhythm and blues," a category that the vast majority of radio stations don't offer on their play lists. Yet, white artists who sound "black" or sing "soul" songs don't have that problem. Their music is considered "pop" or "rock and roll" and it gets the nationwide radio air play, and the millions and millions of dollars in sales that air play brings.

I am proud of my success in crossing over with many records. I have just as many white fans as I do black ones and those white fans have a right to hear all of my music, not just "Midnight Train to Georgia." I am grateful for the play that my songs get on "black" radio stations and on "white" radio stations; I simply wish that there did not have to be barriers and that it could be about the music, not about race, as too many things in our society are. I take it as an insult to my intelligence when anyone tries to tell me that race is not a factor in the music business.

I have been performing for fifty years, yet my records still have to go through the R&B Top Ten in order to cross over to pop radio and even be heard. In 1994, I released an album entitled *Just for You*. When I asked what singles from that album they wanted to promote, I was told that they didn't think there was a single song that a popular music radio station would play!

In general, white pop artists receive much better record deals than black artists. That's why the artist formerly known as Prince was wearing a sign that said "slave" for a while. He was making a point that his record company had not given him the same treatment it gave to white artists. They finally took the point, and let him out of the unfair contract.

There are megastar black artists, of course, who have overcome this racism in the music industry simply through their earning power. Tina Turner and Michael Jackson are a couple who come to mind, maybe Whitney Houston and Luther Vandross too. Dollars mean power, and they have broken through the barriers. I admire them for that. I just wish those barriers were not so high so that far more black artists could reap the same rewards as all those white performers who do not face the same restrictions.

I am extremely grateful for the gift I have been given and the opportunities that it has created for me. I can scarcely believe that I ever asked God to take this precious thing away from me. Now that I understand what a blessing it is, I want to share it, and that is the basis of my frustration with the segregation of my music and that of other performers restricted to the rhythm-and-blues category.

In 1996, I performed again in the "big room" at Madison Square Garden. It was in that same room that I performed at the age of eight, and won the Ted Mack championship. Once again, I could only sense the audience at first in the darkened theater, but when the lights were brought up, the big room proved to be filled to capacity. As they gave me a standing ovation, I was moved to tears. It hit me then just how far I had come, how much I had survived, and how well this gift had served me through it all.

Through all my pain as well as all my glory, I have been blessed.

CHAPTER 20

After my first husband Jimmy died, I had come to believe that the only other man—other than my grown sons—who would ever love me for my true nappy-headed self was my daddy. We had remained close over the years, even after he left Momma and us. He lived for years in a two-bedroom apartment on his meager earnings at Rich's Department Store. When he died, I thought that I would never again have that sort of unconditional love from a man.

For a brief instant, I thought Les Brown might be such a man.

You see me on the cover of this book wearing the ring Les gave me. My plan was to write this concluding chapter as a happy ending in which I found at last a man who loved me for myself. Instead, just as I was preparing to put my final thoughts on paper, the doorbell rang at our home in Las Vegas. I was home alone, as usual, and reluctant to answer it, but when I saw a nicely dressed couple standing outside, I opened the door.

The man and woman were process servers. They handed me divorce papers that had been filed by Les. I don't think I'd even read all the way through those papers before he was issuing a press release announcing our divorce to the media.

I was stunned and hurt by the way in which he engineered it, and the fact that he did it so publicly, but I was not all that surprised. Fairy tale endings, after all, only happen in fairy tales.

With Les, I got to play Cinderella again. Just for a moment. Once again, I bought into the *Once upon a time*. Sadly, before the *happily ever after* really got started, it was over.

I was in Chicago performing at the Regal Theater in 1992, when one of my publicity people, Karen Mayo, called and asked if she could get backstage passes to one of the shows for herself and a Les Brown.

I didn't ask who he was, but she told me anyway. She said he was a big-time motivational speaker. I had never paid much attention to that sort of thing, and I had never heard of the guy, but I got her the backstage passes.

Les Brown showed up backstage with her a few nights later, and when she introduced us, he hugged me like a long-lost friend. I'm not all that big on being squeezed by strangers, but this wasn't bad. In fact, it was some kind of good. My toes felt a little jolt.

A handsome guy with one of those 100-watt man-child smiles, Les seemed to feel the electricity too. We had a nice chat, and as they prepared to go, Les said he looked forward to seeing me perform again some time. I gave him my private telephone number and told him he could call me for tickets. It's something I do for a lot of people, but Les later said that he thought I was encouraging him to call me for other reasons. Actually, I was just trying to be accommodating to a fan, but, as he walked out the door, I did check him out in the mirror, and I looked twice.

Little did I realize then that I had given encouragement to a man who had landed his first job at a radio station by going in every day for months and months and asking the station manager if anybody had quit, been fired, or died. The station manager finally gave in and let him work there.

I was about to get a big serving of that same Les Brown doggedness. He sent telegrams. He sent flowers. He left messages. He had friends leave messages. I think some of his messages left messages.

Somehow, he even tracked down poor Momma.

"Who is this Les Brown?" she asked one day. "He talks so much."

Les had been talking for a living since he talked his way onto a Miami radio station while working as a grass mower for the city's maintenance department. Abandoned at birth in a vacant building in Miami's poorest neighborhood, he was adopted by Miss Mamie Brown, a divorced woman who worked two or three jobs to support all of the children she took in.

Obviously, when Les Brown set his sights on a target, he was a force to be reckoned with, and as I would discover, it often didn't matter who or what was in his way. He nearly wore out every answering machine in my family, to the point that one day, my sister Brenda asked me to return his calls so that she wouldn't have to stall him anymore. She felt I owed him a return call.

I had to admit, I was impressed by his persistence, even if I wasn't particularly interested in giving him any more encouragement. Since he seemed to be more of a talker than a stalker, I gave him a call.

As fate would have it, I got *his* answering machine, and, to my surprise, I felt a little disappointment that he was not there. Of course, he did track me down later, and once he was back on the trail, he was not about to be put off, even when I told him that my focus in life at that point was my children and my career.

His initial bid was for lunch. I declined. Then dinner. I said no. Next he tried a less specific approach.

"What are you doing tomorrow?" That would be a Sunday, and an early, early church service was on the agenda, I said. This man had no fear of the Lord. "Mind if I come along?"

What could I do? It was not a private church. He was a gentleman and, of course, quite the conversationalist. After church we went to one of my favorite soul food restaurants, Roscoe's Chicken and Waffles, where we talked like old neighborhood pals. Then, after lunch, we parked in front of the Hilton and talked another couple hours. I was impressed that he talked like a man who believed in the same traditions that I held dear, family and faith. At least, he definitely knew how to talk that game.

He was interesting, but I was wary.

I ended that day by being honest with him and telling him that I was not looking for anything serious.

"Well, who asked you?" he said.

That was good for a laugh, but I let him know that I wanted to maintain a distance, and he seemed to understand. Before he left, he gave me one of his motivational tapes dealing with relationships. I listened to it later, and he seemed to have all the right things to say. He could talk the talk, no doubt about it, but could he walk the walk? I wasn't sure I wanted to know at that point, but then, maybe I did.

It was several months before I saw him again. I had returned to Chicago to perform for a convention group, the Luster Foundation, and, coincidentally, Les had been hired to speak to them too. My show was on the final night of their meeting, so he decided to stay an extra night to catch it. We sat in my suite and talked and talked the day before my show, and I found myself enjoying the conversation with a man who was willing to talk about things most males avoided—feelings and relationships.

We parted as friends after that encounter, and I was no longer trying to keep him at arm's length. A forearm, maybe, but not an arm.

For more than a year, we nurtured the friendship on the telephone mostly, but if I was going to be near one of his speaking engagements, I'd try to catch it. He would do the same with my performances. In between, we'd talk and talk and talk.

The friendship moved into a dating relationship in February 1993, and Les made it clear he wasn't playing the dating game for long. He was always dropping hints about proposing, or buying a ring, and getting married. At first, I thought he was teasing, but I began to sense that he was serious. He had me interested, but my protective force fields were going up too. I wasn't sure if it was nappy-headed *me*, or Gladys Knight the performer he was so interested in.

Then, in the spring, I was appearing at the Vegas Hilton when Les flew in for a visit. We were walking through the casino hotel lobby one day when he pulled me into a jewelry shop. He said he just wanted to find out what my finger size was. He acted like it was just a lark, so I went along with it. I even tried on a few nice rings from the display for fun. Of course the saleswoman had her own ideas. Seeing how we acted like two school kids in puppy love, she disappeared for a moment and returned with a "simply fabulous" diamond engagement ring.

There is not a woman on this planet who would not have given that ring a test run. The challenge was to keep from running out the door with it still on my finger. I took it off before giving in to that impulse. "It's very nice," I told Les, but I know my smile gave me away.

The very next day, I was supervising as Les was getting a haircut in his hotel suite, when he asked me to bring him a bag that he'd left on the coffee table. I kept my eye on the hairstylist's clippers when I reached into the bag to give Les whatever was inside. "Look at it," he said.

It was a ring box.

"Go on, open it," he said.

It was the "fabulous" ring.

I was so shocked I didn't even take the ring out. Instead I threw the box, ring and all, at Les, and ran into the bedroom for a good cry.

"Baby," Les said, following me into the room. "What are you crying for?"

I caught my breath. "Because nobody has ever given me a ring before," I said, sobbing like a teenager.

I'd been married twice, but neither Jimmy nor Barry had proposed to me, nor had they given me an engagement ring. Les Brown was the first man to do that for me, and it made me cry.

When I told him that, he said he wanted to do it all for me then. He got down on his knees and proposed.

I accepted his proposal, but I still had reservations about marrying him. We discussed, debated, argued, and screamed over reservations that we both had—about being married, about each other, about the impact it would have on our respective families—for the next two years.

Honey, we did not rush into this, believe me. We were like a couple of scarred veterans of the marital wars, reluctantly suiting up for another campaign.

It wasn't a question about our love for each other, really; it was how do we avoid the usual pitfalls that await two people with such hectic and complicated lives. We both carried a lot of baggage. I had three children from two failed marriages. He had six children from two failed marriages, and a well-known reputation as a lady killer.

My family members had heard some things that gave them cause to doubt Les's reliability, and even his sincerity. I listened this time, and I talked to him about their concerns. I think that is one thing that convinced me to go ahead, his willingness to talk to me about his feelings and his insecurities and his mistakes in life.

There was one day, more than a year and a half after we'd gotten engaged, when we were together again in Los Angeles, and we went for a ride to Santa Monica beach. We parked and started walking and talking. The day was so beautiful. We talked about everything: what we were going to do, how we needed to get it together, whether we still had the same goals in mind.

I thought we put it all on the table that day, and by the time we were talked out, we still had not reached a point of saying we were willing to go ahead and get married. We were wary, both of us, of this challenge.

On the walk back to the car, I stopped and told Les: "Whatever we decide to do, I'm in this because I love you, and I'm gonna kiss you right here in front of God and everybody else."

The next evening Les called me. "Look," he said, "this is crazy. What are you going to do, fish or cut bait?"

"Fish," I said.

With that romantic exchange, I accepted Les's proposal.

We were married in a small private ceremony on August 29, 1995, in Las Vegas.

I'm happy to report that this time there were no spills or falls.

In the months that followed, I have to say that Les brought some wonderful gifts to my life. He seemed to fully support my career and he challenged me to do more. He encouraged me to join him in his public speaking, telling me that I had a gift for it.

I refused to believe him. "There is only one speaker in this family," I'd tell him. "And it is not me. You speak. I sing."

As I had already discovered, he was not one to give up. He'd just laugh and keep coming at me: "You have a speaker in you, another whole talent that you don't know about yet."

Then he manipulated me into doing just what he wanted. I would go to his speaking engagements to support him and to be with him, and he would lure me on stage.

He was tricky, no doubt about it.

"I want to introduce you to my wife. Her name is Gladys Knight."

I'd stand up and wave and sit back down.

Next, he started saying, "Would you please meet my wife, Gladys Knight," and he'd look at me and say, "Baby, come on up."

What could I do? I'd go up and take a bow, and then I'd go back and sit in the audience like a good wife. But Les wanted more.

After a while it got to be: "I want you to meet my wife, Ms. Gladys Knight. Baby, come on up. Don't you want to say hello to the people?"

Okay, I said hello, and then headed for my seat again, but he'd try to get me to join in whatever topic he was presenting that day. He wore me down, in part, because he had a point. I liked to talk to people, as well as sing for them, and I even surprised myself by having a lot to say to them. I came to believe that was probably one of the reasons Les was put into my life.

Because of his prompting, I have developed confidence as a speaker, and recently I became a national spokesperson for the American Diabetes Association. Their work is near to my heart since my mother, brother, and several other family members have diabetes.

Les gave me the inspiration and the courage to step out as a speaker and I am grateful for that because, as I mentioned earlier, I've finally learned to take the blessings where I find them in each moment.

I have many blessings to be thankful for as I write this. Leslie Calvin Brown was a blessing to me. I know that I am stronger and better for having known him. Though I may not see the infinite wisdom of it all right now, it will be revealed to me as all things are pertaining to the master plan that He has for each of us. Until then, I'll be still and know that He is with me even when things don't turn out as I envisioned. I will continue striving to be an example for our Heavenly Father through my being, my music, and now, the spoken word. I have learned through this experience even more lessons about life, to help my children and their children find and capitalize on opportunities to make their lives even better. My son Jimmy has prospered as a businessman and continues to grow as my manager. Kenya has overcome some hardships in her life to find her niche as the owner of a chain of bakeries. Shanga, who no longer has a weight problem and is as handsome as could be, like my Jimmy, is embarking on a career as a restaurateur. I still have my mother beside me, thank God, and the love of my ever-growing family. For that I am grateful. For Les, I have only the wish that he, too, can find peace and love, if that is what he so desires.

I think Les loved me as much as Les could love anyone. I know from our intimate talks that he carries enormous anger and hurt from having been abandoned as a child, and I suspect that as a result, Les has developed a pattern of leaving the people he loves because he fears they, too, might abandon him some day. To protect himself, he walks out first.

He did it to others before he did it to me. I would have stayed with him, I think. I know I would have been there to help him through his scare with prostate cancer, but he shut me out and even spread some hurtful words that I had left him because of his cancer. I'm sorry, Les, but I was not planning on abandoning you.

As my family had feared, Les talked the talk but did not walk the walk when it came to relationships and faithfulness. The presence of other women in his life, whether they were just friends or old girl-friends as he protested, was a constant source of friction and one that he did little to alleviate.

As I write this, my heart is still in halves. One half urges me to cry for the failure of yet another marriage, and the man I love; the other tells me to cry for the blessings that still come to me. I am better off today mentally, spiritually, financially, and emotionally than I have ever been before. My children have grown into wonderful, responsible adults. My grandchildren love me for my cooking.

I am not angry or bitter about this most recent pain in my life. I am resigned and at peace because there are many more lines to be written in this life story. I have known loneliness in front of a crowd of thousands, and I have known fulfillment in a night spent alone with a good book, especially a passionate romance novel. I haven't given up on love and I will continue to love the people I care for uncondi-tionally because that is the only way you can receive love uncondition-ally.

I'm a glutton for life.

Bring on the pain. Bring on the glory. I will be in this fight to share my gifts, to enjoy my blessings, and to be loved without any strings attached.

DISCOGRAPHY

1960 GLADYS KNIGHT & THE PIPS
      Gladys Knight & The Pips
      Up Front Records

SIDE 1:	SIDE 2:
Every Beat of My Heart	Room in Your Heart
Love Call	Happiness
What Shall I Do	I Had a Dream Last Night
Queen of Tears	Letter Full of Tears
A Love like Mine	Operator

1962 GLADYS KNIGHT & THE PIPS
      It Hurt So Bad
      Trip Records

SIDE 1:	SIDE 2:
It Hurt So Bad	Queen of Tears
What Will Become of Me	Linda
A Love like Mine	To Whom It May Concern
Darling	Bless the One
Come See about Me	Walking in Circles

1967 GLADYS KNIGHT & THE PIPS
      Silk 'N' Soul
      Soul-Motown Records

SIDE 1:	SIDE 2:
I Wish It Would Rain	Theme from *Valley of the Dolls*
The Look of Love	Baby I Need Your Lovin'
Yesterday	The Tracks of My Tears
Groovin'	You're My Everything
You've Lost That Lovin' Feelin'	Every Little Bit Hurts

1968 GLADYS KNIGHT & THE PIPS
      Tastiest Hits
      Bell Records

SIDE 1:	SIDE 2:
Letter Full of Tears	Giving Up
Either Way I Lose	Stop & Get a Hold of Myself
If Ever I Should Fall In Love	Lovers Always Forgive
Daybreak	Tell Her You're Mine
Maybe, Maybe Baby	Operator
Every Beat of My Heart	

1968   GLADYS KNIGHT & THE PIPS
          Feelin' Bluesy
          Soul-Motown Records

SIDE 1:	SIDE 2:
The End of the Road	Don't Let Her Take Your Love from Me
That's the Way Love Is	It Should Have Been Me
Don't You Miss Me a Little Bit, Baby	Don't Turn Me Away
The Boy from Cross Town	What Good Am I without You
Ain't You Glad You Chose Love	Your Old Standby
I Know Better	It's Time to Go Now

1969   GLADYS KNIGHT & THE PIPS
          Nitty Gritty
          Soul-Motown Records

SIDE 1:	SIDE 2:
Cloud Nine	All I Could Do Was Cry
Runnin' Out	Keep an Eye
Didn't You Know (You'd Have to Cry)	Got Myself a Good Man
(I Know) I'm Losing You	It's Summer
The Nitty Gritty	The Stranger
Ain't No Sun Since You've Been Gone	I Want Him to Say It Again

1970   GLADYS KNIGHT & THE PIPS
          All in a Knight's Work
          Soul-Motown Records

SIDE 1:	SIDE 2:
Cabaret	Everybody Needs Love
The End of the Road	Just in Time
By the Time I Get to Phoenix	Every Beat of My Heart
Fever	Dr. Feelgood
Glory of Love	Letter Full of Tears
Ain't No Sun Since You've Been Gone	I Heard It through the Grapevine
Girl Talk	He'll Guide My Way
Giving Up	
A Love like Mine	

1970   GLADYS KNIGHT & THE PIPS
          Greatest Hits
          Soul-Motown Records

SIDE 1:	SIDE 2:
Every Beat of My Heart	I Wish It Would Rain
Letter Full of Tears	Didn't You Know (You'd Have to Cry
Giving Up	Sometime)

Everybody Needs Love
I Heard It through the Grapevine
The End of the Road

You Need Love like I Do (Don't You)
Friendship Train
The Nitty Gritty
It Should Have Been Me

1971   GLADYS KNIGHT & THE PIPS
Standing Ovation
Soul-Motown Records

SIDE 1:

Make Me the Woman You Come
  Home To
Can You Give Me Love with a
  Guarantee
Fire and Rain
Master of My Mind
He Ain't Heavy He's My Brother
Bridge over Troubled Water

SIDE 2:

It Takes a Whole Lotta Man for a
  Woman Like Me
Help Me Make It through the Night
The Winding Road
If You Gonna Leave (Just Leave)
No One Could Love You More

1971   GLADYS KNIGHT & THE PIPS
If I Were Your Woman
Soul-Motown Records

SIDE 1:

If I Were Your Woman
Feeling Alright
One Less Bell to Answer
Let It Be
I Don't Want to Do Wrong
One Step Away

SIDE 2:

Here I Am Again
How Can You Say That Ain't Love
Is There a Place (In Your Heart for Me)
Everybody Is a Star
Signed Gladys
Your Love's Been Good for Me

1972   GLADYS KNIGHT & THE PIPS
Neither One of Us
Soul-Motown Records

SIDE 1:

Neither One of Us
It's Gotta Be That Way
For Once in My Life
This Child Needs Its Father
Who Is She (And What Is She to You)

SIDE 2:

And This Is Love
Daddy Could Swear, I Declare
Can't Give It Up No More
Don't It Make You Feel Guilty
Operator

1973   GLADYS KNIGHT & THE PIPS
Anthology
Soul-Motown Records

SIDE 1:

Every Beat of My Heart
Letter Full of Tears
Giving Up
Just Walk in My Shoes
Take Me in Your Arms & Love Me
Everybody Needs Love

SIDE 2:

I Heard It through the Grapevine
The End of the Road
It Should Have Been Me
I Wish It Would Rain
Didn't You Know (You'd Have to Cry
    Sometime)
The Nitty Gritty

SIDE 3:

The Friendship Train
The Tracks of My Tears
You Need Love like I Do (Don't You)
Every Little Bit Hurts
If I Were Your Woman
I Don't Want to Do Wrong

SIDE 4:

Make Me the Woman that You Go
    Home To
Help Me Make It through the Night
For Once in My Life
Neither One of Us
Daddy Could Swear, I Declare

1973   GLADYS KNIGHT & THE PIPS
        All I Need Is Time
        Soul-Motown Records

SIDE 1:

I'll Be Here (When You Get Home)
All I Need Is Time
Heavy Makes You Happy
The Only Time You Love Me Is When
    You Are Losing Me
Here I Am Again

SIDE 2:

There's a Lesson to Be Learned
Oh, What a Love I Have Found
The Singer
Thank You

1973   GLADYS KNIGHT & THE PIPS
        Imagination
        Buddah Records

SIDE 1:

Midnight Train to Georgia
I've Got to Use My Imagination
Storms of Troubled Times
Best Thing that Ever Happened to Me
Once in a Lifetime Thing

SIDE 2:

Where Peaceful Waters Flow
I Can See Clearly Now
Perfect Love
Window Raisin' Granny

1974   GLADYS KNIGHT & THE PIPS
        Knight Time
        Buddah Records

SIDE 1:

How Can You Say That Ain't Love
Somebody Stole the Sunshine
Between Her Goodbye and My Hello

SIDE 2:

Ease Me to the Ground
Your Heartaches I Can Surely Heal
Master of My Mind

It's All Over but the Shoutin'
We've Got Such a Mellow Love

Billy, Come On Back as Quick as You
  Can
It Takes a Whole Lot of Human Feeling

1974   GLADYS KNIGHT & THE PIPS
        Claudine
        Buddah Records

SIDE 1:
Mr. Welfare Man
To Be Invisible
On & On
The Makings of You

SIDE 2:
Claudine's Theme (Instrumental)
Hold On
Make Yours a Happy Home

1974   GLADYS KNIGHT & THE PIPS
        I Feel a Song
        Buddah Records

SIDE 1:
I Feel a Song (In My Heart)
Love Finds Its Own Way
Seconds
The Goings Up & Comings Down
The Way We Were

SIDE 2:
Better You Go Your Way
Don't Burn Down the Bridge
The Need to Be
Tenderness Is His Way

1976   GLADYS KNIGHT & THE PIPS
        Pipe Dreams
        Buddah Records

SIDE 1:
So Sad the Song
Alaskan Pipeline
Pot of Jazz
I'll Miss You
Nobody But You

SIDE 2:
Pipe Dream
Find a Way
Follow My Dreams
So Sad the Song (Instrumental)

1977   **The Best of Gladys Knight & The Pips**
        Buddah Records

SIDE 1:
Make Yours a Happy Home
Best Thing That Ever Happened to Me
I Feel a Song (In My Heart)
The Goings Up & Comings Down
Midnight Train to Georgia

SIDE 2:
On & On
Where Peaceful Waters Flow
I've Got to Use My Imagination
I Can See Clearly Now
Try to Remember/The Way We Were

1977   GLADYS KNIGHT & THE PIPS
          Still Together
          Buddah Records

SIDE 1:	SIDE 2:
Love Is Always on Your Mind	Baby Don't Change Your Mind
Home Is Where the Heart Is	Walk Softly
Little Bit of Love	I Love to Feel the Feeling
	To Make a Long Story Short
	You Put a New Life in My Body

1978   GLADYS KNIGHT & THE PIPS
          The One and Only
          Buddah Records

SIDE 1:	SIDE 2:
Sorry Doesn't Always Make It Right	The One and Only
Come Back and Finish What You Started	Saved by the Grace of Love
All the Time	Don't Say No to Me Tonight
It's a Better Than Good Time	Be Yourself
Butterfly	What If I Should Ever Need You

1979   GLADYS KNIGHT
          Gladys Knight
          Columbia/CBS Records

SIDE 1:	SIDE 2:
Am I Too Late	I (Who Have Nothing)
You Bring Out the Best in Me	You Don't Have to Say I Love You
I Just Want to Be with You	The Best Thing We Can Do Is Say Goodbye
If You Ever Need Somebody	It's the Same Old Song
My World	You Loved Away the Pain

1980   GLADYS KNIGHT & THE PIPS
          About Love
          Columbia/CBS Records

SIDE 1:	SIDE 2:
Landlord	Add It Up
Taste of Bitter Love	Bourgie, Bourgie
Still Such a Thing	Friendly Persuasion
Get the Love	We Heed Hearts

1981   GLADYS KNIGHT & THE PIPS
Touch
Columbia/CBS Records

SIDE 1:	SIDE 2:
I Will Fight	God Is
If That'll Make You Happy	Changed
Baby, Baby Don't Waste My Time	Reach High
A Friend of Mine	I Will Survive
Love Was Made for Two	

1982   GLADYS KNIGHT & THE PIPS
That Special Time of Year
Columbia/CBS Records

SIDE 1:	SIDE 2:
That Special Time of Year	It's the Happiest Time of Year
Jingle Bells	I Believe
What Are You Doing New Year's Eve	When a Child Was Born (*with Johnny Mathis*)
This Christmas	The Lord's Prayer
Santa Claus Is Coming to Town	Let There Be Peace on Earth

1983   GLADYS KNIGHT & THE PIPS
Visions
Columbia/CBS Records

SIDE 1:	SIDE 2:
When You're Far Away	Ain't No Greater Love
Just Be My Lover	Seconds
Save the Overtime (For Me)	You're Number One (In My Book)
Heaven Sent	Oh La De Da
Don't Make Me Run Away	Hero (Wind Beneath My Wings)

1985   GLADYS KNIGHT & THE PIPS
Life
Columbia/CBS Records

SIDE 1:	SIDE 2:
Strivin'	My Time
Just Givin' Me Love	Forever
Just Let Me Love You	Do You Wanna Have Some Fun
Life	Straight Up
Till I See You Again	Glitter

1987   GLADYS KNIGHT & THE PIPS
        Love Overboard
        MCA Records

SIDE 1:

Love Overboard
Lovin' on Next to Nothing
Thief in Paradise
You
Let Me Be the One

SIDE 2:

Complete Recovery
Say What You Mean
It's Gonna Take All Our Love
Love Is Fire (Love Is Ice)
Point of View
Overnight Success

1991   GLADYS KNIGHT
        Good Woman
        MCA Records

SIDE 1:

Men
Meet Me in the Middle
Where Would I Be
Superwoman (*with Dionne Warwick and
    Patti LaBelle*)
Give Me a Chance (*with David Peaston*)

SIDE 2:

Good Woman
If You Only Knew
Mr. Love
Waiting on You
In This Life

1994   GLADYS KNIGHT
        Just for You
        MCA Records

SIDE 1:

Next Time
I Don't Want to Know
I'll Fall in Love if You Hang Around
Our Love
Home Alone

SIDE 2:

Choice of Colors
Guilty
Somehow He Loves Me
End of the Road Medley

1996   GLADYS KNIGHT & THE PIPS
        The Lost Live Album
        BMG Music; Distributed by RCA Special Products

SIDE 1:

How Can You Say That Ain't Love
I've Got to Use My Imagination
Best Thing That Ever Happened to Me
Daddy Could Swear, I Declare
Try to Remember/The Way We Were
On & On

SIDE 2:

I Don't Want to Do Wrong
Where Peaceful Waters Flow
Midnight Train to Georgia
Neither One of Us
I Heard It through the Grapevine